Seriously Hexed

Seriously Hexed

TINA CONNOLLY

TOR TEEN

A TOM DOHERTY ASSOCIATES BOOK
NEW YORK

SERIOUSLY HEXED

Copyright © 2017 by Tina Connolly

A Tor Teen Book
Published by Tom Doherty Associates
175 Fifth Avenue
New York, NY 10010

www.tor-forge.com

Tor® is a registered trademark of Macmillan Publishing Group, LLC.

The Library of Congress Cataloging-in-Publication Data is available upon request.

ISBN 978-0-7653-8377-8 (hardcover)
ISBN 978-1-4668-9323-8 (ebook)

Our books may be purchased in bulk for promotional, educational, or business use.
Please contact your local bookseller or the Macmillan Corporate and Premium
Sales Department at 1-800-221-7945, extension 5442, or by email
at MacmillanSpecialMarkets@macmillan.com.

First Edition: November 2017

Printed in the United States of America

0 9 8 7 6 5 4 3 2 1

For Mike and Melissa,
who believe that one person can make a difference

Seriously Hexed

1

Just a Regular Saturday Night, Except for All the Witches

It was a chilly Saturday night at the tail end of spring break, and Jenah and I were sitting at Blue Moon Pizza, watching Devon's band play.

Well, we *had* been watching Devon's band play. The pizza place wasn't exactly the classiest venue. The band had stopped to deal with a power cord that kept falling out of the wall socket. One of the college kids who staffed the place was getting a longer cord to run to the outlet in the restroom.

"Wait wait wait, Cam," Jenah was saying. "You turned him into what?"

"Hush!" I said, waving my packet of Parmesan at her. "I don't want everyone to know."

"That you turned him into a—"

"An *anything*. You know I don't want anyone to know I'm a witch."

"And especially not—"

"A witch who turned her boyfriend into a turnip. Yes. That."

A bubble of laughter escaped Jenah, but she immediately put on a serious face again. "Cross my heart," she said. And then ruined it by adding, "Hope to die; turn me into a turnip if I lie."

Jenah is my best friend. She's tiny and Chinese American and she marches to the beat of a fashion drummer that only she can hear. Today she was wearing a vintage electric-green dress with silver tights.

She's also one of the only people in the world who knows that I live with a mostly wicked witch, and that I'm a very reluctant witch in training. See, 99 percent of all witches are horrible, miserable people who treat people like animals and animals like ingredients. So if I'm going to—maybe, possibly—be a witch, then I have to go down a different path. A good path. An ethical path.

And somehow not turn my boyfriend into a turnip while doing it.

"It's a different world," I grumbled as I tried to tear open my Parmesan. "You don't have to deal with people who have problems that maybe you can fix."

"I don't follow."

"Devon's been dealing with on-again, off-again stage fright for a while. You know."

"Like the time when he forgot all the lyrics to his songs except for the bit about the butter?"

"That was because of some wicked witches casting spells on him."

"Still."

"Still. The point is, I know a spell that can help with stage fright. But I'm not going to use it, since it contains animal parts. So, the last few months I've been researching vegetarian replacements. Finally I tried the finished spell on him, and . . ."

"Turnip?"

"Turnip."

"I'm sure he appreciates it," said Jenah. "Except maybe the ready-to-be-put-in-stew part."

The packet finally opened, scattering Parmesan everywhere. I stared at it glumly. "I should just give up," I said. "Then we could have an actual date night instead of me frantically trying to humanize a root vegetable."

"I'm sure you'll solve it eventually," said Jenah. "I bet you're already working on a new version of the spell."

"I am, but . . ."

"See? You'll get there. You worry too much." She neatly scraped the cheese off her pizza and took a bite of tomato sauce crust.

Despite her show of confidence in me, I frowned at her. "If you have actual power, you *have* to worry how you use it. Like, what if I do something so bad to him that I can't fix it? It would be safer if I never experiment on him again." I brushed the powdered cheese into a pile and reached for a new packet.

"So you finally tried something, and it didn't work, and now you're going to give up?" Jenah looked skeptical.

"I don't want to be a witch. You know that."

"Maybe I don't want to be able to read auras, but I can't turn it off," said Jenah. "Like in auditions last Friday. I could tell that this other girl was going to flub it because her aura was sickly green. And then she puked, so I was right."

"Flu?"

"Your boy isn't the only one with stage fright."

"I don't need any more people to turn into turnips, thank you." The new Parmesan packet opened without trouble. I could finally eat.

Jenah rolled her eyes. "The competition can take care of themselves. Now's the point where you ask me what I'm auditioning for."

I put down my slice of pizza. "I'm sorry." I tended to get wrapped up in my own thoughts, especially when they went all doom and gloom and turnip-shaped. "What are you auditioning for?"

Jenah bounced. "*Cabaret!*"

"Is that the one set in Nazi Germany? About a girl with short hair?"

"Reasonably close."

"Hey, you have short hair."

"I'm not going to get Sally Bowles," Jenah said matter-of-factly. "We're sophomores and the lead is obviously going to a senior. But I *am* hoping to get one of the Kit Kat dancers. Cast list gets posted Monday."

"Well. Good luck," I said, in the hearty way that you cheer someone on about something that is completely incomprehensible to you. I mean, that was okay, though. There were only two people whom I regularly talked to about my home life—Devon and Jenah. Jenah couldn't really understand what it was like to live with a wicked witch, and I couldn't really understand why anyone would want to put on a tutu, or whatever it was that Kit Kat dancers wore, and get up in front of people and have them *look at you.* "It sounds . . . dance-y."

"And sing-y," said Jenah.

"And rehearsally," I said. "In the theater every afternoon." Not that I was one to talk. My afternoons were spent doing things like hanging up snakeskins and watering the deadly nightshade.

"You're thinking about how our lives are diverging," said Jenah, pointing her pizza crust at me. "When the truth is, they won't *unless you let them.*"

"I'm not," I protested. Jenah's uncanny skill at reading people frequently discomfited me.

"I'm here for you, and you're here for me."

"Even if you're not a witch," I agreed. I didn't know what I'd do without Jenah. But, at the same time, there was so much gap in what I was able to explain to her, to share with her. It often tripped me up.

"You could always go hang out with Sparkle," Jenah pointed out.

I rolled my eyes. "She may be the only other teenage witch

in town, but that doesn't mean we'll ever be BFFs again. That ship sailed when we were six."

Up on stage, Devon's band was finally ready to resume. The little pizza joint was right near the high school, and it had long been the place where new high school bands could get their feet wet before moving on to book real gigs.

Or, in the case of Devon's band, allow a shy songwriter a chance to get more confident performing his own material.

Devon was taking the front spot on the tiny plywood stage. I put down my pizza. "This is his song," I whispered to Jenah.

"And he's really going to sing it?"

"Knock on wood."

Devon picked up the mic. "I'm going to sing an old song for you," he said. "'Liontamer.'"

I peered around our booth, scanning the dimly lit pizza place. The dinner rush was long gone and most people had cleared out. There was one family finishing up, a booth with a trio of soccer moms, and a couple tables of high schoolers. They were laughing and chatting and not paying any attention to the trio on stage. I turned back around and shouted, "Woo!"

He gave me a small smile. "Roar," he said into the mic.

Devon is white, with floppy blond hair, and a sweet, shy face. He'd been wrestling with stage fright since before he'd moved to town last October. For a few days, a demon had briefly taken possession of his body, which had given him a crazy amount of cool confidence. But it had quickly been followed by some nasty witches casting spells on him that wrecked his performances, and so his struggle went on.

Nnenna, their drummer, started the opening riff and he launched into the song. "*She's a cool stick of butter . . .*"

The bell over the door clanged and a bunch of guys crowded in, hollering about the college basketball game, their pizza order, and some girl's party later tonight. Devon trailed off.

Maybe he just wasn't cut out to be a performer.

I suppressed that traitorous thought.

The riff looped around again. Devon took a deep breath and lion-roared into the mic. I could see him trying to sell it, trying to put over the casual confidence needed of a rock star.

One of the dudes looked his way and laughed.

It wasn't necessarily a *mean* laugh, but I saw Devon's face crumble. He trailed off.

From the back, Nnenna started into the song. *"She's a cool stick of butter . . ."*

Devon took a deep breath and joined in with Nnenna. *". . . with a warm warm heart."*

The two of them together finished the whole song.

When it was over, Jenah and I applauded heartily. So did a small girl from a high chair. The group of guys had already picked up their pizza order and gallumphed away.

Devon trudged off the plywood platform to our booth as Nnenna and the bassist started packing up their stuff. His sweet face was hangdog.

"Hey, you did your song with Nnenna," I said. "You're a step closer to doing it by yourself."

He just looked at me. "I feel so dumb," he said. "It's like . . . like I can't make our music *matter* anymore. I look at everyone, with their real lives, and I think, how can I make them care about something so silly?"

"Hey now," I said. "The song you wrote for me is not silly."

His face flushed. "I didn't mean—"

"Teasing," I said.

"Nnenna doesn't have that problem," Devon said. "You saw her on the first songs. You could give her 'Old MacDonald' to sing and she'd *make* everyone rock out to it."

Jenah tapped her chin, thinking. "So that's where the stage fright gets a toehold," she said. "As soon as you think it doesn't matter what you're doing, you get self-conscious. And then . . ."

He stared at the table. He was as low as I'd ever seen him. "I'd better help pack up Nnenna's van," he said.

"Come back when you're done," I said cheerfully, trying to jostle him out of his low mood. "Sarmine said I didn't have to be back till ten thirty, if you can believe it. We can still have our date."

He managed a small smile. Then trudged to where Nnenna and the bass player were setting their gear by the bead curtain that led to the back, clearing the platform for the next performer.

The next musician just had a keyboard and stand—no amps or whatever they're called. He had dark hair and brown skin and a very serious beard going. College guy, probably. He dragged a chair over from one of the pizza tables and started right in playing, unbothered by the chaos of Devon's band packing up behind him.

That was the kind of confidence Devon needed, I thought, as I watched the piano player. He was good, actually. Too good for Blue Moon Pizza. I didn't know much about music, but I would assess the piece he was playing as "some kind of tricky jazz thingy." We were seated close enough to the tiny stage that I could clearly see his hands on the keyboard. His fingernails were much longer than I would expect for a piano player.

There was the *dink dink* of the bell over the front door and I turned to see Sparkle and Leo walking in. Leo is a gorgeous sportsball quarterback something or other who looks Middle Eastern. Also, a shifter. Sparkle is tall, half Japanese, and head cheerleader. Also, a witch.

Her eyes were sweeping the restaurant as if looking for somebody. I hoped it wasn't me. I couldn't think how I might have ticked her off lately. Usually she liked to ignore me.

I turned back to the piano player—and saw him frozen, staring at Sparkle.

Well. Guys often did that. Maybe it wasn't too weird.

I watched his eyes get wider and wider as she strode toward him.

But she stopped at our table. "Hey, Cam," she said. "Gotta talk to you."

"*Me* Cam?" I looked around. I was the only Cam in sight.

Sparkle rolled her eyes and sat down in the booth across from me and Jenah. Leo followed behind like a lapdog. Although probably you're not supposed to say that kind of thing about a shifter. Not that witches concerned themselves with tact very often. "It's about your mother."

Oh. "What has my mother done now?"

Sparkle pulled up something on her phone and slid it across to me. "Just look!"

I looked to see an email addressed to "Sparklebarkle, VValdaVelda, PrincessEsmerelda, etc.," with a subject line of "CASCADIA COVEN MEETING CALLED." The body of the email was equally terse—it read "SATURDAY AT 11:30 PM," and gave our address. "SIGNED, SARMINE SCARABOUCHE."

Somehow I wasn't surprised that my mother wrote her emails in all caps.

"What is this?" I said.

"That's what I'm here to ask you," said Sparkle. She lowered her voice. "No one's called a coven meeting in thirteen, fourteen years. What is your mother up to?"

"I don't know," I said. "She didn't invite me."

Eye roll. "Of course not. You have to be a *member*. There are thirteen witches in the coven, and if a meeting is called, we all have to show up, or lose our spot. I just got back from skiing with friends, and Leo and I had *plans* for tonight. That did *not* involve this pizza place, *or* your house." She flipped her hair back. "Ugh, so inconvenient."

"So tedious," I agreed. Sparkle is not wealthy herself, but as top girl in school she has everyone who *is* securely under her thumb. Gotta say, I also would rather be off on some fancy date than dealing with my mother's witch coven. "Why don't you just not go?" I said. "Have fun at your party instead."

"And lose all that power? My old self fought to get that spot." Sparkle picked up a napkin and toyed with it. "I guess it's hard to give that up."

Jenah looked at her intently. Then: "You don't want to step back into your old life."

"I said that."

"I mean . . . they'll have expectations of you."

Sparkle's shoulders slumped. "I wasn't always very nice in my past life," she admitted. "There are certain witches in that coven who may expect me to . . . take their side on things."

I could see how that would be challenging. See, Sparkle was older than she looked. Witches look the age they feel on the inside, and Sparkle was actually about forty. Fifteen years or so ago she had put an amnesia spell on herself to regress to a toddler and live in hiding while she waited for some magical plans to come to fruition. The amnesia spell had been removed last Halloween. But what she hadn't expected is that, after living her childhood over a second time, she would grow up into somebody different.

"Plus, Valda and that Emerald lady will be pretty ticked at you for helping get rid of Malkin last November," pointed out Leo.

"Wait, what?" I said. There had been an episode a few months ago where my mother had invited three particularly nasty witches over for a little reunion. After I had discovered the high school star quarterback was secretly a shape-shifter,

Sparkle and I had to protect him so the wicked witches wouldn't tear him up for their spells. "I thought you were going to make Esmerelda and Valda forget all about that week in November. I gave you a vial of dragon tears to do it."

Sparkle looked defensive. "I forgot how tricky it is to put amnesia on resistant witches. The best I could do was kind of blur the fact that Leo was a shifter. They remembered Malkin was after him but not why."

Ice formed in my stomach. "And they remember that I foiled their plans and let Malkin be eaten by a giant lindworm?" I said.

"Me," said Leo. "I ate her."

"Well. Yes." Sparkle saw my expression and hastened to re-assure me. "Valda and Esmerelda are incredibly lazy. Malkin was always the brains of the operation."

"So you were allies with them before? You hung out with them?"

"No! I mean . . . maybe we voted the same way sometimes. But everyone comes to the coven masked, you know. We certainly weren't *friends*."

"That's why they didn't recognize you last November," I said. "Out of context. Different name. Cheerleading costume."

"And I used to dress like this," said Sparkle. She flipped open her wallet, pulled out a battered, laminated piece of chip-board, and passed it over to me.

"Dude, is that a *trading card*?" said Leo.

It was a picture of an older Sparkle, maybe mid-twenties. But instead of Sparkle's typical ultra-glam appearance, this Sparkle was uber Goth, all in black, with a pale face and heavy black eyeliner that curled around her eyes and cheekbones. Cursive font at the bottom spelled out "Hikari Tanaka."

"Fancy," I said.

"You should do that more often," said Jenah.

Sparkle shot her a look, but I figured Jenah meant it honestly.

"How many people know about your reappearance?" I said.

Sparkle sighed. "Mostly just your mother. Malkin might have realized who I was, but she's gone. I was kind of hoping I wouldn't ever have to get back into it. I just want to be a regular person."

"And protect Leo."

"Sure."

"And magic up new clothes from time to time."

"Obviously."

"And maybe a few more things, like—"

She gave me the side-eye.

"A regular person. Sure. I got it."

It was about then I noticed that the piano music had stopped. I looked up to see the piano player staring straight at the old photo of Sparkle. He glanced up and saw me looking at him.

Then he grabbed his keyboard and stand, jumped off the plywood platform, and booked it through the bead curtain that led to the kitchen and restrooms.

"Uh, where's that dude going?" said Leo.

"I don't know," I said, standing.

"He's been listening in," said Jenah, and then added, "He's cute, in a kind of fuzzy way."

"You should make a move on that," advised Sparkle.

"I'm not interested in dating," Jenah said calmly. "I appreciate cuteness in people, is all."

"And you enjoy setting up other people," I reminded her.

"Purely vicarious," said Jenah.

Sparkle furrowed her brow as she stood. "Cute in a fuzzy way, huh? There *was* something familiar about him. . . ."

She made a move as if to follow the piano player, but just then the door to the pizza place chimed again.

In blew a small woman, white, with short black hair, in a black and white checkered dress. Her eyes scanned the darkened room. I meant to look away from the sweep of those black eyes, but there was something unusual about her face that commanded attention. Her face was magnetic. Arresting. But not because she was so particularly beautiful or anything.

Her face was cold. Like ice.

Behind me, Sparkle swore. I reluctantly pulled my gaze away from the woman, turned to see genuine fear on Sparkle's face.

"Leo. Down," she whispered urgently.

Leo was in the corner of the booth. He couldn't see the woman at the front door.

But he could see Sparkle's expression.

He dove under the booth. And there was a lot of him to dive, so it was not graceful and it involved a lot of Jenah pushing and him grunting.

The woman's gaze swept the dim restaurant, searching for someone.

The family had left. The tables of teenagers looked back at the top girl in school. Sparkle raised black eyebrows at them. "Scatter," she said.

To a person, they did, down to every last tennis player and flautist and Goth girl. They picked up their pizza slices and they all rushed different directions in an attempt to obey Sparkle.

The woman turned, trying to track who went where.

I stood next to Sparkle. I couldn't let her face this person alone—whoever she was.

"Don't be stupid," Sparkle hissed. "I've worked on my shields and you haven't. She'll get anything she wants out of you."

"You mean . . . ?"

"Claudette can *read your thoughts*," said Sparkle.

I could believe that of this strangely magnetic woman.

I pulled a fact from the depths of my memory. "But that was outlawed by the Geneva Coven," I said plaintively.

"Tell that to her."

The woman's—no, the *witch's*—eyes met Sparkle's. She strode to us, chairs scattering out of her path like frightened squirrels.

"Think of Devon," whispered Sparkle as Claudette approached.

"Huh?"

"Romance! Crushes! Strong emotions help shield."

I marshaled my thoughts to think about my boyfriend, who was still in the back of the restaurant somewhere. Unfortunately, most of my current thoughts were not of the strong crushy-love variety and were more of the *poor Devon* variety.

Claudette stopped at our booth and my attention was irresistibly drawn away from thoughts of Devon and back to her. She glanced at me and Jenah and dismissed us, turning to Sparkle. She was not as tall as Sparkle and me, but it didn't matter one bit. I wanted to crawl under the booth myself.

"Where is the . . . the pianist?" she said to Sparkle in a heavy French accent.

"Who?"

"The—Sam. Where did he go?"

"Who's Sam?"

"I do not have the time for this, Hikari," said Claudette. Sparkle tensed at the confirmation that the woman knew who she was. "You have seen the email. Whatever Sarmine has planned, I am not walking into that without preparation. Out with it! *Voyons!* Where did he go?"

Sparkle's chin firmed up as she called upon her everyday hauteur. "I am not interested in your turf wars, Claudette," she said with a sneer. "If you feel you have a claim to the Bigfoot, *you* find him."

Turf wars? *Bigfoot?*

"Eep," said Jenah. I glanced down into the gloom under the table. Just peeping out of the darkness was one small fluffy white rabbit foot.

Oh no. No wonder Sparkle had shoved Leo under the table.

Shifters were in high danger around witches. See, witches—terrible, horrible people as far as I was concerned—were definitely not vegetarian, and they used lots of animal parts in spells. Magical animals—pixies, unicorns, et cetera—had more potency than regular animals. And since shifters, who were extremely magical already, could theoretically change into any animal required for a spell . . . I shuddered. If this ice-faced witch was willing to chase an innocent piano player through a pizza parlor, just imagine what she would do if she found a shifter.

"Eep?" said Claudette, shifting her gaze to the booth.

"Burp?" said Jenah.

"It would be very foolish to be hiding something from me," said Claudette, and her attention was laser-focused on Jenah now. "*Très, très stupide,*" she reiterated in French, apparently to make sure we got it. We got it.

That was when Devon bounded through the bead curtain, his guitar slung over one shoulder and a wide, goofy smile on his face. He pushed himself into the conversation, arms draping over our shoulders. "Yo, girls," he said, in a total stoner-dude voice. "Did you, like, see my set? Ama-a-a-azing, huh? I really killed those songs." He turned to Claudette, who looked slightly stunned. "Whoa, gorgeous. You must be up next, right? You're a singer, yeah? You gotta have some great act. . . ."

My heart melted. Devon was trying to distract the witch from all of us. So brave. So stupid.

Claudette pointed her finger at him. "You. Are not an idle distraction. You have seen the pianist. You are hiding him."

He demurred, backing away. "No, dude, I'm just a—"

She crooked one finger at him. I *saw* him lurch toward her, stumble a half step. His eyes were wide. Her finger beckoned, as if thoughts were coalescing inside his brain and she was going to pull them out, one by one.

"Think of your girlfriend," hissed Sparkle.

His eyes went glassy as the finger kept beckoning.

"She did, eh?" said Claudette, a smirk on her face. "*Très intéressant.* Tell me more. . . ."

The trials and tribulations of our relationship might fill a couple books, but even so, I knew idle gossip wouldn't hold Claudette for long. Not when she got wind of Leo.

I had to do something.

The only thing I had ready to go in my backpack of magical ingredients was the new compound I had been working on for Devon. While it might seem unlikely that an anti–stage fright spell would help Devon at this moment, on the other hand, the Showstopper potion *had* worked once to distract a witch by making her victim completely, irresistibly charming. Same idea, right? And my mental Good Witch Ethics List had determined that it was okay to cast a spell on someone without their permission if it was to save a life.

And this was.

I reached into one of the backpack's pockets and grabbed the ziplock bag of ingredients I had been compounding. No time to do anything fancy like combine it with unicorn hair sanitizer or heat it in a silver bowl or anything else.

Claudette was staring deeper into Devon. "You saw him go through the curtain," she was saying. "And then—"

I blew the compound off my hand and onto Devon. It coated the back of his head. And then—

He was gone.

2

A Seriously Bad Hex

Oh no.

Oh no no no no no.

Claudette blinked. "I was just about to learn—" she said. Her eyes focused on me. "You . . . stupid . . . *épais* . . ." She took a breath. "What did you do to your charming friend? Did you teleport him somewhere?"

My mouth hung open. I had no idea what I did. My heart was going a mile a minute.

"Eughh." She flapped a dismissive hand at me. "It is no matter. I have learned from him where the Bigfoot has gone." She disappeared down the hall toward the restroom, and a few seconds later returned, dragging the much bigger and burlier piano player by his sleeve. His face was a peculiar mixture of angry, frightened, and resigned.

"What's she doing with him?" said Jenah.

"We can't let her take him—" I said.

"Stand back or she'll discover—" hissed Sparkle.

Claudette turned on us. "Yes, *discover*," she said. "Whoever said that, repeat again, *s'il vous plaît*? There was something I was failing to discover. . . ."

Her gaze held mine. Sparkle was right. I had witch blood, but I had no training on how to hold mind-reading shields. I tried to keep her out, but I could feel her thoughts questing into mine, poking around my brain like a little cat tongue.

I tried to hold Sparkle's command in mind, to think of

crushing on Devon. Crazy hard to do when I was filled with frantic worry about what I had done to him. But I had to, if I was going to save—

No. Don't think of that.

I thought about when I had first seen Devon, standing at my bus stop. When he had waited for me on the bus. When we sat on the roof together. Sparkle was right. There was so much emotion in those thoughts that it filled my brain, blocking any other stray thoughts. Sitting beside him, our sleeves barely touching, wondering if he liked me, my breath coming fast—

Claudette's eyes bored into my brain. I held the rooftop image as hard as I could, but I could feel my control slipping. In another moment it would be gone; in another moment I would think of the thing I wasn't supposed to think of, which was right there at the edge of my mind—

That's when the soccer moms stood up from their booth, wands flicked out. "Hand over the Bigfoot," ordered one of them.

What . . .

Claudette turned to face them, her mind releasing mine.

"The *Canadians*," whispered Sparkle. "Live in Vancouver. Always together."

They were advancing now, still looking like some soccer moms that had sat down for pizza. One was black and wore a blue Toronto Maple Leafs sweatshirt. One was white, with frizzy red hair and yoga pants. One looked Indian and was wearing a frumpy blouse and skirt.

"I believe this is not your territory," said Claudette, penciled eyebrows raised. Her grip tightened on the piano player.

"Not yours, either," said Sports Team.

"Hand him over," repeated Leggings.

"You may have noticed there's three of us," said Boring Skirt.

Claudette raised her wand—

The soccer moms raised their wands—

"Epic witch battle," whispered Jenah gleefully—

And then Claudette and her victim disappeared in a puff of smoke. It was pink and smelled like roses.

Sports Team yelled at the thin air. "Stupid teleporting witch!"

Leggings: "You'll pay for this!"

Boring Skirt, in a mumble: "Once we track you down, eh?"

They wheeled and hurried out the front door.

"Ohmigod, you guys can *teleport*?" said Jenah. "Where do you think Claudette went?"

"Who cares about Claudette?" I said.

"*I* care," said Jenah. "That poor piano player—"

"I know, I know," I said, more brusquely than I meant. "But what about Devon?"

Sparkle wheeled on me. "You mean you don't know?"

I was shaking. "Half the people just disappeared and I don't know what happened."

Sparkle rolled her eyes. "It's very simple. Claudette and the Canadians were looking for that piano player, who is obviously one of the Sentient Magicals known as a Bigfoot. He tried to hide because he didn't want them to get his toenails. Claudette snapped her fingers and teleported somewhere. I don't know *how* you do it, but she's known for it. The Canadians will be grouchy at the coven tonight. And Devon—" But there she stopped. "What did you do with Devon?"

I opened my mouth to wail, *I don't know*, but a familiar voice stopped me.

"I'm right here," Devon said.

There was nothing there.

"You invisibled him," said Sparkle. "Except . . ." She sniffed the air. "I don't smell invisible eels." Her face was puzzled.

"There's also that weird vegan invisibility spell, but it doesn't work nearly this well." She poked a finger in the general direction of his head.

"Ouch. My ear," said the nothing.

"Devon," I breathed. "You *are* there." I hadn't disintegrated him, at least. But what had I done?

"Seriously," said Sparkle. "I can't see anything. Leo, can you see anything?"

Leo hopped out from under the table. The white bunny shimmied, and then he was a hawk. He peered at the patch of nothing from one eye, then the other. Then he cawed and shimmied back into a boy.

I sighed and gestured to Jenah. "Clothes," I said.

Laughing, she grabbed them from under the table and tossed them in Leo's direction.

"Dude, I can't even see him with my hawk eyes," Leo said as he got dressed.

"*Or* his clothes," mused Sparkle. "How on earth did you invisible both things?"

"It was a powder?" I said.

She whistled. "That was a seriously good hex."

"Bad hex," I corrected. "Seriously *bad* hex."

"Can't you undo it?" said Jenah.

"I don't know how," I said.

"How did you unturnip him?"

"Sarmine did it," I admitted. I swallowed my pride and looked at my former best friend. "Sparkle, can you try?"

She shook her head. "Not without my ingredients." She looked at my woeful face and slugged me on the shoulder. "Cheer up," she said. "Maybe it won't last that long. You're not a very good witch, after all."

"Thanks," I said glumly.

"How are you going to go to school?" said Leo.

"Makeup," suggested Sparkle.

"All over?"

Jenah slipped around the table and held out a stack of her jelly bracelets. "Try these on," she commanded.

The nothing took the bracelets and hung them in midair.

"A neat party trick," said Sparkle.

"My point is, it's only your current clothes that went invisible," said Jenah. "Makeup plus new clothes might actually work."

"And a wig," said Leo.

Devon didn't say anything, just stood there while they talked around him. I wished I had something useful to add, but I couldn't get my brain to stop worrying about how I had done it and how I would undo it. I wished I could believe Sparkle that the spell would fade, but it seemed just my luck that I would come up with a really good spell at exactly the worst time. Oh, why had I tried my stupid powder on Devon? I *knew* better than to fling untested spells around.

One of the employees finally poked his head through the beaded curtain. College kid. "Uh, you know we're closing soon," he said.

"Okay, dude," said Leo. "We're clearing out."

There was silence as we regarded the nothing in the center of our group. Finally, it said, "Thanks, guys. I guess I'd better go home and try a disguise." By now I knew Devon well enough to know he was feeling pretty discouraged. Lousy performance, didn't stop the witch from kidnapping that piano player, and now his girlfriend had made him invisible. You couldn't blame him.

The nothing gave the bracelets back to Jenah, Leo left some cash on the table to pay for all of us, and we headed out the front door.

"What are we going to do about that piano player?" said

Jenah, as we went to our bikes. "We have to try to rescue him."

Sparkle rounded on her, her face cold with fury. "We do *not*. We have no responsibility to him. This isn't a game, Jenah."

"I didn't think it was."

"His *life* is at stake," Sparkle said, and her finger jabbed at Leo. "You will not jeopardize that, or I will wipe your mind clean, and I don't care how much I mess it up while I'm doing it."

"Okay, okay," said Jenah, holding up her hands.

Sparkle turned, shooting daggers at me. "That goes for you, too." Her glare raked all of us, including the spot where invisible Devon was probably standing. "None of you have shields. You see that witch again, you run the other way. Do you hear me?"

I nodded. So did Jenah.

"Got it," said Devon.

Sparkle nodded curtly at me. "I'll see you in an hour," she said. She and Leo got into his convertible and peeled off.

Jenah's face was still angry. "She's wrong, wrong, wrong."

I shook my head. "As much as she annoys me, this time she's right. We can't face Claudette. Not without risking Leo's life."

"Then *she* should."

I sighed. "Maybe so. But I don't think she's going to."

There was a clatter as a bike detached itself from the bike rack.

"Wait up, Devon," I said. The bike continued to the edge of the parking lot, then stopped there as Jenah and I unlocked ours. I couldn't tell if he was actually waiting for me or just being a gentleman, making sure we got safely on our bikes.

"Let me know what happens," said Jenah.

"I'll try," I said.

She swung her leg over her bike and set off in the opposite direction. I watched the back of her jacket head away. Then I turned back to the bike with the invisible rider. As I did, the pedals swung up, and it, too, started going away from me.

But we had to go the same direction. I followed him down the hills from the pizza place, back toward our neighborhood with the square blocks of old split-levels. A million emotions churned through me as I pedaled down the hill. I was upset and afraid and angry.

I caught up to the empty bike at the last stop sign before our street. "Devon," I said to the thin air. "You know I am so, so sorry. I didn't mean it."

"I know," said the nothing despondently.

"I wouldn't have done it, except—"

He sighed. "Cam, I honestly don't blame you. You made a tough decision in the heat of the moment. I'm not mad."

But now he had to live with it.

"I promise you, the very first thing I'll do is ask my mother to unhex you. We have all day tomorrow before school starts again, and she can do anything."

The nothing squeezed my arm. "I know."

I reached for where I could feel him touching my arm, wanting to cover his fingers with mine. To comfort him. But he released my arm and moved away and I only touched my own sleeve.

"I better get home and figure out how to avoid my parents all day tomorrow," he said. The bike pedals changed positions as he put his invisible foot back on one of them. Then the bike was going, gone.

I sighed. After a few months of dating Devon, I knew that when he was depressed he just wanted to be alone. That he meant it when he said he didn't blame me.

But I blamed myself.

What good was being a witch if I was just going to make everything worse? Sparkle had the right of it. Just give up witchery and live as a normal teenager. I mean, here I'd hexed Devon, and we hadn't even saved the piano player from the witches. Who knew what they were going to do to him? I shuddered as I walked inside.

My mother, Sarmine Scarabouche, was waiting at the door.

Sarmine is tall and white, like me, but with bobbed silver hair. For some reason, she was wearing a long black cape.

"It's about time," she said.

"You said I could have a date," I pointed out.

"A weak moment," she said. "Now sit. I have something very serious to discuss."

I sighed. "I know."

"You do?"

"Sparkle found me and told me you were having some coven meeting tonight. I suppose you want me to buttle or something."

"I want you to join the coven."

"What."

"The coven."

"I heard what you said."

"I want you to join—"

"I am tired of stupid witches and their stupid witch groups," I said.

"Coven," she corrected. "Stupid witch *coven*."

"Evil, rude, spiteful, aggravating—"

"All right, who did you run into?"

"Four witches, just now," I admitted. "Not counting me and Sparkle. Up at the pizza place."

Sarmine narrowed her eyes. "Which ones?"

"Claudette and the Canadians. They were chasing some piano player who Sparkle said was a Bigfoot."

Sarmine sighed. "Up to their old tricks. Claudette probably figured, since she was in the area, she'd do a little shopping."

I shuddered. "It's just, like, they want his toenail clippings, right? Nothing worse?" I seemed to remember Valda talking about that before.

"As far as I know," Sarmine said. "I don't know much about their uses. I've never used them myself."

"And that's not all," I said. "Sparkle said Claudette is a mind reader—"

"She's very dangerous," agreed Sarmine.

"And she was going to discover from Devon that Leo was a shifter, so I—"

"Turned him into a turnip?"

"No!" I hung my head. "I invisibled him. I can't get it off."

"With what, invisible eels?"

"A new spell I was trying, for stage fright. Crushed watermelon seeds, saffron, and unicorn spritzer."

Sarmine furrowed her brow. "And *that* made him invisible? That doesn't seem likely."

"Tell that to Devon." I looked imploring. "Will you help fix him tomorrow? Like you did when I turniped him?"

Sarmine went silent for a second. Then she nodded, appearing to reach a decision. She picked up a black robe and mask that lay the coffee table and held them out to me. "Camellia. You come to the coven for me tonight, and then I will try to fix your boyfriend for you."

"You will?" I very much did not want to go to that coven. It was bad enough that a couple of Sarmine's on-again, off-again witch friends—Esmerelda and Valda—knew that I was beginning to practice spellcraft. I didn't want to out myself to any more wicked witches. I wanted to go along in my little corner of the world, have pizza with my boyfriend, and stay out of the way of nasty people forever.

But for Devon's sake . . .

"I will," I said. "But this isn't going to be a weekly thing, is it?"

"Joining a coven is a tremendous honor, Camellia," said Sarmine in an aggravating tone. "Covens can help set policies for a geographic region."

I looked skeptical. "I've never seen a witch follow rules," I said.

"Change is slow," she admitted. "But if enough witches agree on a law, they can then enforce it and confiscate ingredients from witches who don't follow it. They like that."

"I bet."

"Covens can choose to be forces for good. The Geneva Coven, for example—"

"And I have to go to a bunch of witch meetings when I could be seeing Devon, or . . . ?"

"The Cascadia Coven hasn't been called to order for over a decade," admitted Sarmine, confirming what Sparkle had said.

I counted backwards. "So when? Was my . . . my father on it?"

Her lips tightened. "Yes. Jim was tremendously active in it. He thought we could make changes. He thought—" She sighed. "He was at the next-to-last meeting we had. Same old stuff, trying to protect the rights of shifters and werewolves and so on. He wanted a law granting full rights to Sentient Magicals. A pipe dream. And then . . . you know. He disappeared on us."

That was the way she had always phrased it, transferring her anger onto him for leaving. But . . . "Don't you mean 'and then they got him'?" I said gently.

A tight shake of her head. "Perhaps." She glared at me. "Which means it was his fault for putting himself in jeopardy.

And not being willing to react with enough force, when required."

"I see."

"There was one final meeting, where Malkin and her cronies installed Ulrich Grey in your father's place."

"Ulrich—Wait, isn't he the guy who runs the unicorn ranch?"

"A disgusting, lecherous cheat," Sarmine said, "but not a killer." She shrugged tightly. "After that, there was no way your father's law could get passed. We had been trying to gather support for it—I think one or two might have swung our way—but now it was hopeless. The best I could do all these years was *not* call any coven meetings. It would have only made things worse."

"And nobody else called one either?"

"Why would they? They were happy with the status quo. And then Malkin was off hunting the lindworm for a decade. Even her allies were happy to not see her."

I shook my head. "But then why did you call one now?"

She was very still. Then she said, "Because I have been backed into a corner, Camellia."

And then she did something that made me very worried. Very, very worried.

She hugged me.

After another round of instructions—my mother loves to lecture—Sarmine went out to the RV garage to finish setting up, leaving me to answer the door.

Thirteen witches to make a coven. I let in Valda, short and grumpy and smelling of cigarette smoke. Esmerelda, dressed to the nines in an unseasonably warm white fur coat. Her mother, Rimelda, who was a hundred years old, but looked a spry sixty. The three Canadians. ("You look familiar," said Boring Skirt. I shrugged.) Ulrich Grey, aka the Unicorn Guy, who stared at my black robes in a way that made me glad I was covered in black robes. And a woman I had never met, a tough-looking blonde with a German shepherd by her side. A couple of the witches never came to the front door—Sparkle knew where the RV garage was and went there, and Claudette must have snapped her way to it. I was glad I didn't have to face her mind-reading powers again. Hopefully she wouldn't dare use them in front of a coven full of witches.

Voices on the front step. Hopefully this was the end of the witches. I opened the door.

A middle-aged woman stood there, apparently alone, though I thought I had heard her speaking to someone. I looked around, but I didn't see anyone else in the night. She had dark brown skin and her black curls haloed her head. She was wearing a flowy shirt and skirt, and a silver peace sign charm hung around her neck. She had her black robes in a bundle on her arm, and she smiled at me. That was unusual enough that I smiled back before I thought.

"You must be Camellia," she said, and her eyes were kind behind her wire-rimmed glasses. "I'm Lily. I haven't seen you since you were a baby."

"Cam," I said, and, "Yeah," I said. What do you say to the people who tell you they knew you as a baby? Obviously I didn't know her from Adam. But she was smiling, and that was a pleasant change, to be honest. "Everyone's in the RV garage," I said.

"Thanks, dear." She followed me in, her hand lingering on the door, letting in the chill spring night. Her voice rumbled, warm and wistful. "I haven't been here since . . ."

"Since?" I inquired, as I was supposed to.

She broke off. "Well. Since a very long time," she said.

She let the door swing shut and headed to the back door as if she knew right where to go. She lingered there, too, as if she was looking around at a place she had memories of. I wondered if she and Sarmine had had a falling out. That was remarkably common among witches.

I trailed Lily to the garage and found Sarmine at the side door, smiling and waving everyone through as if she was a glamorous hostess welcoming people in for a cocktail party and not an uptight, recycling-obsessed wicked witch welcoming in a bunch of black-clad hooligans for a little evening of dancing around a cauldron. Or waving incense and myrrh. Or whatever it was that was about to happen.

"Mask," she said to me as I went in, and I obeyed immediately. Apparently coven rules had one good point. Maybe no one would realize that an intruder had joined their circle.

It was approaching midnight and the inside of the garage was quite dark. A low, yellowish fog hung in the air. I wondered if Sarmine had been trying to add atmosphere to what was, after all, a fairly ordinary garage, even if it was painted sky blue. The only light came from the small garage windows—the moon was nearing full and was bright enough to be seen through the soot-smeared panes.

It also stank. It smelled like a swamp—acidic and sulfuric, with pockets of rotten leaf stench leaking out. It was like we were in a haunted bog instead of on a city street of seventies split-levels.

In the middle of the garage was Sarmine's old black cauldron, and placed around it were thirteen glass candleholders—the ones like small glass cups. They appeared to be empty. Circling that were thirteen tall, dark, narrow chairs, each one fantastically carved and decorated. I had no idea where those chairs had come from. I have to admit, I was impressed by our garage.

"We should do this at Halloween," I whispered to Sarmine, as she directed me to stand on her right. "The neighbor kids would love it."

Sarmine, of course, did not answer this suggestion. She seemed unusually tense—but then, anyone would be tense at inviting eleven wicked witches over for a séance. It wasn't making me feel so great myself. The last time she'd had friends over, they'd tried to ruin my high school, and that was just three of them. Now we'd turned the witch dial to eleven.

"Please take your places," said Sarmine.

I guessed that meant me and Unicorn Guy, who was busy trying to creep on one of the witches. I sat down in the chair next to Sarmine. He took the last open place, directly across the circle from Sarmine. I looked around, trying to figure out who was where. But everyone was masked and robed, and it was dim, it was fogged. Classic witches: paranoid and suspicious. Yet, at the same time, I was glad for my own mask. The sooner I could get done with this coven thing, the better. Let them think I was just the butler.

Sarmine was to my left, and the short, black-draped figure next to her, smoking a cigarette, had to be Valda. The woman on my right was too heavily cloaked to identify, but on the other side of her I saw the moonlight glinting off a black halo of curls and identified Lily, the witch who said she had known me as a baby. The German shepherd stood sentinel by the door—perhaps his witch was over there. I remembered the redheaded Canadian and looked for her hair, but many of the robes had hoods, and I couldn't make her out.

There was an unusual air of expectation in the room. A funny, crackling sort of energy. I expected Valda and Esmerelda and so on to be heckling Sarmine, throwing off witticisms. And yet everyone was still. Waiting. It gave me an unusual feeling, as though I had walked into a different witch world than I had previously known.

Sarmine began without preamble. "By the order of Lily Jones, Rimelda Danela, and myself, Sarmine Scarabouche, I call this meeting of the Cascadia Coven to order!" The crack of a gavel sounded, though I saw no gavel and nothing to crack one against. "Now. Women—"

"And men," muttered Unicorn Guy.

"Please initiate your votives so we can begin."

Everyone leaned or kneeled down to their glass candle-holder in front of them, muttering something. Sarmine, on my left, leaned to touch her wand and pronounced her words clearly. "Sarmine Scarabouche."

Ah. I bent forward, but Sarmine stopped me with a motion of her hand.

The others sat back down. My votive looked very obvious, a black spot in the ring of light. I didn't like that.

Sarmine raised one pale hand. "It has been thirteen years since a coven was last called. Too long, perhaps. But we have some . . . unfinished business to deal with tonight."

You could have heard a pin drop in that smoky, boggy room.

"But first," she said, more brightly, "a point of order as we induct a new member into our group. Some of you may have noticed that the witch Malkin Hexenbesen is no longer among us."

Now there were murmurs. Heads turned, looking. I shrank back into my robes as masked eyes turned toward me.

"Ordinarily, of course," said Sarmine, "there is a standard procedure for filling a vacant spot. Any member can nominate a witch, and the coven can vote on the nomination. That happened when the witch James Hexar disappeared thirteen years ago." I started at the mention of my dad. Sarmine was able to say his name so coldly, yet I knew that was not how she really felt. "Ulrich Grey was nominated in his spot, and the motion barely passed." Someone snickered at Sarmine's acidic phrasing.

"But there is another way, far older. It has hardly been used in these more . . . modern times. Yet it is true that if a witch overthrows another witch through combat, she may obtain her place in the coven. As Camellia Hexar overthrew Malkin Hexenbesen, she is now eligible to claim Malkin's place in the circle."

More gasps at that, and the biggest one from me. I didn't mean to have Malkin killed. *She* was the one who had made Leo turn into a giant worm thing. I had merely helped him get free so he could eat her. I definitely wouldn't have done it to obtain this coven spot, and indeed, this seemed like the kind of thing I would have actively avoided. Sarmine really should have said "Do not kill Malkin or you will have to join a coven when you could be making out with your boyfriend." And, anyway, if anyone should get the credit, it should be Leo, for doing the eating. I opened my mouth to say all this, but Sarmine looked ice daggers at me through the holes in her black silk mask.

"Really, Sarmine?" said someone. "We're supposed to accept your word for it? You have more than a little stake in this."

"If my word isn't good enough for you . . ." Sarmine snapped back.

But then a familiar voice spoke up from somewhere around the seven o'clock area of the circle. "I saw and witnessed," it said. *Sparkle.* I craned my head, trying to see.

"Oh, very well," said the first grumpy voice.

"Bad egg anyway," said someone, and there was an uneasy rumble at that. Even these witches had been afraid of formidable Malkin.

"Who admits Camellia Hexar under the old law?" pronounced Sarmine in a deep and resonant voice.

Around the circle the lights went green. Well, not all the lights. Mine stayed dark, and two went red. Apparently two people didn't quite believe Sarmine's story of me ousting Malkin. I wasn't sure I believed it myself.

"Ten to two," said Sarmine impassively. "Motion carries." The cauldron glowed green, accepting the results of the votives. "Now that we are officially thirteen again, we may proceed." I sensed the tiniest bit of relaxing in her tight voice, as if step one of the evening had gone as planned. "Camellia?" She gestured at my votive.

"Camellia Hexar," I told the candleholder as I tapped it, and my glass cup lit up white.

There was silence for a second. I guessed I was now an official member of the coven, like it or not. I wondered if I needed to know a word to turn my light green or red, or if thinking would do it. I wondered if anyone was going to serve snacks.

The cranky voice of Valda broke the silence. "Well, you didn't call a coven meeting after more than a decade just to introduce your daughter to everyone. What else are we here for?"

"Same bee in her bonnet she used to have," muttered someone.

The witch next to me shifted uneasily. "You don't think—"

"Hush."

"Look at her."

Sarmine's face, always rather cold and pointed, had grown even more cold and pointed. Her chin was set. Her eyes were the sort of ice I had long ago learned to associate with Sarmine being a towering inferno of rage.

She paced back and forth at the head of the circle, her black robes swishing, punctuating her anger. In a low voice, she began, "As it happens, my next item does concern the transition of power here tonight." She paused and glared at us. She was really chewing the scenery. I would have been impressed, if I weren't so worried about what was going on. "A couple of days ago, I received a strange box. Label falling off. No return address. When I opened it I saw something strange inside. This knife."

Sarmine held the tiny thing aloft, and I recognized it as the minute ivory dagger Malkin had carried. Cold shuddered down my spine.

"As you all know, sometimes when a witch departs this world, certain spells are set in motion," said Sarmine. "Her last effects are parceled out to allies, relatives . . . other witches. It is one of the reasons I can swear to you that she is dead, and I have brought her last gift here tonight as proof."

She picked up a large cardboard box and balanced it on top of the cauldron. Everyone was tense, but no one made a move to stop her. Curiosity trumped caution.

"You wonder why I haven't opened it all the way yet?" she said. "Because, wrapped around the knife was a letter. With strict instructions not to open the rest of the box until I had summoned a coven and called all of you here. Else she would curse me with guinea pig rabies, blah blah blah. So. Twenty-four hours later, here we are." Sarmine opened the flaps of the box. "Let's see what last surprise the dearly departed Malkin has for us, shall we?"

There was finally a move at that. Lily, the witch two down from me, rose from her seat. "Sarmine, don't!" she shouted. She raised her wand high. Another figure, short and stout, lifting her wand—that was Valda. Automatically I raised mine, and so did another couple of witches—it was hard to see, hard to tell. Were they trying to stop Sarmine or trying to strike while she was distracted by Malkin's "gift"?

I couldn't tell. It was hard to tell anything. Because as we raised our wands, Sarmine touched it, whatever it was, the thing inside the box. A tremendously bright light filled the room, dazzling all our night-adjusted eyes. It crackled and snaked across the room until all our wands were lit by it, like an electrical current. Blinding pain in my eyes—I squinted—the cauldron with the box perched on it was erupting in a tower of green-white flame.

It blazed through the whole RV garage, lighting up the green fog in a nauseating glow, crackling out to all of our wands. Or was it crackling *in* from someone's wand in particular? Everyone was shrieking, the German shepherd was howling, while a rigid Sarmine was shouting desperate words of power at the blazing light. Thunder cracked out of nowhere, and then, with a horrendous, earsplitting *boom*, everything went black.

☾

The lights came on. The swinging lightbulb, bare in the middle of the garage. The fog was gone. The garage was all shelves and paint cans and dustpans. The carved chairs had turned back into our patio chairs and card table chairs and a piano bench.

The cardboard box had fallen off the cauldron. It lay there, turned over, packing peanuts spilling out of it. The glass candleholders still ringed the cauldron, all of them lit white.

No, not all.

The one at the head of the circle, the one in the twelve o'clock position, the one where Sarmine had been standing, was different. It was black, the light snuffed out, gone.

Sarmine had vanished.

3

Vanished, of Course, Never Thinks of Anyone but Herself

Oh no. Oh no. "Sarmine?" I whispered, into the chaos.

Voices clamored around me, fragments reaching my ears:

"That was Malkin."

"What did Malkin send?"

"Definitely Malkin."

"Where's Sarmine?"

Malkin had sent something horrible to Sarmine, hadn't she?

"Disappeared, of course. . . ."

Unless I had done it. I had disappeared Devon, hadn't I? Hexed him, turned him so invisible no one could turn him back.

Had I ever washed that powder off my hands?

I swallowed. "Come back?" I poked my wand into the spot where she had stood next to me. "Mom?"

I felt nothing.

Nothing at all, and order was disintegrating around me. All the witches were running around, accusing everyone else. The brief unity against Malkin had dissolved.

"*You* always hated her."

"Please. *You* took a chance to strike."

"*You* thought no one would notice. . . ."

Reluctantly but firmly, I took my mother's place. I raised my arms and shouted, "That is quite enough." The noise lowered as they looked at me and my hubris. "I don't know what's happened either, but there's no good hollering about it and waking the neighbors. Do you want to have old Mr. McGillicuddy call the police on you?" He had done it seven times so far, if you were counting, and I was.

No, nobody wanted that. "Down with the cops," shouted Valda. She grabbed her broom and hurried to the side door. A flash of pink smoke rose up from the middle of the garage as Claudette winked out of sight. There was a mad stampede from everyone else to follow Valda and get out the door.

And then everyone was gone and the room was down to three. Three black-robed witches who stood there looking stupidly at nothing. At least, I was. I could hardly process it. Sarmine gone. Gone where? If it wasn't my fault, or the fault of one of the other witches, then it was all Malkin, which was entirely believable. She had sent something that vanquished my mother. My mother! The most powerful witch I knew.

What would I do without her?

The door to the garage burst open and no one came through. I started to cross to it, numbly, and then I saw it carefully shut, the doorknob turning. A crack opened in the universe and a girl with chic tortoiseshell glasses and a determined chin poured herself into ours. At least, that's what my brain told me.

"Ugh, why does everyone use invisible eels?" said Sparkle's voice next to me. "I'm sorry, but they stink." She pulled off her mask, shaking out her silky hair.

The new girl looked daggers at the black-clad witch. "I don't see you inventing anything better, *Sparkle*."

Sparkle smirked. "Surprised you're not the only witch at our school, *Poppy*?"

Poppy turned up her nose. "I had my suspicions. I assume that's how you've stayed so popular."

"And *I* assume it's how you made class vice president."

"I would *never*—"

"Wait," I finally said. I recognized this girl now. She was a junior. "Exactly how many witches are there in our high school?"

Poppy shrugged. "Witches cluster where there are lots of magical ingredients."

"And more to the point, what were you doing skulking outside the garage?"

"I was *not*—"

"Girls, focus," said the motherly voice of the other witch. "Poppy, we need to take Camellia back to our house till we can figure out what happened."

I finally turned at that. Behind me was Lily, the witch who had spoken kindly to me at the door. And, of course, Poppy's had been the other voice I'd heard then, the reason Lily had held the door open extra time. My brain was catching up. But why?

"Really, Mom," said Poppy. "I'm sure the *newest coven member* will be fine here." There was acid on those emphasized words.

"Poppy," said her mother sharply. "Where are your manners?"

"Sorry," said Poppy, in a not-terribly-sorry fashion. She pulled out her phone and held it high, walking it around the garage like she was scanning for something. "Garage is clean," she said finally. "We're the only ones here."

While Poppy was checking our garage, Lily had picked up the push broom and was using the handle to delicately poke the cardboard box, which lay on the floor in a pile of packing peanuts. She flipped it over—there was a large hole burned out of the bottom. Some of the peanuts had melted to it, and I now noticed a disgusting burned-Styrofoam smell in with the swamp gas and sulfur. Lily went closer to the cauldron, used the handle of the broom to lift something out of the cauldron. It was a dull bronze object that looked a little like a gravy boat. Lily dropped the broom and stepped back. The gravy boat fell next to the cauldron with a clang.

It didn't mean anything to me, and from the looks of it, it

didn't mean anything to Sparkle or Poppy either. Poppy went back to folding her invisible robes. The material swung around in a disconcerting fashion, disappearing and reappearing parts of her. In contrast to her mother's flowy outfit, Poppy was wearing a button-down tucked into a skirt, with a neat belt. I don't know about you, but belt says "uptight honors student" where I come from. Overall that was a rather cute pink linen suit jacket and a plaid messenger bag, and her hair was pulled up into a curly bun. Rather dressed up for skulking, frankly. It was obvious she was the antithesis of her hippie mom, and equally obvious that she was not at all happy about the idea of me invading her home.

Come to that, I wasn't sure how happy *I* was about going to their house. On the one hand, there was the sweet, sweet relief of letting Lily take over. On the other, Poppy. In addition to the skulking, we weren't exactly in the same social circles, and that was always awkward.

"Honestly," I said, "I'll be fine here. I don't know what's happened, but . . ."

I trailed off. My mother was gone. "I'll be fine" didn't really cover it.

"Nonsense," said Lily. She wrested her gaze away from the fascinating gravy boat. "You are coming with us. Hikari, will you be all right?"

"I'll redo the wards around my grandfather's house," Sparkle reassured Lily. She looked straight at me, her dark eyes boring a message into me by sheer willpower. "It's safer if we all stay at home until this is resolved."

I swallowed. I knew she was thinking of Claudette and Leo.

"Good idea," said Lily.

Sparkle looked down at her feet, unusually hesitant. "I could use a ride though," she admitted. "Leo dropped me off."

"Of course, sweetheart," said Lily, and Poppy rolled her

eyes, presumably less at the fact of Sparkle not having her own transportation and more at the fact of being stuck in the same car with Sparkle. If so, that was remarkably similar to how I generally felt about Sparkle, so that was a good sign.

"I'll have to get Wulfie," I said. The werewolf pup was probably in my bedroom, eating my shoes and hoping I wouldn't find out. "Sparkle, could you round up his food? It's by the basement stairs."

"Dog food stinks," said Sparkle, but went to do it.

We locked up the RV garage and I ran to my room to get my backpack and a couple changes of clothes. I scooped up Wulfie and his dog bed and came down to find Lily, Poppy, and Sparkle all standing around the living room not talking to each other. Sparkle was holding the dog food with a grumpy face, Poppy was examining Sarmine's shelves of witch books, and Lily had a worried look that said she was still running through the events of the evening.

I locked up the house and we piled into Lily's station wagon. She turned on NPR, Sparkle gave directions, and nobody said anything else until we dropped Sparkle off at her grandfather's tiny place.

It was well past one a.m. at this point and after all the excitement I was wiped. Wulfie snored on my lap all the way to Lily and Poppy's house, over in the college district. I'd been up since my usual time of four a.m. to do Sarmine's early-morning chores, and sheer exhaustion was hitting me even while my mind was racing through the same unproductive channels.

My mother was gone.

She might be a witch, she might be terrible to live with, but . . . she was my mother. Our relationship had been improving. We were growing better at understanding each other. Oh, it all sounded so dry and factual, but the truth was, I was worried. Maybe I wasn't good at expressing that, even to myself, but it was true. I needed her back. She was a strange rock, but she was *my* rock.

I staggered inside their house and up some old wooden stairs after Poppy. Settled Wulfie into his dog bed on the floor, changed into the first thing I pulled out of my backpack and, despite the unfamiliar surroundings, fell fast asleep.

I woke Sunday morning with the uncomfortable realization that everything had gone to heck in a handbasket. I remembered right away where I was, but it wasn't my bed, wasn't my room, and that didn't happen very often.

Next to me, Poppy stirred. Sleepy brown eyes blinked open and she registered who I was. Her expression plainly read, *Ugh, what have I gotten myself into.* She rolled out of bed, presumably to get as far away from me as possible. Despite the fact that we had gone to bed at two a.m., after a disastrous evening, she was in a nice set of lavender-striped PJ bottoms and matching lavender tank top, her curly hair held neatly by a silky scarf. I was in a baggy off-white T-shirt gifted by one of Sarmine's suppliers ("Need Newt Nibbles? Try Newt's New *Newt Needums!*") and a pair of old gym shorts. If I knew anything about my hair, it was sticking up in pieces. I don't know that either of us was particularly encouraged by what we saw.

I stood, and we faced each other from opposite sides of the room. Sarmine gone. Who knows where. Can't unhex boyfriend. In charge of Wulfie. Stuck at the house of someone new. A junior. Wearing my Newt Nibbles shirt.

I'm usually good at making plans and getting going. But that morning I didn't know where to start.

Plus, it was totally awkward. I mean, I didn't know Poppy. I knew *of* Poppy. She was one of the popular smart crowd her year. You know them. Not the cheerleaders and jocks and rich kids. No, the ones who run for president and captain the debate team and run the school paper and so on. The ones who are Going Places and Know What They Want to Do with Their Lives and Have it All Together.

About the only thing I had figured out so far was that I didn't want to turn into my mother.

I looked at Poppy, still standing there, considering me. What I managed to say, with my usual grace and charm was, "Need a Newt Nibble?"

Poppy just *looked* at me, like I was the dumbest thing to be in her room in ages. I supposed I probably was. "Look, Camellia."

"Cam."

"Cam," she acknowledged. "History makes strange bedfellows."

"I'm sorry if I kicked," I said. "I'm only used to Wulfie—"

She steamrollered through that. "Stalin and Churchill. Hamilton and Jefferson. Sometimes two warring factions—or, at least, unfamiliar factions—have to join forces to Put Things Right."

"You mean, like, I'm Sherlock Holmes and you're Watson?"

"Let's get one thing straight," she said. "If there's a Sherlock, that's going to be me. You may be Watson if you like."

I wasn't sure I *did* like, but I was willing to set that aside if Poppy was going to help me find my mother. Poppy clearly was a student of True Witchery, like Sarmine was always pushing me to be. "I'm not sure where to start," I admitted. "I don't feel like I have any clues."

"We have loads of clues," Poppy admonished me. "Let's lay out what we know." She put on her vintage glasses and picked up her phone to take notes. "Begin."

Um. Okay. Start at the beginning. "There were thirteen witches in the RV garage last night," I said.

"And one standing just outside it," Poppy added.

"Fourteen," I agreed.

"The witch known as Sarmine Scarabouche . . ." said Poppy.

"Disappeared," I filled in.

"*Appears* to have disappeared," corrected Poppy.

"Oh god, you don't think she . . ." I couldn't bring myself to say it.

Poppy looked severely at me, her dark eyes framed by the heavy plastic rims. "No, I don't think she's dead," she said. "Witches are like cockroaches. Hard to kill them off. And your mother seems like one of the cockroachiest."

I was more relieved than you would expect to hear my mother described as "cockroachiest."

"Now look," said Poppy. "A spell was cast. Probably by Malkin, but possibly by one of the witches in the circle. I saw at least one of the Canadians raising her wand."

"And your mother," I said.

"And you, and several other witches," she said calmly. "And it would be just like any of them to capitalize on your mother's distraction and try to overpower her. Does she have any particular enemies?"

I just looked at Poppy.

"All of them. Right. So the first thing to do is start interviewing witches to obtain further clues. The problem, of course, is that it was dark and everyone was masked. I couldn't see very well through your garage window. I assume your mother keeps it well coated with dragon soot on purpose."

"Naturally," I assured her. Frankly, I assumed I had been supposed to clean it post-dragon and forgot, but I didn't say that. Poppy's certainty about everything made me feel out of my league.

She nodded. "Let's draw up a diagram. Can you tell me where the witches were located in the circle?"

"Located!" I said. "I don't even *know* all of them."

She looked at me, stunned. "This is the *Cascadia Coven*," and though she didn't say it, her tone clearly held the words "you idiot." "That's like not knowing everyone on the Supreme Court."

I didn't tell her that my knowledge of the Supreme Court might not be totally complete.

"They elected you as one of them. *You!*"

I was starting to get annoyed. "Maybe they should have handed out a citizenship test," I retorted.

"When I think of all the hours I've put in. . . ." Poppy took a deep breath. "Focus. The point is finding your mother. Now look. When you have a big school project, you break it down into steps, right?"

"I guess." I tried to stop feeling so prickly. Poppy was trying to help.

"So you don't need to know everyone. Just help me figure out who was standing next to your mother. That would have been a key place to cast a spell on her and miss the others."

I thought carefully back to the witches I had managed to identify. "I was on Sarmine's right," I said slowly. "And on her left . . ." A short figure with a cigarette. . . . "Valda," I said triumphantly. "And she's awful. Likes to drop pianos on people. But this . . . ?" A disappearing witch seemed too subtle for her.

"The first rule is to not rule out anybody," said Poppy. "Even you and me."

That took me aback for a minute. "Why *you*?"

"Oh, I have plenty of motive," Poppy assured me. "I'm applying to Larkspur next year, and one of the application requirements is to complete some impressive magical act. So if I could do something amazing, like disrupt a coven—"

"Wait, are you saying you *did* disrupt the coven?"

"No," she said patiently. "I'm just explaining to you how to think like a detective and not like a pile of mush."

Despite her exasperation, she didn't say it in a mean way, more like she had faith that I could overcome my natural tendency to think like a pile of mush. All the same, I stood up and started pacing. I guess I was kind of stressed out. Yet somehow I had to calmly solve The Mystery of the Missing Mother. It was easy for Poppy. She didn't have a stake in this. I took a deep breath. Then another. Then another and another and—

"Okay, are you hyperventilating on me?" said Poppy. "Here, sit down on the dog bed with Wulfie. Look, I'll solve it without you if you fall apart, so stop fussing."

"Easy for you to say," I said. I may have glared at her. "You don't have a stake in it."

"I do," she said promptly. "If disrupting a coven would be a grand magical act, then surely fixing it would be a greater one. Larkspur will love it."

"Not what I mean. It's. Not. Your. Mother. She's gone, and she's *never* gone, and she was going to fix my hex—"

"Hold up a minute," said Poppy. "What hex?"

I hung my head. "I accidentally hexed Devon last night. Before the coven meeting."

"And Devon is . . . ?"

"Boyf—New boy in school. Sings about butter."

"I've heard the stories. What did you do to him?"

"I've cast like ten spells on him in the last three months." I was gasping those short breaths again. "Trying to fix his stage fright. But the last thing I compounded turned him into a turnip—"

"You're killing me."

"And this time I invisibled him. And I can't visible him again. And he's stuck, and Sarmine was going to help fix it—"

"But she disappeared."

"And, I mean, everyone was raising their wands at the end." I couldn't bear it. "What if some of the not-so-terrible witches were casting a protection spell and I got in the way of it? That spell I cast on Devon was supposed to fix his stage fright, not make him invisible. What if something's wrong with . . . *me?*"

Poppy sucked air across her teeth. "You have a good point."

"I didn't want you to say that."

She began pacing her room while I tried to calm my breathing. Strange, but just talking it all out with Poppy seemed to help. Probably if I could have a good cry I'd feel even better, but I didn't want to cry in front of Poppy.

"Wand," she said, and held out her hand.

"Oh. Yes. Um . . ."

"It's not on you at all times?"

"I was *sleeping*." I rummaged through my backpack.

"I'll check it for hexes. I read of a case like this in *Tattyburr's Magicalle Historey.* Maybe somebody did it to *you.*"

Maybe somebody did this to me. I liked the sound of that. I didn't like the idea that I had an enemy, but I sure liked the idea that it wasn't my fault. My breathing finally slowed as I found the wand, and Poppy got her phone from the charger on her desk. It was a nice room, tidy, in blue and white and wood. One wall was covered in framed certificates.

Poppy grabbed a corner of a geometric blue rug in the middle of the room and began tugging it to the side. I bent to help her and saw that, beneath the rug, the shiny hardwood was stained and pocked, scuffed and worn. "This is where you do your spells, I take it?"

"Mom doesn't care what the floor looks like in the rest of the house, but I do," she said. "Okay, stand in the center, here, and hold your wand." She retrieved chalk from her plaid messenger bag and bent down to trace a pentagram around me.

"Is this going to hurt?"

Poppy was getting impatient again. "Haven't you ever been checked for hexes before? Don't you know anything?"

"For your information, I never wanted to be a witch," I snapped back. I was not going to be lectured by some girl about True Witchery, even if she was a junior. I already had my mother lecturing me.

Poppy stopped drawing the pentagram and stood, her temper rising. "You have the chance to study under one of the most powerful witches around and you don't even care?"

"I don't want any of it," I shot back. "I don't want invisible eels and endless lectures about baby rocs and I most especially don't want to be part of some stupid coven—"

"*Stupid?* Don't you know I'd give my left arm to be part of that coven? And here you are—"

"Oh yeah? So what were you doing there? I mean really."

Poppy folded her arms. "I was trying to get Malkin's old spot in the coven."

"You mean—"

"The spot you got."

"I didn't take it from you!"

"You sort of did, didn't you? Look. We had heard Malkin had disappeared. And good riddance. Her effects were getting sent around to people—like that pretty trick Sarmine got. That doesn't happen unless you had stuff set up to trigger on your death."

I shuddered.

"And you heard your mother. There are two ways to join the coven. A witch sponsors you into an empty seat and you are voted in. Or you take it in combat."

I felt sick. "It wasn't combat, not really."

"I thought if Malkin was really gone, then maybe we had a chance to move before someone worse was put in. That was the only reason Mom allowed me to come. Even she had to

admit that anyone else those goons would put up would be terrible. I promised to stay out of sight until the right moment.
And then—*you* were there."

This was all wrong. "I didn't take it from you on purpose! I
don't want to be part of the coven!"

"You have no idea what you're saying—"

"I hate witches!" I shouted. "I want to be having a normal
weekend like a normal person, eating doughnuts or something,
not checking for hexes and looking for disappearing mothers—"

She shouted right back over me. "That's what I mean! And
just because you're *Sarmine's* daughter, you get this special
place, and you don't deserve it!"

"But I didn't *ask* for it!" I stabbed the air with my wand. "I
hate all this responsibility! I don't want to be a witch!"

Wulfie started howling just as Lily stuck her head in to find
us facing off against each other. Her kind face looked both
worried that we weren't getting along and like she might shortly
order us to get along.

"How are you two doing?" she said, in a tone that said she
knew exactly how.

We lowered our wands and stepped apart.

"All right," I said.

"Fine," Poppy said.

"Thanks so much for taking me in," I said.

Poppy sent a sideways kick at me for sucking up.

"Oh, sweetheart, of course," said Lily. "Now, you two come
eat breakfast while I figure out what to do about this business."

We trailed Lily down the old wooden stairs, Wulfie padding
along behind us. Now that it was light, I could see that the
rest of the house was a well-loved, well-lived-in old craftsman
bungalow, completely stuffed with books and art. Lily's tastes
seemed to run to Americana, and particularly dolls; there
were dolls of all sorts hanging on the walls and propped up

on the bookshelves and mantel. A narrow shelf ran above the curving banister, displaying a collection of black fashion dolls from the sixties and seventies.

"Do you do something with dolls for a living?" I said politely, and Poppy snorted.

"It's just a collection," Lily said kindly. "I teach at the college."

"Her most popular class is called Feminism, Race Relations, and UFO Sightings: A Geopolitical Overview," Poppy put in helpfully. "What? It is."

We sat down at the old wooden kitchen table and Lily passed us a giant bag of rice puffs and a carton of skim milk.

"Isn't there anything with sugar?" groaned Poppy. She hopped back up to poke around the kitchen.

"No," said Lily shortly. She was studying her phone, which was sounding off intermittent text message beeps. "Cam, are you okay with that cereal? We also have bread, if you want toast."

"Much better than what we have at home," I said. Anything was better than homemade beetroot muesli. Poppy shot me a dirty look for sucking up again, but it was true. "I might potentially have a hexed wand, but at least I have breakfast." It felt better to admit it. Maybe I could downshift some of these problems onto an adult. Let the real witches deal with it.

Poppy glared. "I was trying to—"

Lily picked up my wand. She pulled out hers and touched mine with it, checking.

Poppy's face was horrified. "You're supposed to do that in a pentagram."

"Practical advice," agreed Lily. "And you should always follow it, just as I've taught you. But I could tell when I touched it that it wasn't hexed. I have seen hexed wands, and this is not one." She returned it to me.

A disgruntled Poppy closed the cabinet door rather sharply,

relieving her feelings. Lily's phone went off again. "Who are you texting?" said Poppy.

"Your aunt Jonquil," Lily said, her fingers flashing over the phone.

"I'm going to make more coffee," Poppy said. "Mom, do you want the last bit from the pot? . . . Mom?"

Lily's face was ashen. She hurried from the room, her skirts billowing behind her. We heard her clattering up the stairs, and then her voice calling back, "Put it in a travel mug, will you?"

Poppy hurried to obey. She didn't say anything, and I didn't know what to say. I shoveled cereal into my mouth. The coffee-maker percolated.

"Do you think it's something to do with last night?" I finally said in a low voice.

"Unless it's something about Grandma Iris," Poppy said. Her fingers laced around her mug, holding it tight. "But she's only a hundred and fifty; she's still pretty healthy."

"Iris," I said. "Poppy. Lily? *Jonquil?*"

Poppy looked down her nose at me. "Flower names are *very* common among witches," she said, and then added pointedly, *"Camellia."*

"Cam," I said. I hastened to add, "Not that I was criticizing. Just wondering how many more flower girls were going to show up in this story."

"This story?"

"The Story of Camellia and Poppy," I said grandly, "and How They Solved the Disappearance of Wicked Witch Sarmine."

"Poppy and Camellia."

"What?"

"If it's becoming a *story*," said Poppy, "I'm insisting on top billing."

"Then you have to write it out," I said. "I'm not going to be the sidekick of my own story."

"Not your story," whispered Poppy under her breath.

There was clattering on the stairs as Lily hurried down and into the living room. Rummaging noises emanated from that direction. Poppy and I converged on the living room to find Lily whirling about, stuffing things in a satchel and muttering. Poppy looked at the satchel. "Are you going somewhere?"

Lily stopped her examination of the dolls over the hearth. "Oh, Poppy. I can count on you girls to be safe here today— can't I? I know I can. At least your father's traveling, so he's likely out of harm's way—"

"I won't say a word to him," Poppy assured her.

"I know," she said. "Good," she said. "Now—stay inside, girls, okay?" She felt around behind the dolls. "Where did I hide those jackalope whiskers? Not that you would know."

Poppy crossed to the fireplace and picked up a doll sitting on the mantel. "In the pocket of her apron," she said, and handed the small packet to her mother.

Lily narrowed her eyes at Poppy. "Very volatile, jackalope whiskers. Keeping them safe."

"They were safe," said Poppy calmly. "Do you want me to tell you where the attar of roses and powdered claw are, too?"

"Hm," said Lily. "I suppose you'd better."

Poppy crossed to a doll on the bookshelf and procured a small vial from inside a zipper on her back, which kept her cotton fluff inside—and apparently, small vials, too. A third vial was stored in a tiny purse belonging to an old wooden doll. Poppy rolled this last one between her palms, considering. "Jackalope whiskers, attar of roses, and powdered claw. You're teleporting somewhere. You *hate* teleporting."

"You guys know how to *teleport*?" I whispered.

Poppy ignored this. "Is Grandma Iris okay?"

Lily turned. "Oh honey, she's fine," she said. "I didn't mean to make you worry. Now look. I texted your aunt Jonquil, and

I just heard back from her." Lily looked at me. "My sister knows something that might have a bearing on your mother's disappearance." My blood ran cold at that. I mean, obviously I didn't want Poppy's grandmother to be sick, but there had been a moment where I had been able to pretend that things with Sarmine weren't as dire as they seemed, you know? But Lily, who looked like someone unflappable, now looked worried. And it filled my stomach with dread.

"What does she know?" said Poppy.

Lily shook her head. "That's all I'm going to say, Poppy."

"I want to help." Poppy gestured at me. "This is our fight, too."

Lily raised a hand, cut off anything else Poppy might say. "I don't want you girls mixed up in this. I know you've studied and practiced in your room, Poppy, but this isn't one of your carefully planned out spells. The majority of the witches in that coven are repulsive, horrible people. Yes, sometimes magic can push people into doing good. But them? You're fighting a brick wall."

"You always told me never to balk at brick walls," returned Poppy. "Brick walls are made of bricks. And bricks can be—"

"Dismantled, I know," said Lily. Apparently this was an old argument. She sighed. "It's a lot of work to dismantle entitlement, backed up with decades of power. Jonquil thinks—" But there she pressed her lips tight together and cut off that sentence. "I expect you to renew the wards around the house, Poppy, just like we've practiced. I'll be back by tonight." She plucked the vial of powdered claw from Poppy's hand and added a tiny portion of it to a vial in her fanny pack. Then she turned, opening her arms to hug both of us. "Oh, girls. I don't know what I'd do without you, Poppy—and Cam, I know your mother feels the same about you." She squeezed us and let go. "I'll be back soon."

Lily hurried up the curving staircase to work her spell, leaving a mutinous Poppy behind.

I felt a little lost, honestly. I barely knew Lily, but she was an adult—and now she was going. She knew more spells than we did. Had more experience. And she thought there was still more danger on the way. Someone that protective wouldn't be leaving us alone if she didn't think it was absolutely necessary.

Upstairs, there was a clap of thunder. Rose-scented smoke drifted down the stairwell. It was way more dramatic than Claudette's spell. I didn't know if that meant Lily was going farther or that she was less practiced in teleportation.

"When Claudette did it, it didn't have nearly so much smoke," I said, before I thought.

Poppy might be angry at her mother, but that didn't mean I could slam her mother's witch skills. She gave me what might charitably be considered a stare of death. "My mother rarely teleports," she said. "It is *expensive*."

"Jackalope whiskers?" I whistled. "I *bet* they're expensive. Catch *me* working that spell." I was really on a roll.

"And you have some incredibly clever reason for that, from your extensive witch studies?"

It was hard to be pleasant when this know-it-all girl was getting up my nose. "I'm a vegetarian witch," I said. "There are certain ingredients I don't consider ethical."

"For your information, these whiskers came with a certificate of authentication that they were sourced from a jackalope who died of natural causes in the American Southwest."

"Ah."

Poppy snorted. But she looked satisfied that she had cowed me. "Come on," she said gruffly. "You ever renew wards before?"

4

Two Mothers Minus Two Mothers

I followed Poppy around the house, and Wulfie followed me. Poppy used her phone to scan the locks on every window and door. She saw me looking and grudgingly held out the phone so I could see the app. It had a little avatar on it—a cute black guy, his locs held back in a ponytail.

"I programmed it to detect traces of magic," she said. "Phone, tell me how well-warded this window is."

The avatar switched to a frowny face. "Thirty-eight. Percent," he said. The words came out in a robotic monotone with pauses in it, but I was still plenty impressed.

"Wow," I said. "All that and he's cute, too."

Her face lit up. "Mom said as long as I was making an avatar I should think carefully about what I wanted to convey with it, and then Dad said I should make it be a guy because they don't have any good role models in the witch community for studying hard and learning spells, because witch dudes usually give up and go into unicorn selling or whatnot. So I haven't even *made* the app and already it's all symbolic and important, but okay, I get that, that's the way it is around here. So I made a guy. And then Mom was all 'I didn't know you were going to make him look like *that*,' and Dad kind of coughed a bit, but there you have it. I said I didn't see why he couldn't be hot *and* be a good role model, and nobody had any answer to that."

I snort-laughed at Poppy's explanation. Maybe this girl was

someone I could be friends with, after all. If only we hadn't started out on the wrong foot. . . .

"I have to charge it with my wand every day or two," Poppy said. "I'd love to figure out a way to work some elemental power right into the electronics, but the phoenix feather made it run too hot and the dragon milk just soaked it. I lost a perfectly good phone that way. Thirty hours of babysitting down the drain."

Poppy set down the phone on the windowsill. The delight in her face dimmed as she switched over to concentrating on the warding spell. She carefully measured ingredients from her messenger bag straight onto the screen of her phone, using a teaspoon and a pair of tweezers. The app drew yellow circles around her ingredients, turning green when she had measured out the correct amount. In one case, the circle started flashing red. She didn't look at me as she tweezed several grains of powder back off the phone and into the correct vial in her bag.

"Wow, that's precise," I said. She shot me a look like I was being sarcastic, but I wasn't. I could see how devoted she was to True Witchery. Sarmine would have loved having her for a daughter.

Carefully, Poppy got out her wand and touched it to the phone. "You don't have to watch me like I'm going to mess this up," she said.

"I'm not," I protested.

She paused, still not doing the spell. "I'm sure Sarmine has you doing stuff like this all the time."

"She tries to make me," I agreed. "Like last month she filled my room with a mini blizzard and then left her voice on re-peat, shouting the anti-snow spell at me. I had to dig the ingredients out of the drifts."

"Figures," said Poppy.

"Wait, are you saying you've never done this spell?"

She glared at me through her glasses. "It is a very simple spell, and I have done it many times." In a lower voice she muttered, "One of the few I'm allowed to do." She moved her wand through the ingredients and blew the spell onto the window.

Finally she tapped the screen on her phone and a recorded voice spoke the necessary magic words. That seemed clever to me, too. No need to worry about the correct pronunciation.

"What now?" she said suspiciously.

"Automated Witchery is the name of my new band," I said.

She harrumphed and went back to her phone. The avatar popped up, and this time when she scanned the window he said, "Warding. Fully operational."

We moved around the house, Poppy doing her carefully measured spell at each window. More than once I caught her checking her phone for texts, her lips pinched up with worry. I wished we didn't both have to worry about our mothers.

"So, your dad's traveling, huh?" I said, trying to distract her with small talk.

She raised her eyebrows over her phone. "What, did you think he, like, ran off on us or something?"

"No," I floundered. My small talk was terrible. Back to square one.

She sniffed. "For your information, my dad is a poli-sci professor. He's gone this week because he's also a special education advisor to the governor and they had to fly to D.C. It's a big deal for him, and we are *not* going to interrupt him." She looked down at her phone. "Also, he's a regular human, and you've got to work extra hard to keep them safe."

I groped for something to say. "So your mom's been appearing to age along with your dad?"

"She doesn't seem to mind. Catch *me* doing that. I'm going

to marry someone with witch blood. Won't have to make that choice. Or lose him."

I nodded. Living twice as long as everyone else did have some drawbacks. I watched in silence as she measured and combined and blew.

"One hundred. Percent," confirmed the avatar after each spell. "Warding spell. Fully operational."

Finally we worked our way back down to the kitchen. I dug some dog treats out of my backpack for Wulfie and he wolfed them down. It was ten thirty. The idea of staying here all day, just . . . *waiting* to see what Lily found out, was equal parts appealing and terrible. Appealing because Lily was a skilled witch, an adult, and, frankly, we were two teenagers, one with a lot of knowledge and little practical experience and the other with . . . well, neither. Although I did have the turnip spell down pat.

Lily was right—we were safer at home. Besides, the last time I had felt compelled to try to stop some witches, I had known that Sarmine was there, that she had my back. My mother might be irritating and cranky and overfond of horrible punishments, like magically making all my shoes two sizes too small, but she would not have let me actually get destroyed in an epic witch battle.

I had no such illusions about the other witches of the coven.

At the same time, I might go crazy just sitting here, waiting. And Lily was gone, and my mother was missing. Time was of the essence, and Poppy and I were better than nothing.

I looked sideways at Poppy, who was carefully cleaning her phone screen with a small blue cloth. How would she feel about her big detective plans now?

"Come on," said Poppy. She was giving me a mutinous, *I dare you* expression. "Who are we going to go visit first?"

"Oh, thank goodness," I said. "I was afraid you were going to obey."

Poppy rolled her eyes. "And leave this whole mess in the hands of my mother and mopey Aunt Jonquil? They're not even going to *talk* to the other witches. I don't care what Jonquil thinks she knows, I don't see how teleporting across the country is going to help with what happened last night. Besides, if we don't go now, then my mom will get home and stop us from going at all."

"She seems awfully protective for a witch," I ventured.

"Because Grandma Iris was *not* protective and my mom blames her for their youngest sister's death as a teenager."

"Ah," I said. "I'm sorry."

"Long before I was born," said Poppy. She slung her plaid messenger bag over her shoulder. "Look, I'm not an idiot. We're probably in over our heads, too. But I'm not going to stay here. When you have power, any power, no matter how beginning a witch you are"—and here she looked at me, but somehow I didn't take offense—"you have to use it."

"That's remarkably similar to the conclusion I was reaching," I agreed.

Valda lived in a small town about an hour away from us. I had wondered how we would find her address, but Poppy said anything was findable on WitchNet if you did a little digging, and after some creative sleuthing of social media, clickbait articles ("Five Weirdest Backfiring Spells!"), and news ("Witch Caught in Avalanche After Weird Spell Backfires"), she turned up the address to one V. Valda Velda. We let Wulfie out into the fenced-in backyard, with some water and a rubber bone to gnaw on, and we set off.

I wouldn't call the drive there particularly inspiring. Poppy asked me a number of questions about my abilities as a witch. I didn't get the sense that she was impressed by my answers. She still seemed pretty ticked at me getting to be the chosen one of the coven, and I didn't blame her. It would suck to spend your whole life working for something and have someone else who didn't care about it be handed it on a spoon.

After Poppy finished cross-examining me, I stared out the window and worried. So both parts of the drive were equally great.

Valda lived at the end of a dead-end street. In contrast to the normal-looking houses of Sarmine and Lily, Valda's was the first I'd seen that looked like it belonged to a storybook witch. It was a rickety old Victorian with sagging wooden trim and at least five turrets. The whole thing was shrouded in ivy and gloom. Since I knew Valda enjoyed riding around on a broom and favored brute-force methods of witchery like dropping magical anvils on people, I maybe wasn't too surprised.

There was a wrought iron fence, and weeds grew knee high behind and through it. It was a cool, drizzly spring day. I had pulled on my jeans from last night and borrowed one of Poppy's suit jackets. This one was bright yellow. I pulled it tighter as I waded through the weeds to the gate.

"Must not be a homeowners' association around here," sniffed Poppy.

The gate was locked. "Should we ring?"

"I think, if she did do something to Sarmine, then our only hope is surprise," pointed out Poppy. She pulled out her phone and scanned the lock. "Phone, identify spell," she said.

"What good will that do?" I said dutifully. Maybe I really was the sidekick of Poppy's story. Of course, the main character is the usually the one things happen to, and so far *I* was the one with the missing mother and the hexed boyfriend.

Poppy hadn't even gotten to take part in the coven meeting. I cheered up.

"I've been compiling a database of known spells," said Poppy, "which includes as many antidotes as I've uncovered through my research. After he identifies the spell, he theoretically can spit out the spell to reverse it."

The avatar smiled in success and said, "A Verie Moderne and Clever Magnetized Lock."

"Phone, supply antidote," Poppy said.

In his monotone, the avatar rattled off a list of ingredients, which Poppy combined on her phone screen and then blew onto the gate. She touched the wand to the lock and it immediately clicked.

"Technology for the win," she said, a bit smugly, pushing open the gate. It swung inward with a creaking sound.

"I guess we'll go in," I said, taking a step forward.

"Wait," said Poppy, holding her arm in front of me.

A spiked cannonball fastened to a chain came swinging out of nowhere and passed within an inch of my nose.

"Booby traps," said Poppy.

"I should have known," I muttered.

My heart was racing as we made our way up the walk. I had been dumb to think that Valda, of all people, *wouldn't* have booby traps. It was exactly the sort of thing she would enjoy doing. Probably a piano would fall on my head next. I looked up in the sky, checking for pianos.

"At your feet!" shouted Poppy.

I looked down to find a small cartoony bomb had sprouted in the yard in front of me. Its wick was sizzling down.

Poppy yelled at her phone: "Anti-bomb spell! Phone, find anti-bomb spell!"

"Ye Olde Aunty Mame Spell?" said her phone.

"B . . . O . . ."

"A Fancye Beehive Spelle for Manye Bees?"

"*Bomb!*"

"A Verie Explosive Bomb Spelle. Take one pinch cayenne powder—"

I had a water bottle in my backpack. I dumped the entire contents on the cartoon bomb. It fizzled out and then melted into a pile of goo.

Poppy and I looked at each other, panting.

"Technology for the win?" I said, then immediately regretted being snotty. Poppy looked despondent. "It would have worked if you'd had more time," I offered.

"They don't give you time during combat," she said.

"Epic witch battle," I said.

"What?"

"Sounds less scary than combat," I said. "I can handle the idea of an epic witch battle."

Poppy rolled her eyes.

We pressed on, up to the door. It was a massive black door, flanked by diamond-pane windows. I reached for the doorknob and then stopped. See, I could learn not to be a total idiot. "It's probably electrified or something," I said.

Poppy nodded and got out her phone again. She scanned the doorknob with the app.

"Ye Olde Freezing in Place Spelle," the avatar informed us.

"We won't be able to let go of the doorknob," translated Poppy. "Phone, supply antidote."

"One pinch powdered wasabi. One pinch powdered egg. One pinch powdered pixie wing."

"Do you have all those?" I said.

"Yes," she said. "But I don't want to spend next weekend at the creek gathering more sloughed-off pixie wings. I think we should try the doorbell."

The doorbell was large and prominent. So large and

prominent that we simultaneously looked at each other and said, "Booby trap."

It was the first moment we'd done anything in tandem. But I ruined it by saying, "Jinx! You owe me a Coke." Poppy ignored this.

"Okay, no doorbell," she said. She fiddled with her phone.

"Different spell?" I said.

"Megaphone app," she said. Into the phone she said, "Valda, come out. I'm Lily's daughter and this is Sarmine's daughter." The amplified sound boomed around the yard.

"She knows me," I muttered.

"We just want to ask you a few questions," continued Poppy. "Then you can go back to—"

"To dropping anvils on kittens or whatever it is you do," I put in. The megaphone app picked it up pretty well. My words echoed back: "Do-ooh-ooh."

Poppy wrenched the phone away. "You are such a dingbat."

"Valda, come out now. We have cigarettes for you!" I hollered into the phone.

Poppy looked at me as though I were nuts. Which I guess I was, but sometimes your nerves get the best of you. "That is not how you do it, Dr. Watson."

"I suppose you know best, Poppy Sherlock."

The door swung open to reveal the familiar short, stout form of Valda standing there. With the familiar stench of Valda from the lit cigarette in her hand.

"You don't *really* have cigarettes for me, do you?" she said in her grouchy rumble. "I'm running low, and it's so tedious to rub the invisible eels over the broom to fly to the store."

"You could walk," I said under my breath.

Valda coughed contemptuously at me.

"Look," said Poppy. "We're here to talk about last night."

"Not interested," said Valda. She made to close the door.

Poppy stuck a foot in. "Five minutes, Valda."

"Or I'll turn you into a turnip," I said. Poppy shot me a funny expression. It probably wasn't that she was impressed with me, so it must be that she was annoyed that I was taking away the fun of letting her run the show.

"Oh, very well," Valda said with bad grace, and turned away. Poppy grabbed the door before it could close and latch us out, and we trooped into Valda's weird old witch mansion. It absolutely reeked of cigarette smoke. "Back in my day, girls didn't come around pestering their elders," she said. "And definitely not at lunchtime. They had better manners than to interrupt meals."

There was a TV tray set up before one of those ancient, enormous, cube-shaped TVs. The picture was frozen in the middle of an episode of *Demon Hunter*, a trashy soap that Sarmine also enjoyed. And okay, fine, I did too.

"That's the episode where Maria-Elena and Felicia elope to Paris," said Poppy. It seemed like it was everyone's guilty pleasure.

"Well, don't ruin it for me," Valda said. "Get on with it."

"So, Sarmine disappeared last night," I said.

Valda humphed. "And I suppose you think I did it?"

"The thought had crossed our minds," I admitted. "You were standing right next to her."

"How did you know?"

I nodded at the cigarette in her hand. "You're the only one who smokes."

"Hmph," she said. "Back in my day—"

"There were ashtrays everywhere and hostesses offered you boxes of cigarettes when you walked in the door," I said. "But the point is . . ."

"I did not hex your mother," Valda said. "Not that I wouldn't enjoy doing it, mind you. But frankly, it would be too much work. If I tried to hex your mother, she'd fire back, and then we'd be having a battle that nobody wins, and after we're covered in warts and slime I'd still be stuck at the stupid witch coven making stupid laws all night when I just want to get back to *Demon Hunter*." She cast an eye at the TV. "They're getting to the point where Felicia's finally going to dump Zolak."

I didn't know about Poppy, but I believed Valda. Whatever her faults, she would probably come right out and say if she had done it. She didn't believe in beating around the bush. "Do you have any idea who might have done it, then?" I said. "Someone who might dislike Sarmine?"

Valda laughed. "You innocent. *Everyone* dislikes Sarmine."

Poppy snickered, and I glared at her.

I raised my wand threateningly. "Look, Valda, I'd rather you be helpful right now."

Valda shoved my wand out of the way. "She's made more enemies than I have, and that's a lot. The problem is, she's changed over the years. She used to be sensible about things. So when Malkin's mother recruited her to the coven several decades ago—"

"Malkin's *mother*?"

"Well, she recruited Malkin and Sarmine straight off, see? After two elderly witches kicked it under mysterious circumstances involving poisoned mints at a bridge game. Esmerelda and I were brought on later. And Sarmine fell right in line with their goals."

I couldn't imagine Sarmine "falling in line" with anybody, but I definitely could imagine that her ethical code was more flexible than mine and had involved things I would never agree to. "Go on," I said.

"The forties had been a real problematic time, you understand. No one could decide who owned the rights to shifters and weres and so on in their area. By the time Sarmine and

Malkin and Esmerelda and I were in college, things were becoming more sensible. But it still took some activism. Your mom's always been an activist, you know."

"I know."

Valda spread her hands. "So she's the one who spearheaded the laws to divide up the assets fairly. If you laid claim to a shifter, then some other witch couldn't come along and start fighting you. The shifter was yours, fair and square."

I was feeling sick, and Poppy looked nauseous. "You mean . . ." I swallowed. "My mother was in favor of treating people like . . . like that?"

"Hey, she did a good thing," said Valda. "There had been bloodbaths. Now everyone was protected."

"You mean the *witches* were protected," said Poppy.

"Exactly," agreed Valda. "But no sooner had she worked with Malkin to get those laws in place than—"

"Than *what*?" I said, expecting to hear some new atrocity.

"Than she met Jim."

My dad. I tensed, wondering what Valda would say next.

"And what, she changed overnight?" said Poppy. "A love story?"

Valda snorted. "No. But she did change. Became a thorn in everyone's side. Everyone who'd been her ally was now her enemy. And she didn't have much of anyone left to become a new ally. A few hippies, like Jim."

"But you still hang out with her," I said.

"Oh, well. If witches stopped associating with everyone they disagreed with we'd never see anyone at all," Valda said candidly. "There's not a single witch that wouldn't do me in if they had the opportunity, and vice versa. And now—" She broke off. "What was that?"

An ominous rumble was coming from upstairs.

Poppy shrieked as a diamond windowpane shot out of one

of the front windows and streaked past her face, barely missing her. *Pop pop pop* went the rest of the window, and three more diamonds shot themselves at us.

"Is your house firing at us?" I shouted at Valda.

"Thinks there's an intruder—"

"Tell it we're not intruders!" shouted Poppy.

"You are, though," Valda shouted back as she fumbled for her spells. All the lights were going on and off and fan blades were spinning. Probably next they would—yes, there the fan blades went, detaching and shooting themselves toward us. The hall clock was adding to the din, striking noon: *bong bong bong* . . .

"It's like all your defenses are backfiring on you!" I shouted.

Valda whirled. "What did you say?"

"All! Your! Defenses!" I hollered, but then the rumbling grew louder.

"The stairs!" shouted Valda. She gave up on her ingredients, grabbed her broom, and flew out the first window that had popped itself apart.

Leaving me and Poppy standing there like idiots, wondering what was going to come down the stairs.

I ran to the door and tried to wrestle it open. But I realized, too late, that it had rearmed itself. My hand froze to the doorknob. I couldn't move.

"Move!" shouted Poppy, and I turned to see my doom hurtling down the front stairs, straight at me.

5

Hurtling Doom

It was one of those moments where your life passes before your eyes. Or it would, if that sort of thing actually happened. Maybe it only happens in books. I'll tell you what did happen. Everything got all slow. And yet it didn't stop the giant boulder from coming at me like a freight truck. I was about to get smashed into the door that I couldn't let go of.

I didn't know any spells to stop a boulder. Valda surely did, but she had bailed on us. I cursed her. I cursed Sarmine. I cursed the door. I started to curse the boulder, but then I heard another voice shouting something about wasabi—saw a powder dazzle my hand—a flash of light—a person pulling me the other way, away from the door, out of the path of the boulder.

I tumbled down hard, cracking my elbow on the floor and my shoulder on the coffee table. Poppy went into the TV tray, and Valda's tomato soup went all over us. I didn't know it was tomato soup at first, though. I blinked hard through red haze as I watched the boulder splinter that door into smithereens and roll right out the front.

"Ugh," said Poppy as she blotted tomato soup out of her hair. "I literally just washed it. Totally wasted on a coven I couldn't go to and the stupidest haunted house in the world."

"Poppy . . ." I said. I fumbled for words but could only come up with the basic ones. "You saved my life."

"Yeah, well." Her fingers were unsteady as she rubbed her

glasses on her shirt. "I had just looked that antidote up, you know."

"And you *did* it, when it counted."

"I guess so." A slow smile crept onto her face. "You think that counts as an epic witch battle?"

"The first of many," I said dryly.

Poppy flipped open her messenger bag to make sure nothing was broken, and then we hurried out of the ruined house. It was a disaster on the outside, too. Orange smoke was pouring from the upstairs windows. The chimney was disassembling itself brick by brick, each one popping off and crashing to the grass. We ran toward the front gate, which had turned into a gate made of snakes, but was at least hanging open so we could carefully squeeze through.

We stood outside Valda's fence, panting.

"The snakes don't look too happy," I said. "Should we help them?"

Poppy ran her app over them. "They'll revert soon enough," she said. "And I don't want to stay here any longer than necessary. Let's get home and take a shower."

"Dibs on the shower," I said, but Poppy shot me a look of death and I shut up. "Dibs on shotgun?"

"Dear god, what is that?" said Poppy.

"I don't want to know," I said as I turned. A perfectly enormous hailstorm of roofing nails was flying at us.

"Into the car!" shouted Poppy. We dove for it and slammed the doors. A rain of nails hit the car—*tink tink tink*—the first few denting the metal and bouncing off. Then *screech, screech*, as more of them slammed so hard they plunged into the car and stayed there. Poppy slammed her foot on the accelerator and we tore down the street. "Still after us?"

I risked a glance behind me. A cloud of metal nails obscured the back window. I figured it must be a rhetorical question. "Go around the corner," I said. "Maybe we'll lose them."

But the nails kept following, through the streets. Poppy weaved and dodged cars—and blew through several yellow lights—until finally we were on the back highway between the two towns, which was relatively straight and empty. It had only been a couple minutes on city streets but it had seemed like an hour.

Poppy's breathing calmed, although neither of us were what you'd call calm about being tracked by seven thousand roofing nails. "Do you know any spells to stop a cloud of nails?" she said.

"Not unless you think the pear self-defense spell would work," I said.

"Very funny," retorted Poppy, but she was concentrating on the road while a storm of nails followed us, and I forgave her.

I breathed. "Okay. Let's break this down into smaller pieces. When we stop, all those nails are going to catch up with us."

"Thank you, Dr. Watson."

"If we can't stop them, could we at least make them softer somehow?"

Poppy concentrated while she drove at that insane speed. I was glad there was hardly anyone on the back highway. "There's a super-cold freezing spell on my phone that I have the ingredients for," she said. "You'll have to cast it."

"I don't think making them cold will slow them down," I said. "They're not alive."

"It encases them in ice," Poppy explained. "It'll be like a hailstorm, but at least they won't pierce us or the tires. Anyway, do you have a better idea?"

"Ice it is," I said. I picked up her tomato-smelling messenger bag and her phone's avatar directed me through the correct measurements.

"Make sure you get the orange powder, not the red," Poppy said.

"Because . . . ?"

"Instead of frozen nails we'd get superheated ones. Slide right through steel like it was butter."

I shuddered. My hands may have shaken a little as I put the compound together, but I tried to keep that from Poppy.

"We don't have a sunroof," Poppy said, "so you're going to need to lean out the window and throw that powder all over the nails. The avatar will give you a sentence to shout, but this one needs a witch's mental oomph. You have to think hard about where you want that powder to go."

"Easy as pie," I muttered. "All right, then." I took a breath and stirred the ingredients in my hand with my wand, as Poppy directed. Rolled down my window, fist closed tightly over the powder. "Okay. Give me the sentence." I stuck my face out and looked back. There was a nail a few inches from my nose. "Uh, and Poppy? Don't slow down."

"There's a stop sign up ahead!" she shouted at me.

"What?"

"Ick vella du schtott farum!" said the avatar.

"Ick vella du schtott farum!" I shouted, concentrated hard on the circumference of the nails, and flung my powder in their general direction. FYI, it's hard to fling powder over a whirl-wind of nails when everything's moving sixty miles an hour.

"In, in," shouted Poppy.

I turned to see the stop sign rapidly approaching us—and my face. Beyond that, a semi, lumbering through the inter-section. I flung myself back into the seat as Poppy slammed on the brakes.

I ducked. She ducked.

A tremendous hailstorm hit the car. A thunderous

drumming—the roof, the sides, and then, with a tremendous *crack . . .*

"The back window!" Poppy shouted. "Stay down!"

"I wasn't going to look!" I shouted back. And then yelped, as a hailstone bounced off the backseat and hit my elbow. The car was a station wagon, so the trunk and the backseat slowed the hailstones down. Still, I could feel the temperature dropping as ice filled the back and the chill surrounded us. I huddled in Poppy's tomato soup–covered jacket.

Slowly the *crash-bang* died away as the hailstones rolled to a rest. The semi rolled past, the driver not even looking back.

We got out and looked at the car. The back windshield was smashed in. The trunk and backseat were filled with hailstones. I picked one up, marveling at the roofing nail embedded in the middle of it. Poppy had saved us, but the car was a disaster. Also, it smelled like tomato soup.

"Your mom is going to kill us," I said. "What does she do to you for things like this? Sarmine would probably turn me into a solar panel for a week."

Poppy eyed me strangely. "She's not that sort of person," she said. "But she will make us clean it." She looked down at the ice. "We should do that right away, before everything melts and ruins the car."

"We should have gloves," I corrected. "Look at the broken windshield. Plus, we can't leave that stuff here on the road."

"We can't drive like this, either. We'll get pulled over."

"Oh," I said.

"I have an illusion holo I made a while ago, specifically for this car," she said. "It doesn't fool anyone with witch blood, but it'll fool the human police. Hang on while I reactivate it." She pulled out her phone and scrolled to a picture of the car in its pristine state. With her wand, she seemed to draw the holo out of her phone. The holo drifted slowly over the car until it looked like new again—freshly washed, even.

"The glass and nails are still there," Poppy cautioned me. "Blink a couple times and you can see it both ways."

I squinted until I saw what she meant. "That's impressive," I said, sincerely.

"Yeah, well." She sighed. "This holo I can do. I had plenty of time to sit and work on it. But *you* defused the bomb when it was necessary."

"*You* got me loose from the doorknob," I said. "That was an adrenaline-filled kind of situation."

"I'm afraid there's going to be more of those," she said.

"Yeah."

Rather glumly, we got back in the car and Poppy started the engine. "Okay, back to work." I could tell her voice was trying to be cheerful and positive. "What did we learn?"

"Everyone hates my mother."

There was silence for a minute. I pulled my phone out and turned it over and over, thinking how much I'd like to see one of Sarmine's all-cap texts right about now. Or even just to be able to text with Jenah and Devon like a normal person.

"You're fidgeting," said Poppy.

"My mom won't let me have a real phone," I said. I held it out. "I mean, it looks real enough. But it only connects to WitchNet and the witch phone system. I can't call Devon and see if he's looking any better. Er. More visible."

Poppy gave me the side-eye. "Are you saying you want to borrow my phone to talk to your boyfriend?"

"Maybe?"

She passed it over. "Don't do anything dumb like break it."

I put in Devon's number and listened to it ring. No answer. Tried twice more for good measure. Finally I passed the phone back to Poppy.

We drove a little more, and then she said, as if it were being dragged out of her, "Do you want to swing by his house?"

"Can we?"

"I can try to fix him."

"Oh, Poppy!"

"I don't know that I can," she said gruffly. "Don't get too excited yet."

"Thank you," I said. There was a lot of sincerity in that.

"Mm," said Poppy, and we drove the rest of the way in silence.

Devon's parents were backing out of the driveway when we arrived. His mom leaned out the driver's side window and smiled and waved at me.

"Hi, Mrs. Maguire," I said. "This is my friend Poppy. Is Devon home?" I tried to smile and look like Devon would totally be happy to see me, as usual.

"He's up in his room, sweetie," she said. "Been working on some big project all day." She hit the garage door opener button and it went up, revealing a mountain of boxes and stuff that no car would ever fit among. "You kids have fun. We'll be back by dinner."

"Thanks," I said, and waved.

"Why are they looking at the car?" Poppy whispered to me. "They're not witches are they?"

"I think they're looking at us," I said. We were still drenched in tomato soup. I wished I didn't have to visit Devon looking like I had been in a vegetarian bloodbath. But then it finally occurred to me that I didn't. "Unicorn spritzer," I crowed, and retrieved it from my backpack. I sprayed both of us, and immediately we were restored to fresh, pressed, and clean. My shirt still said Newt Nibbles, though. Can't fix everything.

"Not bad," admitted Poppy. "My mom won't keep it in stock

because she hates Ulrich. Do you mind if I spritz the car before I come in? You probably want to see Devon first anyway."

"Fair trade," I said. More cheerful now that I was clean, I entered the garage, walking between all the boxes and junk toward the back door.

I took a deep breath, knocked once, and gently pushed open the door to the kitchen.

No Devon. But would I know?

I moved through the kitchen, took a left toward the stairs. The sounds of his guitar drifted down from his bedroom. "Devon?" I called up. The music stopped.

From far off I heard a door open, and then I saw a pair of jeans and a shirt walk down the stairwell. They stopped near the bottom.

I wrinkled my nose. "Still invisible, huh?"

"Yeah."

I wasn't sure what to say after that. "Working on your music?" I ventured.

"Yeah."

"You've been doing some recordings, haven't you?" I said. "Music videos to put online?"

The empty clothes *looked* at me. I could feel it.

"You can't do that now," I said. "Right."

"Writing a new song," the clothes said. There was silence for a moment, and then he said, "So, your mom . . . ?"

"Ah. Good news and bad news."

The clothes slumped. "Give it to me."

"She said she would come fix you—"

"Yeah?"

"But she disappeared."

"Invisibled, or . . ."

"Gone."

His sleeves tensed. "Those witches?"

I shrugged tightly. "Probably."

The clothes moved at that. Came all the way down the stairs. The shirtsleeves came up and wrapped me in a hug. "I'm so sorry," the shirt collar whispered in my ear.

There was a moment then when I thought I could just forget all my worries and relax into the nothing's arms. Imagine we were finally having that date.

But Devon released me and moved away. The clothes grew stiff and angry. "You get into all these dangerous situations and I can't even protect you. What good am I?"

"You're a musician, not a witch," I said. "I'm the one who's upset I didn't protect *you*." I took a step closer, hoping he would return to my arms.

"And a musician is good for . . ."

"Other things?" I suggested. I waggled my eyebrows, but he didn't seem to take my meaning.

"Entertaining five people having pizza on a Friday night," he scoffed. "At least you can *do* things with your talents."

"Whee," I said. "Look what's already happened to you from witch talents, and that was from a witch who *likes* you."

The clothes slumped at this reminder and turned toward the stairs. "I guess I'll have to try that costume after all," he said. "Jenah texted me that she had a wig and stage makeup I could use. I better get going before my parents get back."

I sighed as he moved away. No invisible kissing for me.

I squelched that thought. That was a seriously unethical take on the situation. You don't go around invisibling boyfriends just so you can invisibly kiss them.

"Before you go," I said to the clothes, "I met a new witch. Well, it's Poppy Jones, if you know her. She's going to try to unhex you first, okay? Then at least we'll have tried everything."

"Couldn't hurt," he said, and he came back. "Tell her I'll wait for her in the kitchen."

"Okay."

"I'll be the invisible one."

"Ha-ha."

I turned just as Poppy came around the corner from the kitchen. She tossed the half-empty bottle of unicorn spritzer to me. "So where's—Oh. Oh, wow."

I made a face, and Poppy hastily put on a calm, competent expression.

"We'll get this figured out," she assured us. She ran her phone over the empty clothes. "Phone, tell me what spell is on here."

There was a long pause. The avatar switched to a puzzled face. "Spell not found in database," he said.

"I didn't make it up!" I said. "I was trying something I found in one of Sarmine's books. It used crushed watermelon seeds, saffron, and unicorn spritzer."

Poppy held up a hand to forestall me. "Phone, tell me what ingredients were used in this spell."

"I just told you—"

"Crushed watermelon seeds, saffron, unicorn spritzer—" said the avatar.

"See?"

"—and an inferior packet of Parmesan cheese."

My eyes went wide. "The cheese. I got it all over my hands. . . . I mixed the ingredients in my hands. . . . Ohmigod."

Poppy raised her eyebrows. She looked like she was barely holding in the words "Always mix on a clean surface" with a supreme effort.

"I know, I know," I said.

"Can you ask that guy if he knows an antidote?" said Devon.

"I programmed him," Poppy explained. "He only knows what I've put in the database."

"Ah," Devon said. "I thought maybe there was a help desk for witches."

"I wish," I said.

"Don't give up yet," said Poppy. "I have some generic anti-dotes stored in here. Let me try them."

"Technology for the win?" I said.

"I hope so," said Poppy.

I trudged outside to the car and tried to lose my worries in the work. The unicorn spritzer had removed all the dirt and some of the scratches, but it hadn't removed the ice, glass, or nails. The ice was melting, and I worked faster on the seat areas, trying to get it out the door before it soaked Poppy's seats. Occasionally I forgot to look with my witch eyes, cut myself on an invisible nail or bit of window glass, and swore.

I had finally swept the last bit of glass from the car and had started filling Devon's trash can when Poppy came out. I straightened, the dustpan falling from my hands. "Did you . . . ?"

But I could tell from her face that she hadn't. "I can't believe I'm saying this, but that's a powerful invisible spell you did," Poppy said. "Invisible eels (A) stink and (B) wear off quickly. This is seriously stuck on him. If you can replicate what you did, you've got something that any witch would die for."

"To be permanently invisible?" I said despairingly. "No one would actually want that."

She looked at me like I was nuts. "It invisibled his clothes, too, remember? Think of it. *Invisible cloaks that don't smell like eels.* I bet you anything this spell is your ticket into Larkspur." She saw my expression and held up her hands. "Or your way to make a million bucks, if that's what you'd rather."

"I *wouldn't* rather," I said. "Not any of it." What if I had invisibled Devon permanently? I could scarcely imagine it. Never going swimming with your friends again. Going through tubs of peachy-tan makeup. And just think of the first time he tried to visit the dentist with invisible teeth!

Poppy must have seen my face, because she said, more kindly, "Just because I can't get it off doesn't mean it's not gettable. Hexes have never been a particular study of mine. Someone will know how to get this off. One of our mothers."

"Which mother? The mother who vanished or the mother who disappeared?"

I expected Poppy to bite back at that, but she merely sighed and said, "Come on. I'll help you scoop the glass into their trash can."

Lily wasn't home yet when we arrived. Poppy checked her phone—no texts or missed calls. That was good as far as fixing the car went, bad as far as having a parental figure around went. I wiped Wulfie's paws and let him inside.

Poppy searched her app for the spell to take dings out of cars. "This is going to be tedious," she said. "We have to cast it on every single dent."

"Why can't anything be simple?"

"Let's stop calling on witches and maybe that will help," said Poppy.

I nobly refrained from reminding her that it was her idea to see if Valda could tell us anything. Besides, she was only trying to help. "We're no closer to solving anything," I said. "And I still have to study American history for tomorrow's quiz."

Poppy perked up at that. "What are you up to?"

"Uh, things and causes leading into World War Two something something?" I said. "I'm so-o-o lost it's not funny." They had recently fired Mrs. Taylor, who let us sit around watching videos, and parceled her classes out among the other teachers.

Saganey had taken over my class, and in addition to the fact that he had high standards for the subject, he also was cranky about losing his lunchtime planning period. It had been rough going for all of us.

"Ooh!" said Poppy, with what I considered to be an inappropriate level of excitement. "I still have the app I made to quiz myself last year. I'll quiz you while we un-ding the car." She saw my face, and her enthusiasm dimmed as she realized that I was not excited by the idea of American history, or an app to quiz me on it.

"That sounds great. Really." I tried to put some cheerfulness into it.

Poppy studied me. "You know what we need," she said. "Reinforcements."

She turned and headed off somewhere while I called after, "Sure you don't have an app for that?"

"I can't hear you," she sang back cheerfully.

She returned a few minutes later with a frozen pepperoni pizza and a couple of frozen candy bars. "My dad hides this stuff from my mom in the deep freeze," she said. "I'm sure she *technically* knows about it, but as long as he keeps the green beans pulled over it, she pretends she doesn't."

"My mood is improving already," I said.

Poppy cooked our pizza and we ate it in the detached garage, by the light of the hanging lightbulb and the faint magical glow as we cast the un-dinging spell over and over. "The pervading idea in the thirties that Americans should concern themselves only with issues of domestic policy is generally referred to as . . ." said Poppy.

"Common sense?" I said.

"Isolationism," Poppy said. "Do you really not like history and politics? It's so fascinating to me."

"You grew up with it," I said. "Anyway, it's not that I don't like it; it's just that it goes in one ear and out the other. It doesn't stick."

"You should come do Model UN with us," said Poppy. "After you've argued about which policies are right or wrong a bunch, it starts to stick."

"Ugh, how boring," I said, before I thought, and then I saw her face fall. No, *fall* isn't the right word. It just . . . closed off, as if she was sorry she had ever suggested inviting me into her world. "I'm sorry," I said. "It's just—I'm more of a science person. I'm in AP biology. I'm not an idiot or anything. I mean, you probably wouldn't want to go to the science fair."

"I've done the science fair every year," Poppy said coldly. "You have to be good at everything to be an all-rounder."

"Right," I said.

We worked in silence for a while after that. I wished Jenah was there; I wished *she* was the one who knew how to cast spells on dents. I could tell her everything that had happened, and then I would feel better. Plus, she always forgave me if I said something stupid, which I did a lot. Whereas I couldn't seem to find the right footing with Poppy. No wonder, though. All her friends were those brilliant, clever juniors and seniors, busy kicking down brick walls and glass ceilings, on the path to success. I didn't know what path I was on, but it sure didn't feel like the success one.

Wulfie trotted up and ate our last piece of pizza. I hoped it wouldn't disagree with him. I didn't have the energy to pull it from his jaws. He minded Sarmine a lot better than me—everybody minded Sarmine. But Sarmine was gone. It might be me and Wulfie forever. The Tale of the Failed Witch Girl and the Tiny Werewolf. Yeah, that was a story I wasn't interested in.

I finished the last dent on my side and let my wand rest on the floor while Poppy finished the last couple on her side. My cheek pressed against the metal door.

Sarmine was gone, and we were no closer to finding her than we had been this morning.

Poppy rounded the car, wand in hand, and stared down at me.

"Feels like midnight," I said finally.

"It's eight," she said, then added, "but we didn't get a lot of sleep."

More silence.

"Tomorrow's a school day," I said.

"Yes," said Poppy.

We picked up, locked the garage, and headed back inside. "I'll be up in a minute," she said. I saw her take out her phone as Wulfie and I trudged upstairs. Where was Lily that she wasn't calling Poppy to explain that she was running late? Off the grid? Out of the country?

Wearily, I changed out of my jeans and back into the gym shorts. Hung up the nice yellow jacket Poppy had let me wear. Thanks to the unicorn spritzer, the Newt Nibbles shirt still had some life in it.

I pulled Wulfie's raggedy, dog-haired bed closer to my side of the bed. It looked woefully out of place in that neat, clean-lined room, with its white paint and blue curtains and walls of framed things. I looked closer at the frames. They turned out to be a selection of awards, report cards, and gifted evaluations. I stood there, listlessly reading something about Poppy's "focus and determination," feeling like a slug dropped in the middle of a Zen garden. This wasn't me. This wasn't where I belonged. Yet, without Sarmine, maybe there was nowhere for me.

A footstep behind me. I turned to see Poppy studying me studying her evaluations. "I like encouragement," she said bluntly. "So sue me." Not bragging, then, but self-motivation. I could understand that.

"Poppy, I . . ." I began. But I had no idea what to say. *I'm sorry you're worried about your mother, too? I'm sure they'll both be fine and that money grows on trees and we'll all get A-pluses this week on our American history quizzes?* I closed my mouth on the lies.

When she saw I wasn't going to say anything, she shrugged tightly, then turned away and started her nighttime routine. I patted the dog bed for Wulfie and he settled his body into it, but he also whined at me. I could feel the tension in his head and neck. Poor boy. He must be wondering why we weren't going back home. It was tough to be in an unfamiliar place. I kept my hand on his head till we both drifted off to sleep.

I woke a couple hours later with the inexplicable feeling that Sarmine needed me. Poppy was sleeping soundly; I didn't want to wake her. Wulfie lifted his head. I patted it and, luckily, he nestled back down and tucked his tail over his nose.

I grabbed the yellow jacket, my house key and shoes, and tiptoed down the old wooden stairs, hugging the railing to make the stairs creak less. The front door was old—it had an ancient door knocker and dead bolt but no modern doorknob with a lock in it. No way to lock it behind me without a key. Well, surely all those wards Poppy and I had done would count for something. Anyone who decided to enter a house with a witch in it would have a nasty surprise.

It was a long walk from the college neighborhood back to my house. An hour, I thought—I'd forgotten my phone. I had no idea what time it was. There were a few cars still on the streets. It couldn't be that late—maybe only eleven. We had gone to bed early and I was thrown off.

The thought went through my mind many times while I walked: What was I doing? Getting out of bed on a school

night on a hunch? On a dream? It was probably an aftereffect
of all that frozen pizza. I should be asleep right now, getting
well rested for that American history quiz tomorrow.

And yet, if Sarmine *did* need me, I couldn't let her down.

I finally turned on our street. Devon's house came first. I
slowed, looking for light from his window. But I saw nothing,
just dark, empty panes of glass.

Another block and I was home.

The house was as dark as Devon's. It didn't particularly look
menacing or creepy. It was its plain old boring ugly split-level
self.

And yet *something* had happened to Sarmine. And *something* could happen to me.

I took a breath and unlocked the door.

Nothing happened. No hexes suddenly firing. No evil
witches lurking in my living room.

One foot inside, the other foot.

Nothing.

I flicked on the living room light.

Still nothing.

The house felt strangely foreign to me, late at night, with
the lights on, with Sarmine gone. Like it wasn't my house anymore. Like I was visiting from my future self, going back to
look at my childhood. Now that I had thought that, my knees
weakened and I sat down hard. I turned my hands over to look
at them, to reassure myself that they were the same teenage
hands they always were. *Witches look the age they feel,* a tiny
voice said inside. *You know how once upon a time a grown-up
Sparkle put an amnesia spell on herself and went back to do
childhood all over again. What if you are old?*

I am not old, I told myself sternly. This house was getting
to me.

I rose and marched firmly to the stairs.

I put my foot on the bottom step, and that's when it hit. An enormous snake—no, not a snake; that thing had a beak and a red comb. It was a gigantic *basilisk*, twice as wide as the stairs and taller than the house.

I shrieked, my mind trying to make sense of the impossibility. Nothing that big could actually fit here. It had to be an illusion, a trick. Maybe Sarmine had warded the house after all—the upstairs, anyway. I frantically cast back to all those study sheets the witch had been making me do for years. Basilisk. An enormous snake with a rooster's head and two stubby chicken feet. Gaze can stun you. Afraid of mutton and mirrors.

Of course. Sarmine wouldn't have a watchdog she couldn't easily subdue. I just needed to do it fast. It had started as an illusion, but it was getting solider by the minute. And once those eyes solidified! . . . Probably would knock me out until Sarmine showed up to unstun me, and who knew when that would be. I ducked as a knobbly chicken foot went past me and took a scrape out of the wall.

A mirror had always hung at the bottom of the stairs. Apparently this was why. I wrenched it from its hook and showed it to the monster. "Go back where you came from!" I shouted. Instantly, the rooster-snake began to vaporize again, shrinking into a wisp of smoke. It went into a picture frame on the landing. Heart beating fast, I studied the picture closer. It was a framed postcard labeled "Visit Beautiful Basel, Switzerland!" I had never paid it much attention. Who knew that it was a house-guarding spell in disguise?

Next to the framed postcard was an ancient wedding photo of Sarmine and Dad, both of them long-haired, Sarmine garlanded in daisies. "How many more surprises do you have for me?" I muttered at it. It didn't answer, of course. Pictures only answer you in books.

I continued up the stairs to the rest of the house, turning on lights as I went. Nothing in the upstairs hall, nothing in my bedroom, nothing in Sarmine's room. I marched all the way through to Sarmine's study, a small room off of her bedroom.

Nothing there, either.

I sat down on the floor, feeling sharply alone. Sarmine was always here—*always*. That house-warding spell must have been set up to trigger on her absence. That would explain why I'd never encountered it. So the house knew she was gone, even if I didn't want to accept it.

Her study was as it always was, a small room filled with bookcases. There was a desk at one end with a bunch of tiny drawers that housed her expensive ingredients she didn't want to store in the basement or garage. One of the bookcases had glass doors, and it, too, held some of her more valuable items.

What was I looking for?

A trace of Sarmine. Some indication as to what had happened to her—if she'd planned her disappearance or if it had been done to her. There were so many questions and, without Sarmine, I was lost.

Break it down, she would say calmly, just like Poppy would say. *Use your brain.* Perhaps she would arch her brow and say, in that superior Sarmine way, *What would I do?*

"Send a basilisk to eat me," I muttered bitterly. I lay back on the rug. I was exhausted. An hour walk, plus fighting a basilisk, plus worry about Sarmine had driven away my strange wakefulness. I could fall asleep instantly. Except then Poppy and Wulfie would wake in the morning to find no Cam. At least one of them would worry about me, I thought.

That's when the front door creaked open.

I sat straight up. My heart was pounding so hard I could barely hear the word called up the stairs.

"Cam?"

It was Poppy. Oh, thank goodness.

Oh, wait. Oh, wait!

I hurried to the hallway. "Don't come up the stairs!"

I was too late; she had already put one foot on the step.

"What the—" was all I heard, as the basilisk rushed toward her.

I hurried, groping for the mirror. No. I had left it on the landing. "Grab the mirror!" I shouted. The basilisk grew bigger, faster this time. Solidifying. "Don't look at it!"

I squeezed past the snake body, tumbling down the stairs before it trapped me in the stairwell. It had caught the strap of Poppy's plaid messenger bag by one hooked chicken claw. She was hollering and trying to pull ingredients out of the bag. She pulled her fist out just as the chicken foot ripped the messenger bag free and sent it sailing through the air. I caught the strap of the bag just before it hit the ground. Now for the mirror. I grabbed Sarmine's—Poppy held aloft her phone—

And then the basilisk exploded into a million tiny basilisk pieces and lay in ruins all around Poppy. She fell to the landing with a hard thump. Slowly she sat up, her eyes round behind her glasses. "What. Was that."

"My mom's watchdog," I said. "What was *that*?"

"Mirror app," said Poppy. She looked sideways at me. "Technology for the win?"

"For the win," I agreed.

Then her eyes widened. "My bag!"

"I caught it."

The relief on her face was tremendous. She might have saved my life, but I had saved her *bag*. She rifled through her messenger bag, checking glass vials and delicate objects. "It's all fine," she said. "Thank you."

"Any time," I said.

"I was worried about you," said Poppy, looking sideways at me. "Disappear in the middle of the night like your mother and all that." I realized then that she had only pulled her pink suit jacket on over her lavender PJ's. Her hair was still in its scarf, now a little disheveled.

"Oh," I said. "I hadn't thought about that." Truthfully, I wasn't used to the idea of a new person caring about me. I mean, I had Jenah, and I sort of had Sarmine, and was trying to rely on Devon liking me because after all he had said it many times, but yeah. I don't know. "I'm sorry."

She shrugged and looked uncomfortable at having admitted that. Maybe she was slow to make friends, too. Or maybe she had been set to dislike me since I had gotten into the coven, and would have preferred to continue happily disliking me forever. Maybe I needed to do a better job at extending the olive branch.

"Did you walk?" I said.

"Oh hell no. I took the station wagon. Did you want to bring back your bike?"

"Poppy," I said, "I am a great admirer of your organization and efficiency. Teach me your ways."

She smiled, genuinely smiled at me. "Help me wipe up the basilisk guts and we'll call it even."

So that was the Saga of How Cam and Poppy Cleaned Up the Second Mess That Day. It was just as riveting as the first. Poppy started to ask if I wanted to be quizzed on American history and then stopped, remembering that that had caused a rift last time. "Please," I said. "Please do help me. I don't want to flunk out of everything this week." So she shot questions at me while we worked. I made a real effort to not sound like an idiot, and she made a real effort to not call me one. It went much better than before.

We finished mopping up and put our tools away.

Poppy looked sideways at me. "And now . . . ?"

"Yes," I said. "The garage."

We crept out the back door, struck out across the yard. The moon was quite full now, and it shone white across the black night, made smaller moons out of Poppy's glasses. I shivered in the spring air, wondering what Poppy would think of my fancies about not knowing what age you truly were. She would probably look at me askance, and I didn't want to disturb our tenuous bond.

I unlocked the RV garage and we went inside. Even though my strongest memory should be of the disastrous coven incident of the night before, I couldn't help thinking of all the years the garage had held a friendly sky-blue dragon. I would rather have her around than any number of covens.

"Cam," said Poppy in an odd voice. She was standing next to the cauldron.

"What now?" I peered into it, expecting to see some bubbling goop perhaps, an unknown spell that had been started after that fiery explosion. But it was empty.

Then I realized what Poppy was pointing at.

"The votives," she said, pointing to the glass cups that had encircled the cauldron. They were scattered now, some pushed under chairs. Sarmine's was still dark; we had seen that last night. But the rest were glowing—weren't they?

"I don't see," I said, and Poppy impatiently pointed, directing me to examine the glass under the chair next to Sarmine's, the glass that stood in place of Valda.

It was not lit at all.

It was shattered into a million pieces.

6

full Moon

I practically jumped out of my skin. I would have jumped into Poppy's arms if I had known her better. Witches seemed to be crowding around me from the shadows, pressing in. Some witch—someone was doing this now. . . . Who was it? . . . Where were they? . . . Surely they were here!

"Deep breathing," said Poppy, who was busy practicing it herself. "Reviewing what we know."

"Sarmine disappeared during the coven meeting."

"And then her glass went dark."

"Then, today, all Valda's traps backfired, and I thought it was just her terrible witchery—"

"But maybe it wasn't," said Poppy. "Because there was that boulder."

"And if we hadn't been there, it would have rolled right through her TV tray."

"Squash," said Poppy.

I shuddered.

"Two in a row," said Poppy. "It could be coincidence. . . ."

"Or?"

She took a breath. "Sarmine said Malkin said to open the box at the coven. If that's true—"

"And who knows, given my mom—"

"Then don't you think it's funny that something happened to the first two people in the circle? Like, in order?"

"Yes?"

"Cam. What if that hex is designed to get every member of the coven?"

I paced back and forth, trying to make my brain work more like Poppy's and less like mush. "Do you think Malkin hexed the votives somehow?" I said. "Squash a candleholder, *poof*, Valda gets squashed?"

Poppy shook her head. "Valda didn't *actually* get squashed, as far as we know," she said. "She was *supposed* to get squashed. I read about a similar case in *Emmetrine's Grimoire*. I bet the glasses are showing the status report on what's *supposed* to be happening with the spell."

"So that's better, right?" I reached down to touch my lit glass.

Poppy grabbed my arm. "I wouldn't," she said. "I trust my logic, but there's a big difference between trusting my logic and having you snuff out your life just to check our work."

I pulled my hand back into my chest. "You have a point."

We walked around the garage, looking at the cauldron, the spill of packing peanuts. The gravy boat still lay buried in the peanuts, but neither of us was going to touch that with a ten-foot pole, or even with a push broom, like Lily.

Finally: "We'd better get home," said Poppy. "It'd be just like my mom to come home at the exact time we're gone."

"What time is it?" I said.

She looked at her phone. "Eleven fifty-nine. Almost—"

"The witching hour. I know, I know." I gathered my wits and walked to the door. At least we could leave this place and go back to Poppy's house. Sleep had never sounded so good.

That's when a shattering sound broke the silence of the night.

This time, I really did jump toward Poppy. I grabbed her shoulder and she grabbed my arm. "What was that?" I said shrilly. I had some excuse for sliding up into shrill, I think.

Poppy dragged me back toward the circle of lights, step by

reluctant step. We peered down at the floor, and what we saw made my blood run cold all over again and my fingers go so numb I no longer knew whether I was gripping Poppy's arm.

The third glass had shattered.

"Ohmigod," I said, and "Run," I said, and though Poppy was more levelheaded than I was, she was sufficiently freaked to agree that was a good idea. I locked the doors with trembling fingers, grabbed my bike, and shoved it through the gaping back windshield hole into Lily's station wagon. The back wheel hung out, but I thought it would hold. We jumped in ourselves and peeled out, all the while feeling like witches were breathing down our necks. The cold air blowing through the missing rear windshield didn't help. Poppy's database hadn't had a spell to fix that. She shivered in her PJ's.

The moon shone into the car, bright and full.

"Midnight," Poppy said as she drove.

"What?"

"The third glass shattered at midnight. And your mother disappearing, last night—that was also midnight."

I thought back to Valda, who had been eating lunch when we arrived. "Valda's clock," I said. "I thought it was just rocking in the spell. But it was chiming noon."

"So whatever these spells are, we just learned something. They're firing every twelve hours."

"Ohmigod," I said. I leaned my head back against the vinyl headrest. The moonlight flashed on a nail that had buried itself in the dash earlier. "And we don't even know who was standing next to Valda. Do you think, whoever it is, they're . . ."

"I don't know," Poppy said grimly. She looked like she was bracing for bad news. "Tell me you have some idea where my mother was standing."

Oh no. "Poppy," I said. "Your mother."

"Where was she?"

I made my mush brain work. I had seen her. I had identified her. "She was standing on my side of the circle," I said firmly. "If Sarmine was twelve o'clock, then I was at eleven o'clock and your mother was at eight or nine o'clock."

"You're sure."

"I am."

Poppy's fierce grip on the wheel relaxed. "If the spell is going clockwise around the circle, then you two will be near the end. That gives Mom time to get back from whatever she's researching. The moment she's in contact again we have to tell her everything we know so far. We'll be able to count down the hours to figure out when her thing is coming. Give us time to stop it."

"This settles it," I added. "If the hex designed to hit everyone, it *must* all be Malkin's doing."

"One last nasty gotcha," Poppy said. She furrowed her brow. "Well, unless one of the witches in the circle gets skipped. Or hexes themselves, too, as a red herring."

"Ugh, stop pointing out loopholes," I said. "This case is complicated enough."

"It is important to think through all the logical possibilities—What?"

"Sparkle," I said, sitting up straight. "Sparkle's a member of the coven, too. And I have no idea where she was in the circle. We've got to warn her."

"We've got to warn all of them," she said.

I might hate all the wicked witches, but in that moment I knew I was in total agreement with Poppy. You could hate someone and still not want them to be shattered into a thousand bits like that glass cup. What calamity did that represent? I shuddered at the thought.

We pulled into Poppy's driveway, got out of the well-ventilated station wagon, and walked to the door. The night was clear and the full moon gave us plenty of light. I thought I knew all our problems at that point. I ticked them off in my head. Missing Mother number 1. Missing Mother number 2. Cascadia Coven Hex. Invisible Boyfriend. That was enough for anybody, right?

And yet . . . I had an uneasy feeling, like I had forgotten something.

Poppy opened the door and felt around for the light. "What the—" she said, for the second time that night.

The kitchen was to the left of the stairs, the living room to the right. Both rooms looked like a tornado had hit them. The kitchen floor was covered in cereal from the bag Poppy and I had left out on the kitchen table. And the living room was worse. All of Lily's dolls were off the shelves—heaped on the chairs and floor. I wouldn't have a clue how to put them back in the right order.

"Do you think this is part of the hex?" I whispered.

"You thought my mom was standing near you!" hissed Poppy.

We crept into the living room, through the piles of dolls, terrified of what we might find. I hadn't seen a disaster of this proportion in a long time. It looked as if a small child had—Oh. Oh dear.

I suddenly remembered exactly what I had forgotten.

Two more steps took me to the armchair. There was a small boy curled up on it. A small boy who, until an hour ago, had been in his shaggy, puppy form.

Wulfie.

Poppy, behind me, *eep*ed at the sight. I didn't blame her. After a night full of surprising things, the cherry on top was finding a small boy in your living room when as far as you knew there were no small boys in your house. "Did you—did you bring a poltergeist with you?" she said.

"That's Wulfie the werewolf," I said grimly. "Around this time every month he changes to boy for a few days. It's horrible—" I caught myself. He was a werewolf, not deaf. "I mean. He's a very good boy and we love him lots and he's, um, a three-year-old. It's exhausting." And then, "Are poltergeists real?"

Poppy straightened up. "Oh jeez. Of course it's Wulfie," she said. "Full moon and all. I—Don't tell anyone I said that. About the poltergeists. It was a joke."

Her lips were pressed firmly together and I didn't push it. "You're exhausted," I said reassuringly.

But our whispering had attracted attention. Wulfie sat up. "Cam!" he said, and bounded off the armchair and through a pile of no doubt valuable and irreplaceable dolls, over to me. "Cam Cam Cam Cam Cam!"

"Oh, sweetie pie," I said, and swept him up in a hug. "What on earth are we going to do with you?"

It took an hour to get Wulfie back to sleep, and even then he refused to sleep in his dog bed. Not because he was in human form but because sometimes he got clingy and refused to curl up anywhere but at my feet, and this was one of those times. It didn't matter to him that Poppy's bed was only a double and we were already squished in there without a squirmy three-year-old boy. I finally got him tucked in on top of my feet, under a spare blanket. I draped a corner of the blanket over his nose to stand in for his tail and then I lay down myself. Of course, I now wanted a drink of water. But I wasn't disturbing Wulfie for anything.

Besides, at this point it was nearly two a.m. on a school night and even wanting a drink wasn't going to keep me awake that long. Poppy picked up some of the dolls before giving up and coming up to bed herself. I ran through the day's woes in my head, bullet points on an imaginary list. Sarmine gone. Lily gone. Almost squashed by boulders and nails and dolls and small boys.

Three witches down.

Who was next?

€

"Esmerelda."

"What? I said groggily. It was early dawn, from the looks of the light, and Poppy was shaking me awake as if we hadn't gotten to sleep well after midnight.

"Esmerelda," she repeated. "It was bugging the back of my mind. I saw the soles of her high heels under her black robes. They were bright green. I remember thinking there was only one person who would have green-soled spike heels."

"That would be her," I said. "But we got four hours of sleep, Poppy. Wouldn't it be nice to let Esmerelda fend for herself?"

"We saw her glass shatter," said Poppy. "Something happened to her, and I feel like it's going to give us a clue about how to stop this before it gets to you and my mom. At the very least, she'll know who was standing next to her, so we can warn them."

"Email," I said. "You can email people from bed."

"Do you have everyone's email?"

"Sparkle does," I said, remembering the message she had shown me. "Except she'll kill us if she finds we're talking to the other witches. She's petrified of Claudette discovering that Leo's a shifter."

"This Leo–Sparkle thing sounds like amazing gossip," said Poppy, "and you should tell me in the car. But right now we've got to go visit Esmerelda, because somebody else's curse goes off at noon and we don't know who. Do you know where she lives?"

"I know where her mother Rimelda lives," I said. I had been at their house for a disastrous pool party once. "We could drive out and ask her, and additionally warn her. She's not a bad sort, for a witch."

Poppy looked at me strangely. "They're not *all* bad, you know. The Geneva Coven actually does a lot of good for the world."

"What, somewhere in Switzerland?" I said. "The ones I've met are terrible."

"My mom. Your mom."

"*My* mom?"

"I mean, she's uptight and cranky. . . ."

"And she wants to take over the world. . . ."

"But she wants to make it better, though?"

I sighed. "I know. She's not the worst." I looked at Poppy. "That doesn't mean we get along."

"I know."

"Mothers."

"Mothers!"

We groaned in unison, and this time I didn't ruin it by saying, "Jinx!"

Poppy looked down at the small boy curled up at our feet. "What about him?"

"We'll have to take him," I said. "Unless you want him to destroy more of your mom's stuff. We should get that cleaned up before your mom gets home."

"Except, school," she said.

"Okay," I said dubiously. "Only, Sarmine would have my head if I left her house like that. I mean, like one time she literally took my head and made it study some horrid witch dictionary while my body cleaned up the study I left messy. She really has a thing about her study."

Poppy rubbed her forehead. "Maybe we can do like thirty minutes of cleaning before Wulfie wakes up."

Which, of course, was his cue to roll over. His eyes popped open, and then with one bound he was across the bed, tackling us.

"Cam Cam Cam Cam Cam!" he shouted, and then, studying Poppy for a second, "Pop Pop Pop Pop Pop!"

"Wulf Wulf Wulf Wulf Wulf!" she hollered back, and tickled him till he shrieked. "All right, let's feed him and get out the door. If all goes well we can check on Esmerelda and still get to school on time."

It was a fine plan. Doable. Except . . .

"And then what do we do with him?" I said slowly. "I mean, *after* we get to school."

We looked at each other blankly. Wulfie had never been a problem as a dog before. And now—he was practically insurmountable.

"What do other people do with three-year-olds?" she said.

"Don't have them," I said.

We discussed and discarded a pile of ideas as we ate breakfast. Spring break was over for the public schools, and there were not a lot of good options for taking care of a small tornado.

Finally I said, "Well, he's my problem. If we can't come up with anything, I'll stay home today."

"Okay," Poppy said. "And I'll stay home tomorrow. Fair?"

"More than," I said.

One thing I'll say for Wulfie: he found the rice puffs all over the kitchen floor vastly entertaining. Chasing and eating them kept him occupied for a good half hour while we got dressed and rounded up our half-done homework.

Once ready to go, we realized we lacked a car seat. But Poppy went down the street to a house where she often baby-sat and came back triumphant with an old one. She buckled it into the wagon, I buckled Wulfie into it, and we set off. Wulfie decided he liked his car seat about as well as a trip to the vet. He started off with a mournful howl, and when that didn't get him released, switched over to shrieking. Since the illusory windshield didn't muffle werewolf shrieks, people turned to look at us.

"Can't you turn him off?" shouted Poppy over the din. "I need my brain to drive."

"You're easier to take as a dog," I told Wulfie. I dug one of the roofing nails out of the dash. I'd like to say the point was rounded down but, frankly, it was still pretty pointy. "Don't poke yourself," I warned. Wulfie immediately became engaged with poking it into the car seat.

"I hope they didn't want that car seat back without holes in it," I said.

"It's all yours," she reassured me.

Poppy followed the rest of my directions and we finally arrived at Rimelda's rambly old house outside of town. Just in time, too, as Wulfie had gotten bored with his nail. We parked on the gravel drive, let the shrieking boy out of his Car Seat of Doom to go run off his energy, and went up to knock on the door.

And again. And again.

Rimelda was either gone or sleeping too soundly to come to the door. It was early for witches to be awake.

"Ugh, wasted errand," I said. "And it's nearly seven. Do you want to try searching on WitchNet for Esmerelda's address?"

Poppy held up her phone, looking for a signal. "We've got

to head back to town," she said. "I'm not getting enough signal to stay online."

"Or should we get you to school? Esmerelda is . . . well. Let's
just say I don't think she'd put herself out for us if she knew
we were in jeopardy."

Poppy sighed and lowered her phone. "I know what she's
like," she said. She pulled her pink linen jacket tighter. "It's
just . . . I only have so much time before my mom gets home,
you know? And she's going to forbid me from helping to stop
this hex before it gets to her. The more information I can gain,
the better equipped she will be. She won't refuse to listen to
what I've already learned."

I could understand that. We both wanted to save our
mothers, even when our mothers made it difficult for us to do
it. "We press on," I agreed. Only . . . how?

It was at this point that I realized we hadn't seen Wulfie
for quite a while. I also knew from last summer that Rimelda
had a pool. I highly doubted that boy-Wulfie had any idea
how to swim. I admit it, I swore—and I wasn't much for
swearing, since Sarmine generally made me scrub out the
cauldron with lye every time I did it. But I was wound up. "I
never had this problem when he was a dog!" I said. "He is
impossible when he's a boy."

"Divide and conquer," Poppy said simply.

We split up, covering the yard. I raced toward the pool area,
scanning it, ears open for splashes. Nothing. I walked its
length, just to be sure. Still nothing. My heart slowed, but
only a little. He was still gone. Rimelda could have as many
defenses as Valda for all I knew.

A shriek from the pool house.

I ran that way, heart racing again. The door was open.

Wulfie was on the couch, shrieking with laughter.

He was not alone.

7

Adventures in Babysitting a Werewolf

"Pink!" I said. "I mean, Primella."

"Cam!" she said, turning from tickling Wulfie. Primella was ten, blonde, and clad in a pink nightgown, pink robe, and pink fuzzy bunny slippers. She was Esmerelda's daughter, and Rimelda's granddaughter. A pillow and quilt suggested she had been sleeping in the guesthouse until a small boy jumped on her. "Is this your werewolf?"

"He's my adopted brother, yeah," I said. My heart rate slowed. Wulfie was safe, and Pink was not a threat. Not unless she'd changed dramatically since I'd met her at Rimelda's pool party last summer, when I helped her outwit a certain double-crossing witch. "How did you know he was a werewolf?"

She shrugged. "I know the signs."

"But what are you doing at your grandmother's?" That was when it occurred to me that she could help us find Esmerelda. "Where's your mother?"

"Home, maybe?" Pink said. "I come out here most week-ends, and it's spring break for me. I like it better than my mom's house," she added wistfully. I was not surprised. There were a lot of bad mothers among witches, but Esmerelda stood head and shoulders above them for bad-motherness. "Grand-mother went into town for doughnuts," Pink said. "I'm sure she'll be back soon, if you want to stay." She tickled Wulfie again. "We're having a good time."

A brilliant idea dawned on me. "I don't suppose you'd be

interested in babysitting?" I said. "My mom disappeared, and we're going crazy trying to figure out what to do with him."

"Oh!" said Pink. She went a little pink. "No one's ever trusted me enough to do that," she said.

Right about that time, Poppy appeared in the door, panting, her linen jacket flapping behind her. "He's not in back," she said. "Oh, good. You found him."

"Poppy, this is Pink—er, Primella," I said. "She might be able to help us out with Wulfie." Right about then, the problem with my bright idea hit me. Money. My face fell. As usual, I didn't have any money, or at least none worth mentioning. I pulled out a quarter and mentioned it.

"I've got thirteen bucks," Poppy said. "But I'm going to need it for fuel if we keep driving everywhere."

Pink looked shyly up at me. "You helped me once," she said. "I'll help you. You don't have to pay me."

I started to say "Are you sure?," but I realized that she meant it and that pushing back would fluster her. So I didn't point out that only crazy people volunteered to babysit a three-year-old werewolf, and instead said, "Thank you, Primella. I can't tell you how much I appreciate this."

She smile-shrugged it off and said, "C'mon, Wulfie, let's go do the rock climbing wall."

He scampered over to it, shouting, "Rock rock rock!" It would be good practice for him to use his hands, I thought—even if he was going to be twice the holy terror after this.

We got Esmerelda's address from Pink and stood to go. "Please tell your grandmother to be on the lookout," I told Pink. "We think there's a hex attacking everyone who was at the coven Saturday night. Probably Malkin's doing. Every twelve hours around the circle."

"I will," Pink promised faithfully. Wulfie whooped with

delight from the top of the wall. We hurried out the door before he could decide he wanted to come with us.

"Well done us," said Poppy as we got back in the car. I could tell she was basking in the same glow of accomplishment that I was. Solving one of our tasks.

"Do you like checking things off too?" I asked as we drove to Esmerelda's. "Writing them down and crossing them off?"

"You know there's an app for that," said Poppy.

But I could tell she was teasing me. Just then I was feeling pretty good about us and how far we'd gotten, all on our own. Sure, pride goeth before a fall and all that. This was no time to start totting up our accomplishments. And yet . . .

"Figured out that all the witches are getting hexed," I said. "Figured out the first two—maybe first three—of them."

"Figured out what time the hexes are firing," said Poppy, who was quick to realize that I was self-buttressing and was happy to join in. "And now to check on Esmerelda and make her cough up the info about who was standing next to her, so we can warn them before noon."

"You know, she and Valda were sort of friends with Malkin," I said.

"Maybe she'll have an insight into what Malkin might have done."

"If she'll share it with us," I said.

Esmerelda lived in a fancy new development around a golf course. Her street was one of those with many huge, identical houses squished together. It probably cost more than both of our houses combined. The lawn—all the lawns—were pristine.

We parked the open-air station wagon on the street and

crept up to the doorbell. I didn't like the hushed street. Mine had a lot more noise, any time of day. Buses going by. Guys on skateboards. People getting into their cars in the driveway, and kids waiting for the school bus and complaining. Here, a grounds crew was working at the other end of the street, three men in one yard running their leaf blowers. But the rest was quiet. Every so often a garage door would open up and disgorge an SUV, then silently close again. I felt like people were inspecting us from behind their window shades.

"Here goes nothing," said Poppy, and she rang.

And rang.

And rang.

"No one is going to let us in," I said. "None of them."

"Because they're all guilty," said Poppy. "Even if they didn't do the hex, they all wish they had." She pulled out her phone and scanned the door. "What happens if we try to force the lock, Phone?"

"Bad hair and ten pounds," came back the robotic voice of the avatar.

I rolled eyes. "Esmerelda."

"Plus, I know there's human eyeballs on us from all those windows," said Poppy. "Ready to dial nine-one-one if we explode her doorknob."

"Let me text Pink," I said, and did, my fingers flying over the phone. The message came back immediately. "Mix two shavings red crayon with one pinch of glue stick. Shake over doormat, tap doorknob with wand. Don't let neighbors see you."

"I have those," said Poppy, who was apparently prepared even in the matter of elementary school supplies. She shook and tapped. Instantly the door opened to a vision of Esmerelda, shining in motherly splendor. I say "vision" because it was immediately obvious to me that this was not the actual Esmerelda. Esmerelda would never have worn that high-necked shirt, or those mom jeans. Esmerelda would never have had a pan of cookies in one hand or leaned down to coo, "Welcome home, darling."

Poppy and I followed the illusion inside the house. It smiled and waved at the blank windows facing the house. Then it shut the door, still smiling and holding the cookies. I wondered what would happen if I tried to eat one. The lock clicked and the vision melted away.

Poppy looked at the door, agape. "Okay, that's an impressive holo for a ten-year-old. My car illusion doesn't wave or speak. We were obviously just activating something Pink has done many times before. I wonder how she created it."

"Poor Pink," I said, imagining her carefully planning out how to transform Esmerelda into the mother she wanted. Sad that she needed to do it at all.

"Probably doesn't want the neighbors to know she's a latch-key kid," said Poppy. "It's not really legal anymore."

"And it's embarrassing, you know. Legal or not." I wasn't the best at understanding people, but this sort of thing I understood perfectly. Covering for your mother's faults. Poppy looked at me strangely, like she didn't understand why I'd be embarrassed about something someone else did, but I just shrugged. "We'd better find Esmerelda," I said. "School starts in twenty-five minutes."

Just like the street, the house was hushed and pristine, all gleaming hardwood and catalog furniture. It made me think of horror movies and jump scares.

I swallowed. "What do you think 'shattered' looks like?"

"Maybe the spell didn't get her," Poppy whispered back. "It missed Valda."

"So if it *did* get her, we try to help her. And if it didn't . . ."

"We make her tell us who's next. And any others she knows."

We finally found Esmerelda in the place we should have expected her: the master bathroom, the one with all the mirrors. What we didn't expect was to find the counters covered with lavender and paprika and elf toenails and everything else, and a fully dressed Esmerelda, who shrieked and covered her face with a bath towel when we walked in.

"What are you doing here?" she shouted. "You little brats, get out of my house!"

"She's not shattered," I said. "You're not shattered."

"Then maybe she's the one who did it," said Poppy.

"Did what?" said Esmerelda, taking the bait. She still wouldn't look at us.

"We found out that the spell that disappeared my mother is still going," I said. "Going off every twelve hours and hexing a new witch. Did something happen to you at midnight?"

"I don't have to tell you what happened at midnight," said Esmerelda. "Now get out of here."

Poppy was stubborn. "At least tell us who was standing next to you. We need to warn everybody, but we don't know who's next."

"They can fend for themselves."

I tapped my phone. "School's in twenty minutes," I said.

"Right," said Poppy. "Time for desperate measures. One . . . two . . ."

On three we each grabbed a corner of the towel and uncovered her face.

Esmerelda, who would like to look twenty, and definitely no more than thirty, looked about a hundred and twenty. She looked older than her mother, Rimelda, and that was saying something, because Rimelda didn't particularly care how she looked. Not only that, Esmerelda didn't even look like an old version of her Barbie doll self. Her ears were big, her nose was hooked, there was a hairy wart on the end of her chin—a more Halloweeny witch could never have been devised. The network of wrinkles that crossed her face reminded me of something—

"Shattering glass," I breathed.

Poppy and I looked at each other. It was clear we could cross Esmerelda off our list. Never in a million years would she have done this to herself. Not even as a red herring.

Esmerelda grabbed for the towel, which Poppy held out of reach. She spat at us. "You little . . . *witches*."

"Answer a few questions and we'll get out of your hair," I said, rising above her insults.

"Horrible, awkward, unfashionable *teenagers*."

Still, how mature did one have to be? I opened my mouth and saw Poppy subtly shake her head at me. Right. We were detectives with a mission.

"Did this happen last night?" said Poppy, gently.

Her tone must have disarmed Esmerelda, whose anger deflated. "Around midnight," she admitted.

"Witch number three," said Poppy, tapping the screen of her phone. "Right on cue."

"The box Sarmine opened seems to have triggered one last spell," I said. "Something from Malkin that's hexing the whole coven."

"Ooh, another possibility is that someone *else* sent that box," said Poppy. "*Pretending* to come from Malkin."

"Seriously, stop pointing out loopholes," I said to Poppy. I turned to Esmerelda. "You've known Malkin since college. Do you think she would have set up a coven-wide hex like this? That would get triggered after she died?"

"She could, of course," said Esmerelda. "But I don't know that she *would*. It's not exactly her style. She always liked to *witness* the damage she inflicted."

I shuddered.

Poppy nodded at Esmerelda. "More to the point, does that particular hex look like Malkin's work?"

I was dubious. Making someone wrinkly seemed too superficial for Malkin.

I pulled out a piece of paper to write down what we knew, but Poppy forestalled me and showed me her phone. She had been busy.

Hexes So Far

1. Sat Midnight: Sarmine. Vanished
2. Sunday Noon: Valda. House tried to destroy her
3. Sun Midnight: Esmerelda. Old and ugly

In that moment I felt a tremendous kinship with Poppy. Staying organized. Making lists.

"That *particular hex*, you said." I tapped the phone thoughtfully. "Do you notice a pattern to these?"

"Besides the one we've already established, of anti-widdershins around the circle?"

"Leaving Sarmine out of it for a minute. Throwing bricks and boulders at someone is exactly the sort of brute-force thing Valda would do. And this mean girl hex"—I gestured at Esmerelda—"is exactly the thing *she* would do."

Poppy pursed her lips. "You might be right. Excellent work, Watson." She eyed Esmerelda. "Is this a favorite spell of yours?"

Esmerelda tossed her gray wisps of hair. "I have too much class," she said loftily. "I wouldn't wish this on my worst enemy." But something about the way she said it made me suspicious.

"Or perhaps," I said, "you *have* wished this on your worst enemy." I considered her. "You do a lot of petty, nasty spells. Is this among them?"

Esmerelda scowled. "Did it once to a girl in college," she said. "Too nasty to do again."

Poppy nudged me. "Anti-widdershins," she said.

"By the way, Esmerelda," I said. "You wouldn't happen to know who was standing next to you, would you?"

"Masked, you morons."

Time to lay on the flattery, and I had a good idea about how to do it. "Ah, but that's exactly why I thought to ask you," I said. "You're the only one of us who knows about fashion and style." Poppy poked me. I figured it meant that she was willing to play along, but she resented the insult to her fashion sense. "Everyone's wearing black robes and masks, sure. But you, of all people, would be able to tell a cheap dime store mask from . . . well, whatever you were wearing."

Esmerelda sniffed. "Like the knockoff robes Ingrid was wearing? All that black market money and what does she buy? Not the real thing, that's for sure."

"Exactly. You can tell."

Indecision warred in Esmerelda's face. She could see right through the flattery, of course. And yet . . . she *did* know, and this was her only chance to show off her knowledge. "*I* was wearing cocktail robes from Gramerina Gris's spring collection, in midnight charcoal," she said, "and a custom, handpainted mask in lacquer black."

Poppy whipped out her phone and made a show of getting all this down.

"That's G . . . R . . . I . . . S," said Esmerelda in a helpful, condescending sort of voice.

Poppy showed admirable restraint in not hexing her, I thought.

"And next to you?"

Esmerelda came to a decision. "On one condition," she said.

"Yes?"

"Give me all your yak fur."

"I don't . . . I don't have any yak fur," I said, thrown. "Poppy?"

Poppy had a suppressed look that said she might break out into laughter at any minute. But she said, perfectly soberly, "I have a standard capsule of it in my bag." She produced it and said, "You tell us what you know, and it's yours."

8

Out of the frying Pan, into the Terrible Teleportation Spell

Poppy and I talked as fast as anything, all the way to school. Our idea that the worst hex you've ever done might now be coming back to bite you seemed extremely plausible. That left us with an ethical dilemma.

Most of the witches deserved what was coming to them.

"Let's review," said Poppy. "First possibility. Malkin did the spell as one last nasty gotcha to the coven. No further rhyme or reason to it, no motive. In that case, we should warn everybody, because Malkin was a piece of work."

"Two, my mom did it," I said. "And she vanished her own self as a red herring. In that case, maybe everyone deserves it and we *shouldn't* warn them. Maybe they—I don't know—didn't do their recycling this week or something. That would be good, because then Sarmine would be safe. But it would be bad because, if Valda was telling us the truth, then our moms were at least tenuous allies in the coven. So why would she have included your mom in the spell?"

"And you," said Poppy.

"And me," I admitted, but I was used to Sarmine coming up with terrible teaching plans. Would I put this whole stunt past her? I couldn't decide.

"Or, three, some other witch did it," said Poppy, "using Malkin's death as a cover. Motive unknown."

"Who's next?" I said. "Is it someone we care about?"

Poppy passed over her phone, where she had been jotting

down the witches around the thirteen points in the circle. I made a couple additions to remind me who was who. And then a couple more notes, just to be a completist.

Hexes So Far

1. Sat Midnight: Sarmine Scarabouche (Cam's mom). Vanished.
2. Sunday Noon: V. Valda Velda (grumpy stompy witch). House tried to destroy her.
3. Sun Midnight: Esmerelda Danela (pissy blonde witch). Old and ugly.
4. Monday Noon: Ingrid Ahlgren (tough blonde with dog)
5. Mon Midnight: Ulrich Grey (creepy Unicorn Guy)
6. Tuesday Noon: Fiona Laraque (Sports Team, Canadian)
7. Tues Midnight: Jen Smith (Leggings, Canadian)
8. Wednesday Noon: Penny Patel (Boring Skirt, Canadian)
9. Weds Midnight: Rimelda Danela (Esmerelda's 100-year-old mother)
10. Thursday Noon: Hikari Tanaka (Sparkle)
11. Thurs Midnight: Lily Jones (Poppy's mom)
12. Friday Noon: Claudette Dupuy (ice-cold French-Canadian witch)
13. Fri Midnight: Camellia Hexar (Cam) (duh.)

"Ingrid Ahlgren," I said.

"And her 'polyester fake fashion.'"

"Aka, the blonde lady with the dog. Can you get her address?"

Poppy nodded. "If not, I'll call Esmerelda and threaten to withhold her yak fur," she quipped.

"What is it with yak fur, anyway?" I said.

Poppy laughed, the first real laughter I'd heard from her. It was the sort of laugh you laugh when your life has been absolute nonsense and you have to either laugh or cry. "Yak fur is a de-escalator," she said. "You use it if you're trying to stop something that's, well, escalating."

"You mean—"

"I mean whatever that terrible hex is she did, it doesn't just cast itself and stop. It keeps going—from bad to worse. She's probably used all her yak fur so far to try to halt it. She'll go through mine and need more. And every moment, she'll appear to get older and uglier." Another gale of laughter. Poppy pushed up her plastic glasses to wipe tears from her eyes and said, "I shouldn't laugh. But if anyone deserves it, it's her. She's the one who thought up that spell in the first place and cast it on someone."

"It's not very feminist," I ventured.

"No," said Poppy, settling her glasses in place. "It's literally not. Whatever traits she decided were ugly—well, *she* decided that, you know? I could argue with her all day about whether it was ugly to have a warty face or wrinkles, but the point is, those are precisely the things *she* thought were the most terrible. Oh, the amazing justice."

We were running so late that the parking lot was nearly full. Poppy headed to the very back, and I crossed my fingers there was a spot for us. Rourke did not like it when I was late to Algebra.

"Do you know Ingrid at all?" said Poppy.

I shook my head.

"So, if my memory is correct, then there's just one problem," said Poppy. "Oh, there's a spot."

"Yes?"

"She lives in the mountains. Like four hours away."

"And we are going to get there during a eighteen-minute lunchtime how?"

Poppy stopped the station wagon and looked me squarely in the face. "How do you feel about teleportation?"

A cold lump formed in my stomach. "I've never done it," I said.

"It's expensive," she admitted. "Mom doesn't like to do it, either. But I brought the supplies. I packed them up yesterday, just in case. We can do it. If you're not too scared."

"I'm not," I said. "I'm just wondering if, you know, if we should even warn this Ingrid. Or not. Maybe 'not' is the answer. Maybe not warn her."

Poppy took a deep breath. "I don't think we should warn her, either," she said.

"Oh good."

"I think we need to sneak up on her."

"Sneak—What—No."

"Invisibly, of course," said Poppy. "I still have my cloak."

"I don't use invisible eels," I said automatically. "Not unless—"

"They were ethically found dead on the side of a creek where they lived their happy, stinky lives. I know," said Poppy. "No. We'll use your new invisibility spell on my cloak. Duh."

"Ah."

"Because I've heard my mom talk about Ingrid. She's a bad one. And you heard what Esmerelda let slip about her, right?"

I thought back. "Something about black market money?"

Poppy seized my hands. "Valda said the main thing that keeps fracturing the coven is the discussion of what to do with Sentient Magicals. What do you think the black market for witches *is*?"

I swallowed, thinking of the magical ingredients that slid

very quickly into unethical territory. Werewolf hairs. Bigfoot claws. And that just scratched the surface. "Things I don't want to think about?"

"Exactly."

"You think she might be the one behind the spell?"

"Well, she's next on the list," said Poppy. "Either we'll rule her out or we'll learn something. Or both."

I grimaced. "Teleporting into a wicked witch's yard."

"I know," said Poppy in frustration. "I just don't see what else we can do. My mom could be in all kinds of trouble and she wouldn't even tell me, just so I wouldn't worry. She treats me like my dad. But I can't sit and do nothing. I hope you have A lunch."

"I do," I said. "And we'll meet—"

"Poppy," hallooed a girl, coming up from the other side of the parking lot. I didn't think Poppy was embarrassed by me—I mean, I'd finally changed out of that Newt Nibbles shirt—but still. We were both people who kept our witch lives secret. We were one person at home. Another at school.

"I'll meet you here," I said.

We nodded and split. Coconspirators to the end.

I was dubious about how I was going to get through my morning with *teleportation* hanging over me, but school had to be gotten through, wicked witches or not.

Devon and I still shared an Algebra class this semester, but Rourke had moved us far apart, so I couldn't sit there and stare at his hair. I mean Devon's hair, not Rourke's.

Devon was already at his desk when I hurried in. I could see from the back that he was wearing visible clothes. A ball cap with some platinum blond hair escaping from it. It was definitely not his usual shade, but I appreciated that Jenah had clearly sacrificed her eighties hair band wig to cut it into Devon's haircut. I was going to have to repay her for that.

I wanted to stop at his desk, but I could see how his shoulders were tensed, how he was trying to casually chat with the guy next to him and ignore me walking in the door. Either he didn't want me to stare too closely at his getup and spoil things, or he simply didn't want to talk to the girl who had hexed him. I made a wide arc around him to my seat.

Jenah came in and perched on the desk next to me. "I have so much to tell you," she said.

"Join the club," I said sourly.

"Lunchtime," Jenah promised. "But I've been dying to tell you one thing since last night. Oh, why don't you have a regular phone?"

"Hey, I can call Sparkle any time I want," I said, holding it up. "Whee."

"Bryan messaged Bobby who texted Olivia who sent me the link. They posted the cast list online. *Early.*"

I suddenly noticed that Jenah was wearing shorts, tights, and hot-pink leg warmers, as if she had a really important dance rehearsal to go to and she couldn't possibly change at any point later in the day. I perked up. I knew how important this was to Jenah. "And you got in?"

"Yes," said Jenah. "You are looking at Rosie, aka Kit Kat girl number one, leader of all the Kit Kats. The three female leads all went to seniors, of course, but I got the best part of any of the sophomore *or* junior girls. I did that thing."

"You. Are awesome," I said. I hugged Jenah and congratulated her, and then the fact that she had said "lunchtime" a few sentences back finally percolated through my brain. "Ugh," I said. "I want to hear the whole story, but I can't join you at lunch. I have, um. Something to do with Poppy."

"Poppy Jones? Captain of the debate team Poppy Jones?"

I nodded. "Let's just say our *mothers are friends.*"

Jenah whistled in understanding at my code. "Her mother? Wow." She leaned closer. "So are you guys going to talk to Sam the piano player? Because I still feel guilty about that." She pulled out a piece of paper and handed it to me. "Look, I called the pizza place yesterday and wormed his name and address out of one of the college kids. We could go check on him and see if he's okay."

She was so close and yet so far. I couldn't even begin to tell her everything that had happened since Saturday evening, not in public, not sitting in the classroom waiting for Algebra to start. And I hadn't thought about Sam since Sarmine disappeared, and that made me irritated at myself.

"You can't go there," I whispered. "You know you can't. That woman is dangerous."

"I know, but . . ."

I could see it in her eyes. Her drive to help could easily overwhelm her common sense. And Sparkle was right—we had to protect Leo from that witch. "Jenah. You *can't.* Just . . . just focus on *Cabaret.*" I put the paper in my backpack, away from her reach. "I'll let you know if you can help."

Jenah drew back, looking a little hurt. "Fine. I can't really leave for lunch anyway. Henny was going to join us for lunch, and she made it into the show too. We have so much to talk over that you might feel left out."

"I wouldn't," I protested, but I did. "Since when does Henny do theater?"

"I told her she should audition so she could hang with me. And then it's a high school show, you know. They cast twenty Kit Kats instead of six. So she's like Kit Kat girl number nineteen, but she is so-o-o happy." She saw my face. "I would have asked you to audition, but you've been busy, you know? And you've said a million times that dancing around in corsets isn't your thing."

"Oh," I said. "It's not," I said. "You crazy kids have fun," I said. And then Rourke *ahem*ed loudly and we had to bust it up and sit down.

Rourke glared at the phone on my desk and I slid it into my pocket. "Miss Hendrix? I trust we are not interrupting your social life any more than necessary?"

"No sir," I said, face flaming red.

His gaze roved the room till he found Devon. "And Mr. Maguire? We are interrupting your busy rock star schedule?" He gestured to Devon's sunglasses and ball cap.

"Dilated eyes, sir," Devon said. "I have a note from the nurse."

"Peculiar," said Rourke with a sniff. He poured himself a mug of root beer while he surveyed the room, looking for something else to complain about. We all waited patiently until he finally said, "Please open your textbooks to page one hundred eighty-three," and sighs of relief went around the room.

I glanced around at my classmates, busy living their ordinary human lives. How I wished the only thing I had to worry about was sarcastic teachers.

If one can hurry in a reluctant fashion, then that is how I got to Poppy's station wagon at lunch. I would much rather be having lunch with Jenah than teleporting to Ingrid's house. Even if Henny was there.

Poppy was already in the car, pulling her cloak out of her messenger bag. It was all visible except for a few blurry patches, and it stunk of eels. "I can't believe I forgot to pull this out and bleach it," she said.

"We've been busy," I said dryly.

"I got you some inferior Parmesan," she said. "So do your stuff."

I was a little nervous, now that I was the one working spells in front of Poppy. My forte was brilliant ideas like pouring water on a magic bomb. Carefully, I combined the ingredients I had used before, but this time added a dusting of Parmesan cheese. I sprinkled it all on Poppy's cloak.

Nothing happened.

Poppy wrinkled her nose, considering. "Did you think of anything in particular while you did it last time? Class Ten and up spells need a significant mental oomph from the witch—"

I raised a hand, forestalling her. Of course. I knew what to do now.

I looked at that cloak and thought about how desperately it needed to disappear. How that was the only thing that could make us safe from Ingrid. How it was the only way we could find our mothers. How *lives* were at stake.

The cloak obediently vanished.

I beamed. Poppy beamed. This was tremendous. We were on fire.

"That was amazing," she said.

"Did you see that?" I said.

"I'm telling you, you could turn that into a business," she said.

"Or *we* could," I said.

"No more babysitting."

"I could get a real phone."

"I wish we could go home and do it right now," Poppy said. "Except . . ."

Except we still had to go to Ingrid's.

Darn it.

I came back to reality with a bump. "Did you get her address?" I said.

"This one was easy," said Poppy, folding the cloak into her messenger bag for safekeeping. "Apparently she runs a dog breeding business called Ingrid's Purebreds. There was a picture of her property on the website, which is important for visualizing. But like I said, it's about four hours from here. In the mountains. Alone. No one around for miles."

"Are you stalling? I feel like you're stalling. I'm stalling. We don't have to do this, right? We could go home and set up our invisible cloak business instead?"

"Teleportation is a perfectly natural process."

"Of what . . . taking your atoms apart and reassembling them halfway across the state?"

"You've been watching too much *Star Trek*. We're going straight through N-space."

"Which is better because . . . ?"

"It's the place where the demons live."

"Yes, much better than splitting us apart and putting us back together."

"It'll be incredibly hot. Witches can only stay in for a split second. But that's enough time to jump through to anywhere you want to go. As long as you keep a mental picture."

"Ugh. I guess we'd better."

Poppy measured out the precious drops of attar of roses and dropped the jackalope whisker into it. Because of the rose oil, she couldn't mix the ingredients on her phone, so she took a small wooden bowl from her messenger bag and put the mixture in there. She rummaged around and pulled out the vial that she and her mother had referred to as containing powdered claw.

Powdered *claw*. And Claudette, the only other witch I knew who could teleport, had been chasing a Bigfoot.

The penny finally dropped. "That's *Bigfoot* claw," I said.

"Just toenail clippings," Poppy said shortly, forestalling my complaint about ethics.

"And the jackalope died of a heart attack . . . I know, I know," I said. But it did explain why everyone wanted to get their hands on Sam the piano player. He was the key to the semisecret teleportation spell. "How did your mom learn about teleportation?" I said.

Poppy shrugged. "Aunt Jonquil, maybe? She does a lot of enforcing for her coven. Hears about weird things." She smeared the oil on my palms and pulled out her wand. She took a deep breath. "Now, in order to not get lost in N-space, you need to think hard about where you're going. Think of Ingrid's house."

"I've never seen her house!"

"Okay, think of me. Look, hold my hand."

"Oh god oh god oh god."

"One . . . two . . . three!"

Flames sprang up around the edges of my vision. They licked the car. They engulfed us. I tried to tell Poppy that I had very much changed my mind, but my words were lost in the fire. It was incredibly hot. Like being under the sun when it's 110 degrees outside. Worse. I could feel the oil smeared on my palms burning off, and as it did, it became hotter and hotter, until if you had asked me I would have screamed that I was actually on fire.

But then, a second later, I saw pine trees in front of me. Mountains. I stumbled forward, still clutching Poppy's hand. We fell out of the flames and onto the cool mountainside. We rolled on pine needles. I wouldn't let go of Poppy's hand for anything. We came to a stop, fetched up against some trees.

"I'm on fire, I'm on fire," I found myself saying over and over. My hands were completely dry again, the protective oil burned away.

Poppy looked rather wide-eyed herself. "That was . . . hotter than I was expecting," she said.

"You've never done it before?"

In a lofty voice she said, "I knew the theory." She picked pine needles out of her curly bun and dropped them to the forest floor. But I saw her fingers trembling. It had been an ordeal for her, too.

"Poppy," I said in a whisper. "Is this her house?"

We slowly stood.

We were on the side of a thickly forested mountain. Below was a pocket valley that, as far as I could tell, must belong entirely to Ingrid. There was a gorgeous, modern-looking mountain house with long clean lines and a billion plate glass windows. Beyond that were a number of outbuildings—a greenhouse, a garage, a beautiful red barn. A ribbon of blue river skated through the valley. It would, in fact, be a lovely place to have a dog breeding business. I imagined them running over the fields below, yapping their silly heads off, like Wulfie. It was so peaceful, so green. No other houses anywhere in sight.

"Do you think she teleports in and out all the time?" I said.

"That or helicopters," said Poppy, pointing.

"Ah."

Poppy pulled the invisible cloak from her messenger bag and we wrapped it around us. It had been made for someone larger than either of us, which helped, but I wouldn't call it ideal. Also it was still a little whiffy from the eels.

"Next case we solve, we'll bring an invisible bedsheet," I said.

"Two bedsheets," said Poppy.

We inched closer to Ingrid's house, my heart racing. I mean, at least I *knew* Valda and Esmerelda. They were terrible people, sure, but I knew what sort of terrors they might do.

But if Poppy was right, then Ingrid was way worse than Valda or Esmerelda.

And I had no idea what she might do to us.

"Let's peek in the side door," whispered Poppy.

It was dead silent in the middle of nowhere. "Maybe the hex has already got her," I whispered back.

Poppy silently tapped her phone. It was only 11:52. She held it up inside the cloak, scanning the door for defensive spells.

I remembered the hex that struck Valda's house and felt a little jumpy. "What if the hex thinks Ingrid is at home, but she isn't? But we are."

"That would be an amateur sort of hex," said Poppy, her voice still low. Quietly, she reached for the doorknob. "No spells I can see. Being out here in the wilderness must make you careless."

"Oh, it does, does it?"

I turned to find myself looking into the eyes of the large German shepherd I had seen at my house the other night. But now he was rigid, his nose pointing straight at us. I could sense that he was only held in check by the woman standing next to him.

"Rover," said Ingrid. "Cloak."

The dog sniffed again, and then, with one swing of his head, got a sturdy mouthful of eely cloak. Another swing and he had pulled the whole thing out of our nerveless grasp. It landed on him, disappearing him for a second. He wriggled out of it, looking disdainful.

Ingrid stood there in overalls and boots, shovel in hand. "Care to explain what you're doing here?"

Poppy was much smoother than I was. She fell back on her debating skills and rose to the occasion, while my brain was still going *dog dog teeth dog witch shovel dog.*

"We're here to warn you about the spell that happened

at the coven Saturday night," she said, massaging the truth a wee bit.

Ingrid laughed in our faces. "You mean Sarmine disappearing? It's a shame, of course, but I don't see what it has to do with me." She felt around in the grass, picked up the cloak from where the dog had dropped it. He growled at the smell. "Ugh, kids and their invisible eels," she said, tossing it our direction. "Heel, Rover."

Poppy grabbed the cloak out of the air and tucked it safely in her messenger bag. "Sarmine wasn't the only victim," she said to Ingrid.

"Is that so?" Ingrid said, dusting dirt from her hands. "What a shame. I'm sorry for . . . who did you say disappeared next?"

"*Nobody* disappeared next," I said. "It's actually the worst spell you've ever done, coming back to bite you. And soon. So you need to think quickly: What's the worst thing you've ever done?"

"Ha," Ingrid said. "You think you can catch me out with that?"

Poppy and I looked at each other. "We're not making it up," I said. "We just saw it happen to Valda and Esmerelda."

"To—What on earth are you talking about?" Ingrid shook her head. "This is nonsense. Those two nitwits probably did their own backfiring spells. Valda in particular is a menace. Now, if you'll excuse me, I have actual work to do." She scraped her boots on the mat, whistled to Rover, and watched as he obediently wiped his paws. "I'll thank you two junior scouts to get going before I call your mothers." She snorted laughter. "That is, *mother*."

"Now look," said Poppy. "In about two minutes, the worst spell you've ever done is going to backfire on you. We are *warning* you. We are trying to *help*."

"Or Lily sent you to find out if I was the one who blew up

Vera Quatch's house when she was in it," Ingrid said dryly. "She's always suspected me, with no reason. It would be like her and Jonquil to concoct a harebrained strategy for digging up the past and make you saps believe in it. Now, if you'll excuse me, I've got important work to do."

She slammed the side door in our faces, and Poppy and I went glumly down the porch steps. "That was fun," I said.

Poppy's mouth was set. "I know this was my stupid idea. *And* I forgot to bleach the cloak."

"It could have been helpful," I consoled.

"We are detectives!" said Poppy. "We are saving our mothers! We are not responsible for saving a bunch of terrible awful witches who never did anything for anybody."

"Well," I began—and I guess I'll never know exactly what I intended to say, because at that moment the house exploded.

9

Witches Are Positively Ungrateful

Poppy and I dove for cover. I barely had the wits to protect my head, but Poppy grabbed a fistful of ingredients from her messenger bag and flung it over us, shouting something. Immediately we were enveloped in an invisible dome. I could tell it was there because I saw a flaming board hit solid air a foot away from my head and bounce off.

"I've had that protection spell prepped and ready to go for two years," panted Poppy. "Mom said, 'What makes you think you'll randomly be near an exploding building?' and I said—"

"That liar! I can't believe she stood there lying to us!"

"So you haven't been around witches your whole life or anything?" Poppy said dryly.

"We were trying to help her!"

"And she was a big jerk, so yay burny house."

I scrubbed the dirt and soot off my face as I watched the house burn. "Do you think she made it out okay?"

"Witches are cockroaches," Poppy said succinctly, and indeed, through the smoky haze at the back of the house, I watched a figure, enveloped in an enormous black cloak, totter through the wreckage toward the helicopter, dog racing along at her side.

"Do you think we should see if she's okay?"

"And have her hex us for 'starting the fire'?"

"Good point."

But the fleeing form was not headed for the helicopter. She was headed toward the barn.

And the explosions were not finished.

Halfway down the hill, the greenhouse exploded, a shower of glass and metal. We ducked, covering our heads. As we rose, it was clear that Poppy and I were having the same worry.

"The barn," I said. "She's a dog breeder."

"That must be where she keeps them," said Poppy.

We ran around the house, around the fire and smoke, looking for a good path down the hill. Down below, Ingrid was coming out of the barn, lugging two wriggling puppies in her arms, and now running for the helicopter, her German shepherd herding them all on board.

One of the sheds exploded.

Wind swept the fire toward us as the helicopter took off. There was smoke and soot in my eyes. But through the crackling and the blades I heard—yes, I was sure I heard howling down below.

Ingrid hadn't rescued them all.

We found a safe path down the terraced mountainside, going as quickly as we could around the rubble of the destroyed buildings. The second shed exploded as we went. There wasn't much left to go, except that barn.

Halfway down, Poppy grabbed my arm.

I looked down to see the barn cracking open, as if a giant hand had twisted it. The mournful sound rose louder, and my heart clenched tight, thinking of Wulfie howling his heart out in a barn like that.

"I don't see any fire," Poppy murmured. "Maybe she has a protection spell on the barn."

I hoped with all my might that Poppy was right, as, wands out, we made our way down to the barn. There was a giant hole in its side, but torn boards and broken glass lay across the hole, blocking our entrance. Poppy scanned it with her app.

The avatar began to list off the spells in his monotone. "A Verie Good Protection Spelle for Large Outbuildings. A Nice Spelle for Containing That Which Does Not Wish to Be Contained. . . ."

"What *doesn't* she have on this?" Poppy said.

"They probably hate her so much she has to hex them to stay in," I said. "Poor things."

We moved as one to disassemble the boards. "Wait," Poppy said. "Let me cast a glove protection spell on us." She did, and then we began pulling apart the cracked and twisted lumber. I could feel a nasty buzzing sensation in my fingers, even through her defensive spell.

As we pulled the boards away, I could see inside—a barn full of fuzzy gray puppies, tumbling over each other . . . well, four of them, anyway, though they were active enough to look like twenty. Their conditions looked adequate if not exciting; I suppose Ingrid couldn't scare away the buyers by leaving them in squalor. Still. They were puppies. They should be out running in the field, not shut up in this barn.

Poppy grimaced. "There's a big containment section here," she said. "Set up to zap them anytime they tried to escape. Here, grab one end of the spell and start pulling." The pocket of her pink linen jacket had snagged on something—it was ripped. Dirt caked my shirt and hands. We ripped and tore at the wood and the spell, and the buzzing sensation slowly dissipated as a great gash opened up in the spell on the barn.

The puppies hung back for a moment, not knowing if they would get zapped again.

"Come on," said Poppy. "Who's a good boy? Come on."

First one, then another—the four puppies tumbled out and onto the field.

Six puppies total, and Ingrid had only bothered to grab two? She hadn't even left the door open to let them run to safety. It made me livid.

One of the puppies tore out and back and then jumped on me, knocking me over. He licked my face and I let him. It reminded me of my brother, in his sweet puppy form and not his current crazy monkey form.

Slowly a thought percolated through my brain. Poppy was probably right that it was mush. In my defense, I had been dealing with flaming houses for the last fifteen minutes and it didn't leave a lot of room for thinking sharp and incisive thoughts.

"Poppy," I said slowly. "Are these really dogs?"

Poppy sat down hard next to me. "Werewolves?" she said, shock in her voice. Another puppy immediately jumped on her, licking her all over. Through puppy kisses she said, "But it's the full moon. They would be people. Your brother is."

"Of course," I said. "I'm being dumb."

But Poppy shook her head. She wasn't dismissing my idea. She pulled out her phone and scanned the puppy on top of her. The avatar shook his ponytail. "No spells found," he said, and again and again with the same inflection, as Poppy checked the other puppies and their collars. "No spells found."

"Even witches have to earn a living," I said. "So she raises dogs."

"And what better way to smuggle werewolves around than to raise them alongside actual dogs?" Poppy said. "I bet you anything those were the two she rescued." She went back to the barn and found several more collars hanging on a hook.

Nothing, nothing . . . and then the avatar paused. "Unknown spell detected," he said calmly. "Ingredients used: wheatgrass, wolfsbane, words of power . . ."

Poppy's face sobered, and it hadn't been cheerful before.

"It's a spell I don't have in my database. And I have lots of spells in my database." She took her glasses off, absentmindedly cleaning them with her dirty shirt while she sorted out the implications. "Wheatgrass is used in several different spells that involve repressing physical change. And wolfsbane . . ."

But I could make an educated guess. "You may not be a werewolf, but we love you just the way you are," I told the puppy licking my face. I set him down. "Run, little one." The four of them tore around as Poppy and I looked at each other. "We can't leave them here." I was certain on that point.

"I wouldn't leave a fly I cared about with her," said Poppy.

"But can they go through N-space with us?" I said.

"If we had a firm grasp on them, sure," said Poppy.

I looked dubiously at the four frisky pups. "What happens if our grasp is not so firm?"

Poppy made a face. "Bad things. Getting lost in N-space, in the demon lair. Unable to get back out. The oil burns off quickly. If you dropped a pup, we *might* be able to find him again, if we were quick and he didn't go anywhere. But you'd only have a couple seconds before you'd burned through all your traveling juice. And then all the books say that you'd be stuck. In . . . well, in limbo, almost literally."

I shuddered. "But you'd be able to come find me, right?"

Poppy shook her head. "It's like you're traveling through another dimension. Even if I turned around and came right back to Ingrid's, it wouldn't be the same path. The only way I could find you would be to make a deal with . . ."

Ah. "A demon."

"Yeah."

"Let's stick together."

"Yeah."

"Not let any puppies go off the path."

"Right."

Poppy flipped open her messenger bag to pull out the ingredients. "Oh no," she said. "No no no."

"I don't like the sound of that."

She faced the bag toward me. Something had leaked all over it.

"I landed on my bag during the explosion," mourned Poppy. "I didn't have a spot for the attar of roses so I put it with the carrot juice. And now . . ." That did explain the carroty smell.

We looked at each other, uncomprehending. A moment ago we had been discussing how to get four puppies home with us. And now—without the proper ingredients for teleportation we were stuck here. On a witch's mountain. Four hours from home. "What are we going to do?" I said.

Poppy sighed. "We can try my mom again. But (A) she hasn't been answering, and (B) I'm going to be grounded for life if she finds out I'm on Ingrid's mountain instead of safely at school."

"The SUVs," I said. "There were three of them in the driveway. Maybe one has the keys."

We found four leashes in the barn, tackled and clipped them to the puppies one by one, and finally clambered back up to the smoking wreckage of Ingrid's house, debating the merits of grand theft auto all the way.

One of them *did* have the keys. There were benefits to living on a mountain by yourself. Except . . .

"I'm not really up for stealing cars," said Poppy. "I know what happens if you get pulled over for that."

"Then I'll steal it," I said. "I'll drive."

"I'm maybe more worried about that, if that's possible."

"We aren't stealing it," I said. "We're borrowing it. Not just to save ourselves—to save the puppies."

"That is true," said Poppy. "Maybe I can change the tags."

In the end she changed the tags *and* the color, flicked a "do not notice us" spell on the car, and we headed down the twisty road out of the mountains, with four puppies happily exploring the backseat.

"This counts as playing hooky from school, you know," she said.

I sighed. "I know." There went my American history quiz.

"And the car is bugging me big-time. I don't want that on my record when I'm applying to Larkspur."

"You said that name before. It's a college, I take it?"

"You've never heard of—"

"No, I've never heard of! Stop lecturing me on everything I haven't heard of!"

There was a pause, and then Poppy said, "It's the Larkspur College of Applied Witchcraft and Theoretical Sorcery, it's *the* top school for witches in the U.S., and I'm sorry."

"I'm sorry, too," I said, my anger cooling immediately. "I shouldn't have yelled. Sarmine's probably mentioned it."

"I think your mom went to the state university," she said. "Like mine, only my mom's a bit younger. They have secret classes you can take, along with your regular education."

"So what *do* you want to do?" I said. "At this Larkspur."

"Nuh-uh," said Poppy. "That's not the point."

"I thought the point of going to college was to major in something, blah blah."

"Nonsense," said Poppy. "I mean state school, sure. The point of going to a top school is to meet the other people who are there, going to a top school. It is irrelevant what you actually major in."

I tried a different tack. "So what do you want to do with your life? Is that irrelevant too?"

"No," she said. "But it is indeterminate."

I was tired of not being able to follow half of what Poppy said. I just waited.

"Graduation is an impermeable barrier," she said. "The line between high school and college—I can't see that far, and I know I can't. I'll be transcending. It is as incomprehensible to me what I will want five years from now as high school was to me when I was three. Can you imagine picking out your high school classes when you were three? The job of Current Poppy is to strategize me into the position from which I will have the maximum amount of opportunities to optimize my future. Future Poppy will take over when her time comes."

"That's actually reasonably brilliant," I said.

"It's challenging to stay focused and yet flexible," she said. "I maintain a sort of tunnel vision for exactly that reason. All that Present Poppy has to do is complete one grand magical working to be accepted into Larkspur and stay in the right direction for the future. Future Poppy will worry about what I do when I get there."

I wondered what Future Cam would think about what Present Cam was doing. It probably depended on whether or not I got Present Cam killed.

I texted Pink to tell her we would be late to get Wulfie. She texted back that he was busy jumping on all of Rimelda's beds.

"Too bad Pink can't make a hologram for us so your 'mom' could call school and say we got sick," I said. "You don't have anything like that already, do you?"

"Never needed it," Poppy said. Then: "Ooh, ask Pink if Rimelda would call in and cover for us. I bet she'd do it. She'd love to get one up on some random authority figure."

It was worth trying anything at this point. I texted the idea to Pink and got a smiley face in reply.

Three hours and forty-two minutes to go, or so said Poppy's phone. Plus or minus traffic, of course. I looked sideways at Poppy. She was concentrating on the road.

"The hexes are *definitely* striking in order," I said.

"Check."

"The nastiest spell you've ever done, backfiring on you."

"Check."

"It's *got* to be Malkin's hex," I said. "Ingrid didn't even have an escape plan. Neither she nor Valda nor Esmerelda would have intentionally suffered through the hex they got."

"Maybe we're looking at it backwards," said Poppy. "What if the witch who cast it is someone who isn't till the very end? And they plan to stop the hex before it gets to them, after they knock everybody else out? Who was at the other end of the circle?"

"Me," I said.

"Oh."

"But on my right was that French lady," I said.

"Claudette," said Poppy. "I think she technically lives in British Columbia, but she's got, like, places in Quebec and L.A. and the South of France. She teleports a lot."

"I'll say," I said. "Did you know she was chasing a Bigfoot Saturday night? Before the coven, I mean." I filled Poppy in on our pizza place adventure, which made me abruptly think of Jenah. I wished I could tell her about everything that had happened. But sometimes it was tough to get her alone.

"I'm sure Claudette would be happy to have Sarmine out of the way," said Poppy. "But would she turn on the others like that? Maybe."

Mostly, I was glad Claudette was near the end of the circle and we could put her off for a bit. "How are your mind-reading shields?" I said.

"I know the theory," Poppy said ruefully.

We kept wrangling through witches and circle placement and spell stoppages until we had run ourselves in circles. The car fell silent, except for the panting of one eager puppy who was particularly enjoying running back and forth between the windows.

Now that we were pretty sure that the hex the witches were getting was the worst thing they'd ever done, it set me free to imagine dire things about my mother. I mean, was vanishing someone really the worst thing Sarmine Scarabouche had ever done? She'd done twenty worse things to her own daughter before breakfast.

I finally just had to say it, to lance the wound by putting the words out there. "Did my mother really vanish?"

"As opposed to . . . ?"

"If she didn't cast the hex, then she *got* the hex. The worst spell she ever cast, coming back to bite her. What if it wasn't vanishing?"

"What, you think she vaporized somebody?"

I couldn't decide. "Maybe, if she thought they deserved it."

"*Or* maybe the worst thing she ever did was teleport somebody to some terrible locale," said Poppy. "She moved them to Death Valley. That's why she vanished. And as soon as your mom finds some jackalope whiskers, et cetera, et cetera, she'll pop right back."

"Yeah," I said. I didn't think my mom had ever done the teleporting spell, but I didn't say that.

Poppy put a comforting hand on my arm. And she wasn't a touchy-feely person like her mother, so that touch was like the equivalent of a bear hug. "Look. How about after dinner we'll go back to your house. We'll see if we can find any more clues. Okay?"

I guess I needed to hear a plan, a concrete plan, because that cheered me up a bit. "Okay," I said, with more energy.

Poppy, who also liked concrete plans, put both hands back on the wheel. "And now," she said, "back to our other problem."

"There's only one?"

"*One* of our other problems," she amended. "*What is the worst thing you've ever done?*"

The good thing about being a beginning witch is that I haven't actually done that much. I shook my head, listing off the few things I'd managed. "Self-defense," I said. "The basic one that just stops a bad spell."

"Oh, with the pears?" She nodded. "Go on."

"Power spell. Charisma spell. Some random practice spells for Sarmine. Love potion."

She raised her eyebrows.

"Long story."

"I'm not seeing a lot of bad ways these spells could be used against you," she said. "Maybe you'll be fine."

But then my heart sank. "Oh, wait. Turning Devon invisible."

"Could be worse."

"Turning him into a turnip."

"Definitely worse." She tossed me her phone. "Will you write that down? Cam might get a backfiring hex." Her aplomb was admirable. "Oh, and you're certain about where my mother was standing, right? Esmerelda wasn't lying or anything?"

She said the thing about her mother in an equally callous tone, but I knew how Poppy felt about her mom. Which led me to think that she wasn't just being callous about my backfiring hex. See, I could do this "understanding people" thing, too.

"Your mom was near the end," I assured her, and I opened up her notebook app and notated it, then read it off to Poppy.

Hexes So Far

1. Sat Midnight: Sarmine Scarabouche (Cam's mom). Vanished.
2. Sunday Noon: V. Valda Velda (grumpy stompy witch). House tried to destroy her.

3. Sun Midnight: Esmerelda Danela (pissy blonde witch). Old and ugly.
4. Monday Noon: Ingrid Ahlgren (tough blonde with dog). House exploded.
5. Mon Midnight: Ulrich Grey (Unicorn Guy)
6. Tuesday Noon: Fiona Laraque (Sports Team, Canadian)
7. Tues Midnight: Jen Smith (Leggings, Canadian)
8. Wednesday Noon: Penny Patel (Boring Skirt, Canadian)
9. Weds Midnight: Rimelda Danela (Esmerelda's 100-year-old mother)
10. Thursday Noon: Hikari Tanaka (Sparkle)
11. Thurs Midnight: Lily Jones (Poppy's mom)
12. Friday Noon: Claudette Dupuy (ice-cold French-Canadian witch)
13. Fri Midnight: Camellia Hexar (Cam) (duh.) Might get a backfiring hex ??

"That's three whole days till your mom," I said. "And four till me."

"And two and a half till Sparkle, and Unicorn Guy is tonight," she said. "Ugh, the thought of going out to his place to warn him slash check on him is killing me."

"He is such a creeper," I agreed.

"Ooh, wait," said Poppy. "Sparkle."

"Two birds with one stone?" I said.

"High five," said Poppy.

I dialed Sparkle's number and put her on speakerphone. "She's probably in fourth hour already," I said. But she picked up. I could hear the echo of the gymnasium and the thumps of balls in the background.

"This better be important, Cam," she said.

"Because you're getting in trouble for us?"

"No, because I don't want anything to do with W-I-T-C-H stuff when there are regular people around. You know that."

"I know that spelling it probably doesn't help," I said.

"Listen up," said Poppy. "That hex that got Sarmine? It's not just her. It's hexing every single witch who was at the coven, with the worst spell you've ever done. Yours is coming Thursday noon."

"Thursday noon?" said Sparkle. If I hadn't known her better, I would have said she said it in a small voice. But Sparkle is never small-voiced. Anyway, the next second she said dryly, "It's almost worth it to see some of them get one-upped. I can only imagine what happened to Esmerelda."

"It was rather awesome," said Poppy.

"Sparkle," I put in. "What's the worst thing you've ever done?"

Sparkle snorted. "Too many to list. I'm screwed if that hex gets to me."

"But have you ever killed anyone?" said Poppy.

There was silence while Sparkle thought about this, which wasn't super encouraging. "No," she said.

"Not even Past Sparkle?"

"Past Sparkle once hexed the food at the cul—at the place she lived, so everyone got terrible food poisoning," Sparkle said. "But no one died from it. Also I never went by 'Sparkle' the first time around, so it's weird to call that person 'Past Sparkle.' She usually went by 'Kari.'"

"Past Kari was nasty," said Poppy.

"Look, however many people you are, the point is you're going to be extremely unhappy but you won't die," I said. "Correct?"

"I think so, yes," said Sparkle. Her lack of certainty was irritating. I kind of like to be more certain about how many people I have and haven't killed, and I also like that number to be zero. "Can I get back to volleyball now? My team is losing without me."

"One more thing," I said. "Can you warn Unicorn Guy? He's next on the list."

"Ugh," said Sparkle. "I loathe Unicorn Guy. He's creepy *and* fetishy."

"We know," Poppy and I said in unison.

"Please?" I said. "We warned *you.* Just leave a note on his door if you want. Tell him Ingrid's house exploded. That'll convince him."

"You promise you're not going to do anything dumb like talk to Claudette?"

"Not without you," I said.

"Oh, all right," said Sparkle. "I guess I can weasel some unicorn hairs out of him while I'm there. Where are you calling from, anyway?"

"Long story," I said. "We'll tell you tomorrow."

"I'd just as soon you didn't," said Sparkle, and hung up.

I went back to Poppy's notebook app. "So, do I write that down for Sparkle's possible hex?" I said. "Maybe food poisoning, maybe murder, IDK, who, like, cares and stuff?"

"Might as well," said Poppy.

I studied the list again. "It's a good thing you *weren't* part of the coven, or you'd be on here, too."

"Yeah, I've been thinking that."

"What if, though? What do you think would happen to you? You've been working spells a lot longer than I have."

"That's the thing," Poppy said. "Are these spells measuring the nastiness of the intent? Or just the spell, period? Because I haven't done many mean things—" She blushed.

"Except . . . ?"

"Well. I was eight and just learned I was a witch. So

don't hold it against me?" Her voice was suddenly soft and pleading.

"Cross my heart," I said.

"I depantsed someone."

"You . . . what?"

"Depantsed someone."

I doubled over laughing. "Boy or girl?"

"Boy. They deserved it."

"I'm sure they did."

"I had braids at the time. He kept pulling them. *Extremely* inappropriate."

"This is so *Anne of Green Gables*. Did you hit him with your slate?"

"No, I told you, I depantsed him." She was laughing now. "I would love to see Anne do that to Gilbert."

"What would Marilla say?"

"Marilla! No, that neighbor lady, what's-her-name, she would have said send me back to the orphanage."

"You can't leave me hanging. How did it go down?"

"He was in the cafeteria. . . . It was still really mean. I shouldn't have done it."

"I forgive Past Poppy," I said.

"And I had been researching this spell at home, because I was so mad, but I wasn't actually going to do it, just hold my ingredients and imagine how satisfying it would be—"

"And he did it one more time."

"No. He did it to my friend!" She wiped away tears of laughter. "I still can't decide if I was angry on her behalf or jealous that he'd switched targets. Eight-year-old Poppy was maybe not as feminist as she could be."

"So then . . ."

"Right in front of everyone. Right next to the steamed carrots. Boom. Depantsed."

"And he was humiliated."

"Yeah. And I was satisfied *and* guilty. You know."

"Yeah."

Poppy sobered up. "I guess, if that *did* happen to me, then I had it coming."

"It's a little worse to happen in high school than grade school," I said. "And to a girl."

"It has severe feminist implications," she said. "This is bigger than me. Now we *really* gotta stop this spell." There was an edge of hysteria in her laugh, like she knew depantsing was nothing, set against what the other witches might have done.

"Maybe that's not the worst thing?" I said. "Is there anything else?"

Poppy shook her head. "Do you ever have—I don't know, this sounds stupid. But kind of . . . *teaching moments* in your life?"

"I don't know," I said. "Explain?"

"Well, that was one for me," she said. "I felt so good about what I'd done—and so bad about feeling good. It really stopped me from going to a bad place with magic."

"Yeah," I said, nodding slowly. "I think I know what you mean."

"So I do know," she said. "This is the worst thing. Most of the spells I've practiced have been under my mom's supervision, you know? And none of them were bad. And the things I've done in secret aren't terrible either. This . . . well, it wasn't even that horrible to him. He did deserve it, and it didn't turn him into an outcast, just made people laugh for a couple days. But for me, it was the one thing. And I think . . . I think this spell might be sort of centering in on things like that."

"I don't think Ingrid felt guilty about blowing up that lady's house," I said.

"Except she did, kinda, because she knew instantly what her thing was," Poppy said. "She brought it up, not us."

I nodded. Maybe some witches did feel guilt, after all.

Maybe that guilt was coming home to roost.

It was a long drive, made worse, first, by stopping a hundred times to let puppies do their business, and second, by rush hour traffic once we hit town. I won't say we got along perfectly—Poppy insisted on quizzing me in American history some more, on the theory that I would get to retake the quiz tomorrow, and after her app buzzed at me for the tenth wrong answer, and I told her I wasn't doing it anymore and I didn't care if I flunked, she got all huffy. Then she made me read her calculus problems while she tried to solve them in her head. And look, it's not my fault that I don't know what all the slashes and symbols are called. I'm barely keeping up in algebra. I thought we could talk about, like, anything else in the world, but Poppy insisted that calculus was the only thing that was going to take her mind off her problems, so there we were.

But even long drives come to an end. Poppy parked Ingrid's SUV on one of the side streets near the school. We loaded four squirmy puppies into Lily's open-air station wagon and headed off to Rimelda's. All four puppies stuck their heads out of the busted rear window. I wasn't sure how well that illusion would fool people if puppy heads were coming through it.

"Ugh, did someone throw their lunch wrappers through the back window?" I said.

"I wish you could drive," moaned Poppy. "My back is killing me."

We were flat-out wiped. I dreaded what Wulfie was going to be like when we found him. But then we had the first pleasant surprise of the evening: Pink was in the pool house, sitting next to a conked-out Wulfie, looking mighty pleased with herself.

"I ran him around the house fifteen times," she said. "And we did the rock wall like fifty times probably, and jumped on every bed, and went swimming twice."

"I can't thank you enough," I said.

"You are awesome," said Poppy.

Pink pinkened. "I am?" She looked shyly up at us. "I guess I did a pretty good job, huh?"

"Amazing," I assured her. "Do you want to watch four puppies next? I suspect they'll be easier than Wulfie."

"All right," she said, proud and grinning. "I'll have Grandmother get dog food. We've got it covered."

Poppy and I handed off the puppies to Pink, then loaded the sleeping Wulfie into the backseat and got back in the car for the millionth time. The sun had set and the twilight was shading into dark. "Maybe he'll stay asleep," I said. "Wouldn't that be amazing?"

Poppy, who had more experience with babysitting small children, looked dubious. "At any rate, I'm not waking him," she said. "Even if we regret it tonight."

"He looks so sweet when he's asleep," I mused. "Not like a holy terror at all."

"Same with puppies," she said.

"True."

We drove back to Poppy's home in silence. The stars were out, and the cool spring air filled the car. Wulfie's moon shone brightly down on us. Poppy turned on the heat, letting it fight back against the wind. I would have nodded off if Poppy hadn't told me at the beginning of the drive that I was under no circumstances to flunk my duties as driver-keeper-awaker.

We pulled into the driveway, drove down its long path into the garage at the back of the lot. Wulfie was snoring softly. Poppy carried our backpacks, and I picked up my brother, cradling him against my chest. He really was a sweet boy. It was funny how mixed up my feelings for him were. I knew he wasn't just a puppy dog, but I mostly only saw him that way. It made it hard to think of him as a person. But person or puppy, he was still my brother. I kissed his forehead gently, careful not to wake him.

We walked through the fenced backyard, up to the back door. I hadn't noticed before that their back door had a fancy door knocker—a bitey, eagley looking thing. "Did I leave the kitchen light on?" said Poppy as she reached for the doorknob.

I suddenly remembered what we had been doing yesterday morning. "The wards!" I shouted, too late.

As her fingers touched the doorknob, a roar sounded out of nowhere. Not nowhere—there was a transparent lion-eagle thing, as big as the house, suddenly swooping down on us with a giant hooked beak. Another guardian, like Sarmine's, only Sarmine hadn't drilled me in how to disarm this one.

"Poppy!" I shrieked. "What is in those wards of yours?"

"Gryphon!" she shouted back. She was busy digging for ingredients. "Carrot juice everywhere . . . Glass everywhere—Ow!"

Wulfie stirred in my arms. His eyes popped open. "Cam!" he squealed, clambering up my shoulder.

"Afraid of mice," panted Poppy. "Afraid of . . ." She combined and threw some mixture all over the gryphon. It turned into a shower of tiny mice as it fell. The gryphon reared back in horror and shrank away, turning back into a plain brass door knocker on the door.

"You are definitely improving on doing spells in the heat of the moment," I said.

"You really think so?" A smile flickered over her face. "Practice helps, huh?"

Wulfie bounded off of me and began chasing the mice through the grass. "I thought you were a wolf, not a cat," I said.

"There goes that nap," said Poppy.

But the mice were way too fast for his boy form, and he zoomed back, knocking me over. "Cam Cam Cam!" He started to lick my face, and I laughed and gently rolled him away, tickling him instead. Wulfie might technically be a three-year-old, but he didn't speak like one, undoubtedly due to spending so much time in puppy form. Whatever he was trying to tell me about his day with Pink, it came out in monosyllables. "Cam!" he said as I stood up. "Pink!" Then: "Cam Cam Pink Pink Cam!" He clambered up me like I was Pink's rock wall.

"Wulf Wulf Wulf," I hollered back, as he lodged one foot on my elbow and swung a leg onto my shoulders. Puppies with hands are a bad combo, I tell you.

"Uh-oh," said Poppy.

"Pop mom," said Wulfie.

"Pop mom" was right. Lily stood in the kitchen doorway, in a billowy cotton nightgown. Her arms were folded and her expression was severe. She didn't look quite so loosey-goosey and hippie at the moment. There was a tense moment where I imagined everything Sarmine would do to me if she found me disobeying her like this.

And then Poppy ran to her mother and hugged her tight. "I was so worried about you," she said. Lily squeezed her daughter, and I saw her melt for a moment. "You didn't even answer the phone."

Lily stiffened up and drew back. "Speaking of that, I've been home for twenty minutes. And where were you girls? I've been calling and texting."

Uh-oh. "Uh, that's my fault," I said. "Poppy's app wouldn't stop buzzing at me, so I shoved it in my backpack." I pulled it out and saw eleven missed messages. I handed it to Poppy with a grimace of apology.

She sighed. "Cam, I know you're not my daughter, but I do feel responsible for you right now. And Poppy . . . Poppy, I was very clear about my expectations while I was gone. Fix the wards and *stay behind them.*"

Poppy grimaced. "We did the wards," she said, gesturing at the door knocker. "But we couldn't sit here and do nothing. You know that."

Lily rubbed her forehead. She looked worn out. "I can't have anything happening to you girls. You don't understand. This is how . . ."

She looked at me, and my heart beat faster. This was how *what?*

Her eyes fell and she turned away, headed into the kitchen. We trailed along behind her, Wulfie on my shoulders. "This is how it begins," Lily said. "This is how it always begins. The coven starts to disagree. People stand up for what they believe in. And you think you're having a civil discussion, and then people start disappearing. Jim—a thorn in their side from day one—vanished. My sister Jonquil, advocating on behalf of her girlfriend Mélusine for better rights for mermaids—so they just vanish Mélusine. Jonquil gets depressed and moves to New Hampshire. Bam, bam—inconvenient people drop off the face of the earth and—Surprise!—new people are installed into the coven." She wrung her hands, pacing. "But what is it this time? The only thing Sarmine did was try to install Cam." She looked at me. "Unless someone else coveted that spot. Someone besides Poppy."

"Sit down," said Poppy. "You're not making sense. Who else wanted that spot?"

Lily shook her head. "I don't know."

Poppy flicked a glance at me. Though I barely knew Lily, I had never seen her this flustered. I bet Poppy hadn't, either. I swung Wulfie down from my shoulders and handed him a chew toy. I hoped that would keep him occupied for a few minutes. "What did you find out?" Poppy said.

Lily took off her glasses and rubbed the bridge of her nose. Finally, she appeared to come to a decision. "If I tell you, perhaps then you'll understand the danger," she said. "I went to talk to your aunt Jonquil. I'm sorry I wasn't able to text you. We ended up having to summon . . . well . . ."

Poppy's eyes were big. "You summoned a demon? You're always telling me never to mess with them."

Lily shook her head. "We had questions to ask. Anyway, I didn't dare leave Jonquil alone with him to check my phone. Never turn your attention away from demons. You don't know how tricky they are."

"I know," I murmured, having seen them in action. It was probably the one bit of knowledge I had over Poppy.

"But why did you run off to talk to Aunt Jonquil anyway?"

In response, Lily went to the living room and came back with her satchel. She didn't even make any fuss about the dolls, which is how I could tell how distracted she was. She pulled out a large coffee table book titled *Antiquities & Artefacts*. "It took a long time to convince the demon to give up the information," she said. "But finally Jonquil traded him one hour inhabiting the local weatherman—I know, I know—and he produced this book." Lily put her glasses back on, then flipped through the book till she found what she was looking for. She slid the book over to us.

There on the page was a grainy picture of the exact gravy boat that Sarmine had produced during the ceremony. No, not a gravy boat at all. "Bronze lamp, 225 BCE," I said, reading

the caption. "Continually misplaced, current whereabouts unknown. Useful for storing—"

But I didn't like the looks of the last word, and my tongue
just stopped.

Poppy whispered it into the silence. "Demons."

10

Lily Puts Her Foot Down

"Are you saying . . ." I said. I gulped and tried again. "Are you saying a demon was in that thing? *That* was the green flame that came out? A *demon* took Sarmine?"

"Oh, Cam," said Lily. She gave me a hug, as tight as she had given Poppy. But the hug couldn't change what she had learned. "I'm afraid . . . I'm afraid that's a possibility we're going to have to consider." She looked at my stunned face. "Let me get you girls some hot chocolate. Wulfie, would you like some cereal?"

Poppy tugged on my arm. "Sit down," she said. "You look like you're going to fall over at any minute." She moved me to a kitchen chair.

I had not realized until then how much I had hoped this was just one of Sarmine's crazy stunts. Make yourself disappear under suspicious circumstances. Hex all the witches you hate. I had half thought the curse would peter out by the time it reached our side of the circle.

"Teaching activity," I muttered. "I'm supposed to level up, or something." I groped for a way to make it familiar, make it all okay.

"What was that?" said Lily.

I buried my face in my hands. Much like Esmerelda would never have hexed herself with that particular curse, not even for a red herring, Sarmine would never have let herself be seized by a demon. She just wouldn't. She couldn't give up her power like that. She couldn't stand to not be in control. The only way she would have let a demon seize her is if she had no choice. No warning. No nothing.

"But how *do* death triggers work?" Poppy was asking her mother. "Like, was Malkin's package set up to go specifically to Sarmine, or was it set to go more generally to the witch that *caused her death*—" She broke off, looking wide-eyed at me. "I didn't mean—"

I wailed, I admit it. "Do you think that lamp was meant for *me*?"

I dug my fists into my eyes. Lily was right. Poppy and I didn't know what we were up against. We had started on a lark, really—the junior detectives go around on an Easter egg hunt to all the witches. Sarmine was missing, but surely if we followed the steps of her treasure hunt we would solve the clues and bring her home.

And now I was facing down the reality that she really had been stolen, by an evil elemental.

And it was all my fault.

Lily set the hot chocolate down in front of us. "Cam," she said, "I want you to listen to me." Her kind face was stiff with worry. "You did not cause your mother's disappearance. You are not responsible for all the evil in the world."

"No," said Poppy softly from the other end of the table. "But we are responsible for fighting to make it better."

Her mother flicked her a glance. It was clear this was an old argument. "Yes, *when* you have taken care of yourself and your family first, *when* you are fully trained, *when* you are an adult."

"Evil doesn't always wait for good to be prepared," said Poppy.

"*Evil* can take my family from me," said Lily, strain in her voice.

Poppy crossed to her mother and seized her hands. "You don't know everything we've learned. We've been sleuthing. We can be a team, Mom."

"We aren't a *team*; I'm your mother, and I'm responsible for keeping you safe." There was a warning hint of danger in her voice. When you live with someone who regularly threatens to turn you into a rechargeable battery, you are on high alert for those things. I could sense a temper about to blow from ten feet away.

Poppy could not. "But you were *gone*," she said. "And we had to drive out to Rimelda's anyway. We had to get someone to babysit Wulfie."

"Rimelda babysat Wulfie?"

"No, her granddaughter did," said Poppy. "And you know Rimelda wouldn't hurt us. She's grumpy, but not mean. And we checked on Esmerelda—but of course we could handle *her*, Mom. And it was worth it, because we learned—" She broke off, remembering what we had learned. We stared at Lily, fearful of what she would tell us when we told her what we had learned.

"What did you learn?" Lily said evenly.

Poppy fidgeted with her phone. I closed my hands on my hot chocolate. Neither of us wanted to come out and say it, because then we were going to learn something, and that was going to change everything.

But it was Poppy's mother. It was my turn to help Poppy. "So, uh, we think the spell might be homing in on something bad you did once." I stumbled through the words. "Like, the worst spell you ever cast on someone. Because, uh, Esmerelda was old and ugly and getting older and uglier by the minute and she, uh, confessed that she did that to someone once."

Lily said, "But that could be coincidence."

My eyes met Poppy's. Our other confirmed example was

Ingrid, but I didn't think we wanted to tell Lily we had been teleporting.

"We drove to Valda's, too," said Poppy. "Her house attacked us. It shot all its windows at us, and then an enormous boulder—"

"Came hurtling down the stairs at you?" said Lily. Her voice was remarkably even, like she was super controlling it.

"Yeah!" I said. "Hey, how did you know?"

Poppy shot a look at me that told me my brain was being mushy again. "We thought we'd better warn everybody. Bad things are happening to people, Mom. Every twelve hours, going around the circle, starting with Sarmine, Saturday midnight. We didn't know they were things that they *deserved*."

"Deserved!" said Lily, with a funny catch in her voice. "Yes, I suppose they are that."

There was silence in the old kitchen as I thought through the ethics of a karma hex, of people getting exactly what they deserved, smack out of the blue. Were Poppy and I supposed to keep intervening, now that we knew? Or were we supposed to stand back and let justice be served? My Good Witch Ethics List didn't have anything about this.

Poppy stared at her mother until the question finally had the strength to slip from her lips. "So what have you done?" Poppy said in a tiny voice.

Lily was still. Too still. Too not answering us immediately with a laugh and a joke. If the answer was "Nothing," wouldn't she come right out and say it?

She raised her head and seemed to recall that we were watching and waiting. A smile pasted itself on her face and she said with a laugh, "Oh, well, there was that time when I was seventeen that I lost my temper and turned my obnoxious ex-boyfriend purple. That's not too bad, right? I can take being purple for a few days. I remember it wearing off pretty quickly. It was a lovely shade."

"Mom," said Poppy.

Lily rose from the table. "Now you two need to be in bed. Hex or no hex, school goes on. Good thing the college is still on spring break—I can watch that boy of yours tomorrow." Lily puttered around the kitchen like everything was normal, wiping the counters with a dishrag. "After Jonquil finishes shepherding the weatherman–demon business, she's flying out to help. She'll be here Friday morning, and then, purple or no purple, we'll go find Sarmine and this whole business will be solved."

"*Mom.*"

"I'll email the coven and tell them to be on the watch for things at—what did you say? Midnight and noon? They won't believe me, but we'll have done what we can." Wulfie looked up from his dish and yawned. "Are you done with your rice puffs, honey?"

"Mom!" said Poppy.

"What is it?" said Lily. The chatter of words ceased and danger was back in her tone.

"You can't do this," said Poppy. "*Something* is going to get you on Thursday midnight. Even if Aunt Jonquil is coming, it will be too late. You *have* to let me help you. You can't fight this alone."

"I do not have to do any such thing," Lily said, eyes flashing. "Now get to bed, both of you."

"You know I'm capable," Poppy said, not moving. "You know how hard I work to learn everything I need to know. You know—Gah! Your *mother* wouldn't have kept you from helping."

Lily flung the rag in the sink and turned on us with blazing eyes. "And that is exactly why Jonquil and I no longer have a little sister. Because my mother never lifted a finger to protect us. Because she wanted us to go out there and defend ourselves against the witch world."

The anger was plain in her voice. Wulfie dropped his rice puffs and ran to clamber up into my arms.

Poppy closed her eyes. She looked like she knew she had taken her argument one step too far. "I'm sorry."

"Do you think this is fun for me?"

"No," said Poppy, and a flash of the fire returned. "But keeping me safe behind some window wards won't do any good either. It won't make the bad things go away. And you know this."

Lily shook her head and crossed to Poppy. "Car keys," she said. Poppy looked back, mutiny in her eyes, and Lily waved her hand impatiently. "You should be glad I'm not taking your wand."

Shock and anger. "You wouldn't."

Danger in Lily's tone. "I will if you cross me," she said. "I'm doing this for your own good."

"No, you're doing it for Rose's," said Poppy as she dropped the keys in Lily's palm. "And she can't come back to thank you for it."

Poppy stormed upstairs, and Lily dropped heavily in her chair.

I shifted from side to side, unsure what to do or say. "I'm sorry Wulfie destroyed your house," is what I settled on.

"I can fix it," she said. She looked up at me shouldering the squirming three-year-old. "Here, give him to me."

"Oh, I'm sure I can . . ." I demurred, but Wulfie slid off of me and onto her lap.

"I remember how exhausting it is to have a little one," she said. "And you girls need sleep." She looked at Wulfie, who was busy reaching for the salt shaker. "Come on, you," she said.

"You're going to run around the living room twenty times and then we'll try B-E-D again."

I dropped a kiss on Wulfie's thick hair, grateful for Lily's help with him.

Slowly I went up the curving stairs, mindlessly straightening plastic dolls as I went. My heart seemed to have exploded in my chest. If a demon had taken Sarmine, what could I do? How could I get her back? Not only that, but something terrible was going to happen to Lily in three days. You could tell from her story about the purple boyfriend.

I found Poppy in her room, her back to me, staring through the wall of certificates. Her arms were wrapped around herself and she was whispering something. I moved closer and found it was, "She's lying, she's lying, she's lying."

I didn't know what to say. Because the problem is, Lily *was*.

I am not really any better at hugs than Poppy. I tentatively put my hand on her shoulder. She turned, and suddenly we were hugging. You couldn't squeeze the worry away. But you could try. She drew back, scrubbing her eyes with the back of her hand. "Ugh, Cam, what are we going to *do*?"

"Do you think—" The words broke off. My voice fell to a whisper. "Do you think she killed someone?" I hastened to add, "I'm sure it was only in self-defense or something."

"If not that, why wouldn't she *tell* us?" said Poppy. "If she had exploded someone's house, like Ingrid, then we could move to your house for a few days. If she made someone ugly, like Esmerelda's hex, she'd tell us and we could laugh about it. Like the purple thing, I guess, except I didn't believe that for a minute. Maybe she did it, but it certainly wasn't the worst thing. She was lying. She's *lying*."

"You said in the car you thought the hex was zeroing in on something you felt guilty about," I said. "Maybe, if it was self-defense . . . ?"

"I'd still feel guilty about that, wouldn't you?" said Poppy.

"Yeah."

"Oh, Cam," she said. She sat down hard on the floor, as if she couldn't even make it to a chair. "What are we going to do about our mothers?"

I sat down next to her. Her question seemed unanswerable. "She wouldn't really take away your wand, would she?" I said tentatively.

"She's done it once before," said Poppy. "Worst week of my life. I had no way to protect myself. It's . . . it's criminal."

"Hey, at least your mom didn't turn us into refrigerator magnets for disobeying her," I said. "My mom would have done that." My mom, who was kidnapped by a demon. "I wonder what your mom will say when she sees the car. We shouldn't have made her mad, I guess."

Poppy's brown eyes snapped open and she looked at me with disbelief. "I'm not *trying* to make her mad. But I'm going to speak my mind if I think she's wrong. What else would I do?"

"Maybe you couldn't tell her temper was about to go," I ventured.

"Oh, I could tell." She thumped her fist against the bed. "What's she going to do, turn me into a newt?"

"'Horrible punishments are the established method for rearing young witches,'" I quoted.

"Not in this house." There was silence for a moment while I thought about the time that Sarmine punished me by making me gather one thousand perfect dandelion puffs under a full moon and bring them home without a single one going to seed.

Poppy studied my face. In a less gruff voice she said, "I suppose I have heard the stories. You just *know* Esmerelda's like that. And I guess even Grandma Iris, from what my mom says. You talk about having to be tough to survive; you should talk to *her* sometime. But times change."

"Not fast enough," I said.

She had a look like she wanted to say something, and didn't want it to be the wrong thing. "I know you want to find your mother. I expect . . . it's also hard when you have a challenging relationship. Was it . . . different when your dad was around?"

"He disappeared so long ago I don't really remember him," I said. I spread my hands and considered them. "Everyone says he was nice. *Too nice,* Sarmine always said. But then Sarmine thinks you've gotta be tough. Put yourself first. Who knows, she'd probably tell me not to try to save her, like your mom." I shrugged. "I want to save her anyway."

"I know," said Poppy.

"After that . . ." There was a pit in my stomach as I said it, but I was wondering if it was the right course of action. "Maybe I'll step away from witch things permanently. All I've done is make things worse." I tried to fix Devon and it backfired on him. I tried to stop Malkin and now my mother was gone. "I never wanted to be a witch. . . . I thought I could be a good one. . . . Maybe it's best to not be one at all."

There was silence for a moment. Poppy was looking at me sympathetically, but she also wasn't saying anything like "Don't do that, Cam. The witch world needs you." Maybe she didn't know what to say.

She stood and held out a hand to me. "C'mon, let's go to sleep. Maybe things will look better in the morning."

"Maybe we'll find out that Unicorn Guy got what's coming to him," I muttered.

"Cam," hissed a voice in my ear. "Cam. *Camellia.*"

"I will not go hang up the stupid snakeskins," I growled at the voice. "I am *done* hanging up your snakeskins."

"Cam," the voice said again. "I have an idea."

I forced my eyes open to see Poppy shaking me awake. The bedside clock said it was four a.m. "Why do all your ideas happen at night?"

"My subconscious mind does its best work then," said Poppy. "Now look. If my mom is right, then that lamp loosed a demon. The demon took Sarmine somewhere. But then what?"

"But then what *what*?" I said.

"Where did the demon go? He doesn't have a body, so he can't wander around long without losing all his substance and disintegrating. Demons have to have a physical place to live while on earth—that's why they try to get a human. But he doesn't have a human. He has some sort of enchanted lamp."

"Maybe his task was done, so he got to go home," I said. "I wouldn't want to hang out in a gravy boat."

"Or maybe his task was *not* done," said Poppy. "Someone's busy breaking those votives and setting houses on fire."

I shuddered. "But you scanned the garage with your phone," I said feebly. "It was just you, me, Sparkle, and your mom."

"Because he was busy taking Sarmine somewhere," Poppy said triumphantly. "You see? If my theory is true, he's back in the lamp, back in your garage. He's been hanging out there the whole time."

I closed my eyes and hoped against hope that this was all a dream. "You are not seriously going to say the next thing you're going to say. Are you?"

"We have to go to your house," said Poppy, "and summon him from the lamp."

11

I Am Not a fan of Poppy's four A.M. Ideas

I had thought we already found the rock bottom of things I wanted to do this week. Join a coven. Teleport onto a witch's mountain. Study for one of Saganey's American history quizzes.

But it turned out there was a new depth I hadn't found.

"You want to summon an evil elemental, who is lurking in an ancient gravy boat except when he's busy hexing us one by one, and sit him down for a pleasant chat?"

"Yes, and we'll go right now," said Poppy, springing out of bed. "It's four o'clock. Good time for sneaking out. No time like the present."

"Couldn't we sleep until, like, four thirty?" I said. "Dawn light and all that?"

"Come on."

We crept downstairs as quietly as possible. Poppy disarmed the wards on the back door and we slipped through. The chill of predawn spring made the hairs on my arms stand on end. I have experienced a lot of four a.m.'s doing chores for Sarmine Scarabouche and have never learned to like them. There is something positively hateful about four a.m.

Poppy unlocked the garage and we slipped inside. "Now, I've never actually summoned a demon," she explained blithely, "but I think he's in the lamp, not in N-space, so theoretically it will be easier. Summoning a demon from N-space involves making complicated passes with your hands in and out of the other dimension."

"But you know the theory," I said dryly.

"Exactly," she agreed.

The station wagon was no longer an option, but we had our bikes. Which was good, because there wasn't time to walk there and back without Lily waking up and catching us. My bike was leaning against the wall and Poppy's was hanging from a hook in the ceiling. "Probably has two flat tires," she said as she lifted it down and checked them. "It's been ages since I rode anywhere." But no, they were fully aired up.

"Right about now I'd usually be dusting the enchanted obelisks or something," I said with a yawn. "What?"

"The tires," Poppy said suspiciously. "I don't buy it."

"Nice of your mom to do it?" I hazarded.

"And what else did she do?" said Poppy. She ran her phone over the bike.

The avatar yawned—she must have programmed that in—and announced, "Ye Ancient Bike-Tyre Fixing Spell. Bethylyn's Impressive Mud-Removeth Spell. . . ."

"Maybe she can do mine next," I said.

"And Poppy's Super-Cool GPS Tracking App," he finished, and shut his eyes again.

"Um, what?" I said.

Poppy was livid. "I freaking *made* her that GPS app." She gave the bike an angry shove and it fell against the wall. "We can't take my bike to your house. She'll *know*."

It was a quiet morning in the old bungalow. Lily told Poppy she had fixed her tires, and I saw from her searching expression that she was hoping it would mend things between them. Poppy just glowered. Rice puffs were never eaten more tensely.

We biked to school and locked them up. Yet again, I missed

Jenah at our locker. I looked for her in Algebra, but she wasn't there, either. I desperately wanted to see her. I hoped she had listened to me and Sparkle and not gone chasing after that piano player. I had enough to worry about.

Foremost on my mind, of course, was the terrible feeling that my mother might not be coming back. I told that feeling to go away, tried to concentrate on algebra. But it is very hard to solve for x when you only want to solve for Sarmine. Across the room I saw Devon, looking not so hot himself. His stocking cap was pulled down to his sunglasses. He was wearing his winter gloves, his fingers tapping out whatever song he was working on.

I firmed up my resolve. Sarmine wasn't going to be back anytime soon, and I still had an obligation to fix Devon. Even if I was going to quit the witch business forever, I couldn't hang up my witch hat until that was done. I scribbled out a note and, when Rourke's back was turned, passed it across the classroom to Devon. It said, "Am so sorry I've failed you. Poppy & I aren't the only game in town. We'll try P's mom next." He tried to smile my direction, but it wasn't very convincing. I shook my head. As soon as school was over, I was going to find Devon and drag him to see Lily. She was a strong witch—surely she could fix him.

Right about the time I was watching Devon try to fake a smile at me, a runner arrived with a note for me to come to the principal's office. Rourke looked disdainful as he read it out loud. Several members of the class giggled. Suck-ups.

I gathered my things and went. What kind of trouble was I in now? It occurred to me that it might have something to do with our absence from school yesterday afternoon. Maybe Rimelda hadn't called in after all. Or worse, maybe she had said something that was about to get me suspended.

I stopped at the secretary's desk. "Um, Camellia Hendrix?"

I said. Heads swiveled toward me and the secretary drew back from my mere presence.

"I trust you are feeling better today?" said the secretary.

"Yes?"

"Your grandmother's description of your stomach illness was quite . . . graphic."

"It was terrible," I assured her. "But it's all over now."

"Good," said the secretary. "You have some paperwork or something here; just let me find it. . . ." She bent down to look for whatever it was, and I turned to see a familiar face.

Jenah.

Sitting on the chair inside the door, spine straight, looking as if she was about to spit nails, and gleeful about it. Jenah always did like a good righteous anger.

"Jenah?" I said, and I could feel my spirits lifting at the sight of her. "What are you doing here? Is that a *sweatband* in your hair?"

"Ah, yes. A letter came in the mail for you," the secretary said, sliding it across the counter. She withdrew her fingers immediately, wary of the nonexistent stomach bug. I picked the manila envelope up, absently noting the typewritten label made out to my nonwitch name, Camellia Hendrix, c/o Hal Headley High. Probably some information about science camp scholarships. Mrs. Bell had said she would send my name in.

"Well," said Jenah, "it's like this. . . ."

"Jenah Lee?" said the secretary. "The principal will see you now."

Jenah stood and I noticed that the sweatband look extended to the rest of her outfit. Yesterday the leg warmers had been paired with regular street clothes. But today she was in a shiny electric-green leotard and neon-orange leggings, with the hot-pink leg warmers over that. White socks and black character shoes completed the ensemble. She looked like she was about to star in one of those dreadful ballet movies she made me watch with her.

"Were you doing cartwheels in the hallway?" I said dryly.

Jenah drew herself up to her full height of extremely short. "I," she said with great dignity, "have been dress coded."

"For this?" I said with surprise. The leotard was not low cut or anything. "What about the time you wore all those feathers and you kept shedding bits every time you went to the board in Algebra? Or the time you came as Anna Karenina for English and you covered yourself in train track markings? You didn't get coded for any of that."

"It is a Feminist Travesty," said Jenah, "and I Will Not Stand for it."

"Jenah Lee?" the secretary said, with more impatience this time.

"I'm coming," Jenah said calmly. But her dark eyes were snapping fire. She picked up her pink duffel—of course Jenah had abandoned her backpack for a ballerina's duffel today—and walked with grave and shiny dignity back to the principal's office.

"Miss Hendrix? Is there anything else I can assist you with?" the secretary said.

"Er. No." I turned and fled back to Algebra, worrying about Jenah all the way.

☾

Jenah never made it back to Algebra. I spent French and English worrying about, in order, Sarmine, Devon, Jenah, Lily, and the fate of the world if left to the devices of the wicked witches. I say "in order," but the truth is that Jenah kept bubbling to the top, partly because I was worried about her, and partly because of the thoroughly selfish reason that I wanted to tell Jenah about all my *other* worries. Jenah had told me so many times that I needed to share things with her and stop trying to do everything myself, and I was slowly getting better at it.

After English, I hurried down to the cafeteria, hoping to finally catch up with my best friend instead of teleporting somewhere with a stranger. Although, I admonished myself, Poppy wasn't really a stranger anymore, was she? She was at *least* an acquaintance. We had saved each other's lives a few times, and that counted for something, right? Sherlock and Watson were getting used to each other.

But she wasn't Jenah.

Jenah wasn't alone. She was talking to a familiar black-clad curvy girl. Henny was there—aka Henrietta Santiago-Smith, occasionally lovelorn cartoonist and Kit Kat girl number nineteen.

Well, that wasn't so bad. Henny had been involved in the dramatic incident in November when we had saved Leo the shifter from Malkin the Terrible. Thereby kick-starting this new disaster, apparently. I liked her well enough, but she had a disturbing habit of sizing me up like I could be the center-piece of her next big comic. The rest of the time, she was off in the throes of artistic vision, eating a sandwich while sketch-ing the skateboarders or something.

Still. Jenah was there, and that was key. I *had* to tell her my worries about Sarmine. She was the only one who knew my long, complicated history with my mother. Maybe I could trust Henny not to include this in her comic. I sat down next to the cartoonist and said hi.

Jenah had changed into an entirely different outfit, which she had apparently stored in our locker just for this occasion, and was ranting about her dress coding. "Ooh, it makes me so mad," she said. "Nobody fussed when I dressed up as Queen

Elizabeth for a day, and that was way more distracting. That giant ruff." She nodded at me. "Hi, Cam."

"Are you all right?" I said. "You didn't get suspended?"

"Well . . ." Jenah began, and in the middle of that dramatic pause, another girl came and plonked her tray down on the other side of Jenah. She was white, with short, bleached white-and-pink hair and a rainbow T.

"It's total BS," the new girl said. "I'm sorry, but if the VP has the nerve to say it's 'distracting,' then he's the one with the problem."

"Ladies and gentlemen, Olivia. Olivia, everybody."

Olivia flashed a smile full of braces at us. I couldn't decide if she had more metal on her teeth or in her ears. "Kit Kat girl number three," she said.

"I'm Cam," I said. "Kit Kat girl number zero." To Jenah, I added, "So it was the VP who turned you in? I was wondering if it was Rourke."

"Stopped me before I even got to class," said Jenah. "And no, not suspended, but definitely reprimanded."

Two boys sat down next to Henny. One was dark, with a quirky smile and bright yellow suspenders. The other was pale, with sleepy blue eyes and an eyebrow piercing.

"Ugh, we heard about the dress coding," said the first.

"Terrible," said the other.

"Kit Kat boys number thirteen and fourteen," said Jenah. "Aka Bryan and Bobby. Also, dating." She looked at them. "Wait, *are* you dating this week?"

"Yes," said Bryan.

"This week," said Bobby.

They grinned, and Bryan stuck his hand around the back of Henny to shake mine. "Don't mind us," he said. "It's actually very nice to meet you."

The problem was, it *was* nice to meet them, too. Jenah had a knack for making friends, and she had a knack for sitting with one person or twenty and making it feel like a party. Our high school was so huge I barely knew anyone. Sure, these people looked familiar, but they were *new*.

And none of them knew that I was different from all of them. None of them knew that I had a horrible witchy home life and that I just needed a quiet place alone with my one real friend to process it. I mean, why *would* they know they were intruding? They were all theater people, like Jenah. They were all friendly and loud and prone to breaking into funny accents at the slightest provocation. Even now, Olivia was busy telling a humiliating story about the time she was dress coded in kindergarten for taking her overalls off to use the restroom and then *forgetting to put them back on*. And, I mean, I would have died before I told that story to a group of people I barely knew. Morosely, I pushed my kale around on my plate. The kale didn't care about my existential crisis. It went on being disgusting.

"Nobody tells the *boys* what they can and can't wear," said Henny.

"We do have a rule against baggy pants that show your underwear," said Bryan.

"Sadly," said Bobby.

"So the boys have one rule," said Jenah. "*One*. I looked up all the rules for girls. No yoga pants. No spaghetti straps. No midriffs. And a really ancient one that says the teachers can have you kneel down to check the length of your skirt."

"Catch *me* kneeling to anyone," said Olivia.

"You break that one at least once a week," I put in. I meant it as a joke, but I found that when it left my mouth it came out shrill, like I was trying to claim a history with Jenah over all these new people.

"True," said Jenah easily. "They've never enforced that. But then why have it? It should be gone. And none of these laws should apply to *just* girls. No baggy pants for all, fine. No midriffs for all, fine. It makes me mad."

"It should," said Henny.

"Hear, hear," said Olivia.

"The question is, what can we *do* about it?"

Across the room I saw Poppy sitting with her junior friends, the ones who were Going Places. Talking and laughing and apparently having the time of her life. Able to hide all her worries. Able to put everything from the weekend aside. How could she compartmentalize so well? She was way better at this than I was. I was lousy. She didn't even glance at me.

I stood up abruptly. "I, uh. Better go," I said.

Jenah waved absentmindedly at me as she listened to Olivia recount some involved story about a protest she went to once.

I ran outside, rather blindly. I had this terrible feeling that I was going to burst into tears at any moment, and I did not want that to happen in the middle of the Kit Kat revelry.

I made it to a private corner of the hedge. Of course, there, the tears did not come. There was a terrible tight feeling around my temples, all through my sinuses. I felt like a good cry would help, and I equally felt that I did not want to be caught having one. I looked in my messy backpack for something to make the headache go away and instead found the manila envelope from the principal's office this morning. I had forgotten it, in the distraction of seeing Jenah get dress coded.

Numbly I opened it. I had hoped to convince Sarmine to let me do something with my summer this year, something other than hanging snakeskins and dusting Gila monster skeletons. I had hoped a scholarship would sway her. Now there was no reason to even think of science camp. Sarmine was gone, maybe for a long time, maybe forever. I could see my summers stretching out, me searching for her like she had searched for my dad. And where would I live, anyway? Go back home with Wulfie; resign myself to missing school three days out of every month? Have Pink make me a holo of Sarmine to answer the door and smile at the neighbors?

I looked at the scholarship form for a long time before I realized that it was not, in point of fact, a scholarship form. It read:

> *Dear Camellia,*
>
> *If you receive this, then the worst may have happened. Enclosed is a record of my Class Thirteen spells. It may give you a clue as to what has happened to me. If you can find me, do. If you cannot, please do not waste your life moaning about it. I wasted entirely too much time searching for your father and I do not intend you to repeat the same mistake.*
>
> *The house, of course, is yours, as well as the contents of my storage locker, Moonfire, and care of the small burden known as Wulfie.*
>
> *Sincerely,*
> *Sarmine Scarabouche*

There were a number of oddities about this letter, but the one that really got me was the sign-off. "Sincerely?" I said. "*Sincerely?*" No one answered my question, though, so I breathed, counted to ten, and read the letter again. The real strangeness was in the last sentence. Moonfire the dragon—she had left us last Halloween. And the final phrase—"care of the small burden known as Wulfie"—that part was written in, in blue ballpoint. The rest of the letter was typewritten, the page bumpy with it. Yet I hadn't seen her typewriter in years.

I turned the page over, but it was empty on the other side. I reached into the manila envelope, shook it, and out fell one other thing: a black square, about five inches by five inches, with a hole in the center. I picked it up. It was floppy. No, not just floppy. This was literally an old floppy disk, wasn't it? I had seen pictures in computer class last year. I hoped Sarmine didn't expect me to track down a forty-year-old computer to run it on.

There was a white label on the disk—it had the notations for a brief spell.

Honestly, if you had told me a giant man-eating sloth was liable to pop out of the bushes as soon as I cast that spell, I still would have done it. The spell required three ingredients. I had those three ingredients in the pockets I had painstakingly stitched into my backpack.

I combined the ingredients and touched my wand to them. With a breath that caught in my throat, I blew on the powder in my hand. It coated the floppy disk. A light shot up from the circle of the disk, filling the hedge.

A life-size picture of Sarmine flickered into sight.

12

The first Recording

I *knew* it was some sort of recording, and yet that didn't stop the flicker of hope. Stupid hope.

It was Sarmine, but a much younger Sarmine. A Sarmine in a T-shirt and long hair—a Sarmine from forty years ago. She was smiling, and she said, "This is for Jim, who is off in Africa saving the whales or something and says I have to leave a record of any Class Thirteen spells I perform, in case things go wrong." A familiar dry arch to the eyebrows. "Of course, my spells never go wrong, so this is nonsense." She reached out to me and I jumped back. She must have been picking up the floppy disk, because the view swung away from her, around her workshop, while she said, "As you can see, I'm working on Ye Olde De-Smoggifying Spell to help clean up the city. I will leave this recording running, in case anything goes wrong." Eyebrows. "I think what is far more likely is that someone will crack this holo and uncover my secrets. Is that you, Jim? Is this all a ruse?" She grinned and turned back to her spell.

Voices in real life, behind me. A wave of kids running by, and the hologram was playing right out there in the open. Before I could think what to do, they ran right through it, as if they didn't see or hear it.

I sank back, heart beating. The holo was still streaming from the disk, young Sarmine laughing and chatting away.

This was something only I could see.

It was something sent to me, coded for me.

It had been set up long ago.

Something really *had* happened to Sarmine. This was what the witches had been talking about at the coven, with Malkin's nasty surprise. Some witches had spells set up to trigger on their deaths, like human wills. Sending things around to people.

This wasn't anything Sarmine had planned out this week. The letter wouldn't have mentioned Moonfire if it were.

Sarmine really was gone.

I desperately needed to cry, but the tears were stuck too tight to get them out. I flung myself facedown in the grass, in the hedge, wanting to press myself right into the ground and never come out. Above me, Sarmine kept prattling on about beetle wings and the proper use of sunflower petals and I just let her.

Noon came and went, and the sixth witch got a hex, and I didn't care.

The bell rang for the end of A lunch, but I didn't go.

Saganey's terrible American History class could carry on without me, I thought, but in truth it wasn't even as conscious as that.

I lay there, and when I got tired of the ants trying to crawl in my nose, I rolled over. But then I could see Sarmine's holo, with happy, young Sarmine. I told it to pause, and it obeyed me instantly. The tears finally started to come, but now I didn't want them. I rolled back into the dirt, refusing to cry.

That was Sarmine before she had lost my dad. Before *he* had vanished mysteriously and she had tried everything to get him back, and failed. She had told me long ago to accept that he was dead. And now she was basically telling me to accept the same thing about her.

A light touch on my shoulder roused me from one of the times I was facedown. I sat up, wiping dirt from my face. Jenah was looking down at me with a concerned expression. "Hey," she said. "Do you need my help?"

This was my chance, my moment. Here Jenah was, and here no Kit Kats were. I tried to find words to tell Jenah what was going on. But I am not good at sharing things. I knew this, and Jenah knew this. So it didn't matter how much I wanted to tell her things. All the words still had to get together, deep inside, and form sentences, and the sentences had to coordinate into a reasonable paragraph and come marching out of my mouth.

And I could not do that with Henny coming up behind her. And Olivia behind that. What, were they following Jenah around from class to class now?

I stood up, brushing off my shirt, putting my mother's floppy disk back into the manila envelope, where its glow (to me, anyway) was muffled.

"I saw you from Latin class," Henny said breathlessly, pointing at the windows above us. "And I texted Jenah to see if you were dead, and *she* didn't know, so we figured we'd better check on you at break."

"I said it was pretty thrilling to cut class in front of the whole school like that, and maybe you were protesting something," said Olivia, braces flashing. "End sleeplessness! Naps for all!"

"Or you were attacked by a wit—" Henny said, with far too much excitement and far too little tact. She broke off. "Attacked by bees. Maybe you were attacked by bees."

"I am sorry to disappoint you," I said coldly, "but I was not attacked by anything."

Henny shrugged. "It would make a good comic."

Olivia said, "If you *do* want to join our protest, Jenah's making plans for a sing-along tomorrow. You can come be an honorary Kit Kat and join with us as we support her cause."

I looked at Jenah. She was looking at me. "Take a stand with me?" she said.

I couldn't be one of her sidekicks, one of her hangers-on. Jenah's story was a funny little comedy, a lighthearted journey of optimism and punk rock and leg warmers. Mine was a tragedy, with orphans and witches and a nasty rock bottom. We neither of us fit into the other's story, not now, maybe not ever.

I turned away from my best friend. "I gotta get back to class," I said.

I told the office the final remnants of the food poisoning had reared its ugly head during lunch, and I think between how ghastly I looked and the reports that had trickled in of me lying in the shrubbery, the secretary believed me and marked my fourth period as excused. I told her I didn't need to see the nurse and thought I could make it through the rest of the day.

I probably should have taken her offer to lie down. I wasn't any good in AP Biology, and I was unspeakably terrible at volleyball in gym, two things I usually do very well and passably well in, respectively. I finally asked the gym teacher if I could sit down for the second half of class, and maybe she had also heard the horror stories, because she took pity on my pale face and red-rimmed eyes and let me sit down. I was calling in all my good girl favors this week, all my street cred I had built up over so long juggling everything at once. I had found my breaking point, and maybe it was going to stay broken.

I retrieved the floppy disk from my backpack and sat down on the bleachers. Whispered to it to play. Was it true that no one could see it? But no one pointed at me, no one looked around.

While I had been lying facedown in the dirt, the holos had been moving inexorably forward, year by year. I told the disk to play at twice the speed, and it obeyed me. A couple of the scenes were in the RV garage—I slowed it down, heart in mouth, when I saw a demon appear—but it was only that time when Sarmine had summoned a minor demon to heal Moonfire's wing. I had heard that story but had not seen it.

I stopped the recording suddenly. There was another figure moving around in the background—who was that? I told the recording to pause, looked hard at the blurry image.

Dad.

It was Dad. I had never seen a video of him. He kneeled by Moonfire, soothing her as the demon Nikorzeth mended the torn wing. The segment went briefly white, showing that the scene was ended, and then Dad was gone again. Too soon. I replayed that section, waiting for that small glimpse of my father.

He had loved that dragon. I had loved that dragon. She had known both of us, and I had never really thought about it. Sarmine darted around, keeping an eye on Nikorzeth, making sure everything was going smoothly, but *Dad* was the one talking to Moonfire, telling her she would be all right. Somehow it brought him home to me in a way that stories hadn't. This was someone I had missed knowing, because of some malevolent witch business. He had dedicated his life to "foolishness" like helping shifters get to safety, and it had done him in.

Damn witches anyway.

I suddenly wondered if I would see myself on these videos. We must be close to my birth. Would I see me as a baby, sitting in a carrier, watching Sarmine? I could imagine her cooing to me about pentagrams and demons while I waved a rattle.

The next holo started.

Sarmine ran into the room, clothing disheveled, face white. I sat up straighter, looking at the details. Had we skipped to this week? Was I about to learn something? She started a mixture going in the cauldron, something that was silver and mirrored, and I heard her mutter something about a scrying pool. Why, when I most wanted her to narrate, was she doing nothing?

She peered into the cauldron, and it suddenly hit me who she was looking for.

My father.

This was his disappearance. Thirteen years ago . . . I would have been two. Where was I? Asleep, perhaps, or simply left to my own devices upstairs.

It was clear from her expression that the scrying pool was doing her no good. She could not find him.

The holos grew repetitive after that—Sarmine in a different outfit on each new day, trying some new spell. The lines in her face grew deeper. Her black hair turned salt-and-pepper as the months went by.

Finally, she tried the worst spell of all. A spell where she actually sacrificed a small animal in a smear of crimson blood. It was the spell that Sparkle and I had seen when I was five. We had squeezed into the window well, peered through the small basement window to spy on my mother's secrets. I had been excited, I remembered with shame. Sure, deep down, there were really no secrets to be found. And then . . . we had seen *that*. I had been horrified. Sparkle, trying to repress forgotten witch memories herself, had also been appalled. Together we had concocted a new story, blocked out that horror, disassociated ourselves from witches and my mom forever. Even our own friendship had fractured—the beginning of its end.

I could hardly bear to watch that spell from a different

vantage point. It had already been burned in my eyes once
before.

But all that happened was that the spell ended and she had
still found no sign of Dad. I knew, from things she had said
since, that that was the day she gave up looking for him. Three
years of searching. Done.

The volleyballs thumped. The sneakers squeaked.

Sarmine still went into the basement, she still worked spells,
but she no longer spoke of Dad. Her face became drawn, lined.
Her hair went silver. I told the disk to speed up by two and
watched the moments of her life flicker by.

Sarmine was aging now. Aging faster since Dad had disappeared. I didn't know for sure what year any of these were.
I could occasionally make a guess by her hair or clothes.

I slowed the holo to regular speed. This Sarmine looked
like the one I remembered from middle school. Hard to narrow it down further. I scanned the background, searching for
clues—and then I saw that one of our sofa cushions lay on
the basement floor. A small lump lay in it.

"Roses," Sarmine was saying as she picked up ingredients.
"Eye of newt. Shredded basil."

The lump lifted its head and whined. I recognized that
whimper, even in its newborn puppy state.

Wulfie.

I clapped a trembling hand to my mouth. *What was she
doing to Wulfie?*

Sarmine crisscrossed the room, narrating as she found ingredients. From the daylight streaming in the small basement window, it must be day. I must be at school—seventh
grade. Yes, I remembered coming home from school one
day in September and finding that she had brought home a
puppy. Typical Sarmine, she didn't explain what he really
was until a couple weeks later, when the full moon hit and

he suddenly became an infant for three days. I was woken from a sound sleep and dispatched to the grocery store for formula and diapers.

"*Homo sapiens werewolficus*," Sarmine was saying to the recording. "Most of the time you'll be a shaggy gray puppy. Easy enough to hide. But those three days around the full moon . . . we're going to have our hands full, aren't we."

I knew all that. But why did she have him in her workroom? Sarmine always had ulterior motives. She had rescued our dragon in large part so she would have a steady supply of dragon tears. That easy access to an elemental's power had increased her own power, and trading them had been a comfortable source of income all these years.

She had always told me that Wulfie was a stray she had adopted. But, looking at him with the perspective of time, it was clear that this tiny pup was too young to leave its mother. Had she stolen Wulfie from his mother in order to use him?

I paused the holo. Was Sarmine actually in league with Ingrid? I couldn't believe that my mother would be on the side of true evil when it came to Sentient Magicals. I knew her ethics were more . . . flexible than mine, but still. Was this recording about to show me that Sarmine had been a terrible person, give a reason that someone on the side of good might have been willing to hex her this week?

I grimaced. In that case, the answer might well be *Lily*, meaning she had been lying to us all the time. I didn't want to believe that, either.

Volleyballs thumped on fists, on the floor. Shouts of laughter.

If I found out the worst, then at least I would know the truth. I unpaused the holo, heart in mouth.

"This will delete your tracking spell," Sarmine said to the shivering pup. "They'll never be able to find you."

"Who?" I said silently. "Who won't? His mom?" I stared into

the holo as if it would answer me. "Why *did* you adopt Wulfie?" I whispered.

She turned from the puppy, as if she could hear me. I was sure she couldn't, but it still made me catch my breath.

"Why am I risking myself for you?" Sarmine mused. She sank to the floor, awkward in her usual pencil skirt, studying the tiny puppy curled on the sofa cushion. As if she couldn't help herself, she reached out a hand to stroke his fur.

He lifted his head weakly, gave her a grateful lick.

Sarmine stroked him again, then stopped, picked something off his fur. "Damned puppy mills," she said, and her lips tightened. "Jim would have never stood for it. Would have broken his own neck if he had to, to try to save your whole litter. I'm not that foolish."

I sucked in breath. Sarmine was trying to *save* him. It was like Dad trying to rescue Leo's mom, the shape-shifter, so many years ago. Werewolves were not as in jeopardy as shape-shifters—only their hairs were valuable. There would be no point in killing a werewolf, no pressing need for us to keep Wulfie hidden, but I wouldn't be surprised if other witches had guessed his nature and surreptitiously swiped werewolf hairs off the couch the few times they came over.

"Did you steal him from Ingrid?" I said to the light. "Tell me how you saved him, Mom. Tell me what you risked."

She didn't answer, of course. She balanced a small saucer of something on the sofa cushion. "You'd better eat that," she said sternly. "I'm not in the mood to hand-feed any puppies."

Wulfie made a valiant effort to lap up the milk, or whatever it was. It clearly was hard for him.

Sarmine sighed and tapped her wand into the saucer. A stream of milk rose up and went into the small puppy mouth. He sucked on it greedily. A minute or two and he stopped whimpering, but seemed too exhausted to continue.

"You want your mother, don't you," whispered Sarmine. "I told you, I'm not that foolish." She reached down and unbuckled his collar—pulled it off and dropped it. I caught the flash of words as it fell. *Ingrid's Purebreds.*

There was a sound, and Sarmine suddenly tensed, looking around. Her fingers stilled. "Damn fool anyway." She stood, arms wide. There was a sudden flash of green light, followed immediately by the scene going white, ending.

Except, this time, the white stayed. No new scenes cued up. "Don't tell me this is the end of the disk," I said to the empty air. As usual, there was no answer. Surely that was not the last time she had recorded something. She had worked at least one Class Thirteen spell since then—the demon that she summoned last October. Had she given up on running the recording, knowing that my dad was never coming back to check her work? And who would try to save her, if she failed? She didn't have any real friends.

I suddenly shuddered. Was this my future if I stayed in the witch business? Was this what I was destined to become? Angry and alone, my only friends some paranoid witches? You couldn't call them friends, not like Jenah.

Maybe my mother had never had a Jenah. Maybe you *couldn't* have a Jenah, not if you were a witch. A Jenah could never understand your world, nor you hers. All the more reason to leave the witch world behind. Make that choice.

Sarmine had only had my dad to trust; he had been everything, and now he was gone.

But my father had disappeared when I was little, and she was still making these recordings. Who did she expect to come save her?

I admit, there was that small flicker of hope that said, What if my dad were still alive? What if she held out hope that he would come back? I mean, I knew he couldn't be. It's not the way the world works, not in real life. It's only in stories where you have a joyful family reunion, the family restored, everyone happy. No, Sarmine and I had had to learn to get along without him. We had reacted badly. I had retreated into denial. Sarmine had gotten cold. But we had come to accept it.

No, she wasn't still making these for my dad.

I stared through the white holo, out into the thump and squeak of volleyball.

I knew the answer. I had that letter. I knew why she was still making these videos, even if I wasn't ready to face what it meant. It was all wrong to learn this kind of thing too late. To see that I *did* mean something to her, that I had meant something to her for a long time. To tell her that she meant something to me.

Because my dad had disappeared, and Sarmine had kept on going. She had still had someone to believe in, someone to fight for, and who she hoped would fight for her in return.

Sarmine had me.

After school, Poppy found me at the bike rack. "Ready?" she said. She looked suspiciously cheerful and my miserable self resented it.

"Ready for what?" I said grouchily. "Ready to go back to your place and fuss over things like American history quizzes and calc derivative thingies while our moms get taken by demons? No, wait, I'll just imagine I'm normal. Now I can worry about things like dress codes and cast lists instead of despairing that I'm now an orphan in charge of a werewolf. Awesome."

Poppy raised eyebrows at me. "Do you want to talk about whatever that was?" she said.

"Poppy," I said, and the words came tumbling out in a way

they hadn't been able to with Jenah. "I got a recording from my mother. Something she had triggered to go on her . . ." I couldn't say it. "You know, like she got the gravy boat from Malkin." I pulled out the letter from the envelope. "See, she wrote it ages ago."

Poppy's face was serious. I could tell she was trying to spin her answer so I didn't lose all hope. "This means it's even more important that we go to your garage," she said. "We have to ask the demon where he took her—"

"Or what he did to her—"

"Uh-uh-uh. *Where he took her,* and why that would have caused this letter to trigger." She pulled out her phone. "And here's the other reason we have to go. Look what I found on WitchNet this afternoon, all over social media." She started a video, and I focused my misery to pay attention.

It was someone's cell phone footage, set against the gray backdrops of city buildings. A blurry figure was running down the street, hollering, as an enormous grizzly bear ran behind her. As she turned the corner, I thought I caught a flash of the maple leaf emblem. Sports Team. "The Canadians were next in the circle, weren't they?" I said.

"And that's not all." Poppy restarted it. "Look at that rainbow flash, zipping out of frame, just there. That's not a hex firing. Someone *put* that bear there."

"The demon," I said.

"Our guess was right," she said. "He's not *just* hanging out in the lamp in your garage. He is actually the one performing these hexes."

"Pretend my brain is mush and explain to me why you're so excited by that."

"I thought one witch had set in motion thirteen hexes, and Sarmine getting disappeared—"

"Destroyed—"

"*Disappeared* by a demon was just one of those hexes. All set up in advance by the witch. But no. One witch has made a deal with this demon to carry out the thirteen hexes."

"Slightly different," I conceded.

"So, for one, it explains why the hexes are firing every twelve hours," she said. "Demons can't live on earth without bodies for more than five, ten minutes at a time. That lamp was specially crafted to be a demon container, like the book said. So it can hold him. But he can only stay out for a few minutes. Then he has to go back and recharge. It must take him half a day to build up to full power again."

"And for two . . . ?"

Poppy's eyes lit up as she seized my arm. "It means the hexes aren't inevitable. We have the chance to stop him."

Somehow we had progressed from having a chat with a demon to overpowering him. The escalation was making me dizzy. Besides, would overpowering him bring back Sarmine? "How do we do that?" I said warily.

"Pentagram, of course."

Poppy thought one more witch would be a valuable addition, so we went down to the football field to collect her, even though I would rather have gone home to bed. What was the point of doing anything anymore? Sarmine was gone, and had been gone from the moment that demon took her on Saturday. The only thing I could do now was get myself in trouble as well, and then who would watch Wulfie?

No, that wasn't true, I sternly reminded myself. I had Devon to unhex. And I had to help Poppy rescue her mother. She couldn't do it alone, and I couldn't quit now. Besides, maybe the Sarmine holo was a clue after all. There was the episode with tiny Wulfie that had ended abruptly—and Poppy and I had just seen Ingrid's black market puppies. Maybe Ingrid was the mastermind of all of it, striking back for Sarmine's long-ago theft. And even if we couldn't find Sarmine, we could find the puppies and bring Ingrid to justice.

Except why would Ingrid have destroyed her own house? No, it was all a dead end. Everything was a dead end.

I will tell you right now that it is very hard to buck up if you think your mother might be gone forever. Even if she's a wicked witch with whom you are frequently extremely annoyed. But for the sake of the others I made the effort. There was still time to help them.

I told Poppy some of what I had seen on Sarmine's recording as we headed to the locker rooms. Sparkle had admitted via text that that's where she was, and of course Sparkle was not going to go to the trouble of walking out to meet us, so we were going in.

Voices from the back, one high, one low. Laughter. Low rumbles. Music? Someone must have their iPod on.

"Ugh," I said. "I am not in the mood to see a Sparkle make-out session that she totally could have stopped. She had oceans of warning." I hollered down the hall. "Sparkle!"

A low song, drifting out: *"Each drop of rain will raise the sea . . ."*

No scuffles, no bodies jumping apart. We rounded the corner into the open area. I saw Devon's backpack on the floor, saw his guitar hanging in the air. He was clearly sitting there, strumming it, even if I couldn't see him. And did that mean he was wearing his invisible clothes, or no clothes at all?

Because sitting on the bench, an inch away from the invisible boy-band boy, was Sparkle.

13

Superior Witch Is Superior

"Well," I managed, as the song came to a sudden stop.

Sparkle rolled her eyes at me. "It's not what you're thinking, so don't be a nitwit. Unless what you're thinking is that a *superior* witch is trying to take off the curse you hexed him with."

"That's what I was thinking," helpfully put in Poppy.

I glared at Poppy, who was supposed to be on my side. Back to Sparkle: "I remember asking you for help at the pizza parlor, thank you very much. I thought you were through being a witch."

"I can't resist the call of a young man in distress," drawled Sparkle, clearly enjoying this.

"I asked her for help," put in Devon. "She told me to bring my invisible clothes to wear."

"Spoilsport," said Sparkle.

"Charming," I conceded. "Well, did the superior witch manage to take off my inferior little curse?"

She looked disgruntled. "No. It's like you glued it on. I've never seen anything like it."

"She's been working really hard at it too," said a deep voice. I looked up to see Leo watching the whole thing with an amused expression. I could see that Sparkle and Devon's closeness didn't bother him one whit, and I wished I could feel as manly and secure as he obviously did.

Sparkle, meanwhile, was looking at me with an expectant expression. I knew what she wanted.

"Thank you for trying to break my hex," I muttered, my humiliation complete.

"Any time," she said grandly.

"In the meantime, we have something you can definitely help us with," said Poppy. She outlined what we had figured out so far. "So we want to, first, make a pentagram, and second, summon the demon out of the lamp. I figure the more witches, the better."

But Sparkle's face was grim. "I'll go," she said, "if only to stop you two idiots from destroying all of us. But Leo is absolutely staying here."

"And Devon," I put in. "You'd better stay here, too."

"Now wait a minute," said Leo in a rumble.

The guitar rose as invisible Devon stood up. "I'm not staying behind."

"Leo," said Sparkle. "You don't understand. If anyone finds out what you really are—"

"*What* I really am?" said Leo, his eyebrows raised.

"I mean—"

He forestalled his girlfriend. "It's only the witches who want to get me. Demons don't care, right? They don't cast spells?"

"No," Sparkle admitted.

"Then I'm coming with." He crossed his arms in a way that said it was final.

"And I'm invisible," said Devon. "He won't even know I'm there."

I could see we were being overruled. "If you promise to stay safe," I said.

"I will," promised Devon.

"You know what happened last time," I said.

"What happened last time?" said Poppy.

"Demon took over his body," I said.

"Briefly the most popular boy in school," said Devon.

"Devon . . ."

"I'm kidding. I'll be careful."

Leo had a convertible, but it wouldn't fit five. We piled into Ingrid's SUV. Sparkle took one look at the dog hair all over the backseat and called shotgun. I got in the back, sandwiched between the two boys. Given that the football player took up more than his fair share of the backseat, and Devon didn't appear to be there at all, anyone who looked at us would probably have thought I was intentionally cuddling with Leo. Sparkle, content in the front seat, didn't seem to feel threatened by this a bit.

I sighed and leaned my head against invisible Devon's shoulder. For the first time since I had hexed him, he didn't pull away. An invisible hand stroked my hair.

"I really do forgive you, you know," he said in a low voice.

"You do?"

"I know it goes with the territory. Besides, I've been thinking."

"You have?"

"I have to have something to do while applying a heavy layer of base each morning. How do girls manage it?"

"I don't," said Poppy from the front.

"I enjoy it," said Sparkle. "Speaking of . . ." She pulled some glittery eye shadow out of her purse and began reapplying it in the mirror.

"Turn on the music, will you?" said Devon. "I want to talk to Cam."

Poppy laughed. "We'll talk about demons. Sparkle, have you summoned one?"

"No, but I know the theory. . . ."

"Anyway," said Devon, his voice low and in my ear, "the point is, I know I have to solve this myself. The stage fright part, I mean. It's always been true, and it's still true. It's not your problem to solve."

"I'm only trying to help—" I started to sit up, but he gently pulled me back to him.

"And I appreciate it. But you have enough going on. Sparkle caught me up on everything. I should be helping *you*."

"You do?"

"I've been doing a lot of thinking this week. I can't sit around singing about butter and ignoring everything going on around me. I want to help."

"Too dangerous."

"You never know," he said, and I could hear the amusement in his voice. "Invisible guys might be useful." Invisible lips brushed my cheek and I blushed.

"Can't you save the invisible kissing till after we trap the demon?" drawled Sparkle. She was looking at me in the mirror.

"You're just jealous," Devon told her, amusement in his voice.

"Fighting words," Leo admonished Devon, but I could tell he was laughing too.

"Don't make me pull over," said Poppy.

I snuggled closer into Devon's arm, and for a moment just let myself imagine that none of us were witches or shifters or invisibly hexed. Friends, hanging out together. Off to get ice cream or go skiing or do any of the things that normal people did.

Sparkle sniffed. "So sue me that I don't want to encounter this stupid coven hex. That food poisoning spell I did made everyone sick for a week."

"I'll hold your hair, babe," promised Leo.

Or maybe, in some way, it was *better* that we all had this bond. We all knew what it was like to deal with the witch world. We understood things about each other that no one else ever would.

I wondered if the coven had ever been like that, once upon

a time. A group of witches that actually cared about each other, had the same goals.

And I didn't mean goals like taking over the world.

"Was it always terrible?" I said to Sparkle. "The Cascadia Coven?"

"Sure," she said. "Only I enjoyed that, the first time around."

"Wait, how are you still on the coven anyway?" I said. "If the last time they met was right after my father disappeared, then I would have been three-ish and you four-ish. Hadn't you already taken your amnesia spell and regressed to being a kid?"

"I gave my grandfather my proxy vote," Sparkle said. "So I wouldn't lose my place."

"Proxy vote?"

"Ooh, ooh," said Poppy, briefly putting her hand up. "I get to explain something."

Sparkle rolled her eyes.

"There are strict attendance rules to keep your spot," said Poppy, "because otherwise everyone would be too lazy to attend. It takes three witches to call a coven, and then, if someone doesn't show, they get to vote in someone else."

"Like when my father didn't show up, they could put Unicorn Guy in his place," I said.

"Right. So the loophole is, if you can't go to a meeting—"

"Because you're off hunting baby rocs in Paraguay—"

"You can send someone you trust to vote for you."

"I bet that always goes over really well, with no backstabbing," I said dryly.

"Yup," said Poppy.

"Still. Thirteen years without any meetings."

"Witches live a long time," chorused Poppy and Sparkle from the front.

"I guess we do," I said.

We turned into my neighborhood. The invisible figure next

to me tensed as we neared my house. I couldn't blame him. It had been the site of too many dangers for him.

Maybe it wasn't just the witch world that would be better off without me. Probably Devon would be, too. He could find some other girl who didn't continually drag him into jeopardy.

Because danger seemed to go hand in hand with dating a witch.

My father, Jim—vanished trying to help people to safety. Lily was protecting Poppy's dad by not informing him of anything going down this week. Leo's bio parents were long gone. And Sparkle's grandmother—what about her?

I leaned toward the front seat. "Did your grandmother, um, pass away before we were born?" I said to Sparkle.

"Not before *I* was born," said Sparkle. "Obviously."

"Ah, right, I forgot," I said, and helpfully explained to Poppy, "It's a long story."

"I call the person I live with my grandfather," said Sparkle, "but he's actually my father. I'm on my second round of growing up."

"So who's the witch? Your mom or your dad?"

"My dad has witch blood, but he kept it secret. My mom was straight human. When I was four the first time, my mom was shocked by the magic coming out. She ran off with me and joined a cult. They said they could train it out of me."

She said this quite matter-of-factly. Poppy and I caught each other's eyes in the rearview mirror and looked at each other in horror. "Are you kidding me?" I said.

"We were there till I was eleven," Sparkle continued, "and then my father found me and took me home. She stayed. But I gather I was unmanageable, and he's not a practicing witch. So he sent me to live with my great-aunt up in Seattle and she trained me for real, but she was totally paranoid, certain everyone was out to get us and we'd better get them first. It was just the two of us in this tiny basement apartment festooned with booby traps and skulls—super unhealthy."

"I take it that's how we got GothSparkle," I said.

"Yeah. I was researching elementals and I found out about the power of the phoenix rebirth that was coming up in the next couple decades. Later on, after I had left her—wrangled my way into the coven and all that—I ran across the amnesia spell. And my life kind of hard-core sucked at the time, so I made an extraordinarily good plan"—this was said with a lot of sarcasm—"to go crawling back to Dad, take a dozen years out of my memory, and forget who I was until it was time to remember and harness the phoenix."

"It was a good plan, babe," said Leo. "Because now you're with me." He didn't seem surprised by her story, which must mean that Sparkle had finally confessed to him that she was—shudder—old.

"True," conceded Sparkle.

"And then no one got the phoenix power," I explained to Poppy. "Well, I helped our dragon go off and find some companions with it. But the witches made off with a few feathers is all."

"Man," said Poppy. "I had heard about some phoenix stuff going down last fall but I did not know the whole story." She glanced at Sparkle. "And I cannot believe you hid it that well. Up until recently, I thought you were just a cheerleader. But I guess *you* mostly thought that too."

Sparkle stared off into the rearview mirror. "The thing is, I got to live my real life this time around. Not my crazy mom one that set me on a bad path. A second chance. It's not something everyone gets to do." Her eyes met mine in the mirror. "I even had some better friends, this time around." She smiled, almost wistfully, and I had a sudden sharp memory of us playing together in grade school. When she was loyal to you, she was fanatically loyal. Like the way she was with Leo. The friendship had had its good points.

For the first time in a long time, I regretted that we had grown apart.

I wondered if it was anything that could be put back together.

Because it wasn't just me and Sparkle. There was an unusual sensation in the car; I could feel it. A growing bond. I had never been part of a group like this. Poppy. Sparkle. Leo. Devon. Me. It was weird and strange and amazing. Frightening—it could slip away and I wouldn't understand how to make it stay. How could I capture it? How could I keep it?

How much had I missed by being a loner all those years, turning only to Jenah for friendship, keeping even her at arm's length about my home life?

Maybe second chances were possible for more than just Sparkle.

We were pulling up to our house now, and Poppy parked the SUV in our driveway. She turned to face us and, as one, we waited expectantly.

"Okay, everybody," Poppy said. She eyed each of us in turn. "We're going to trap the demon in a pentagram."

"With what?" Sparkle said.

"I will now take your brainstorms," said Poppy.

"Chalk on the garage floor," I said immediately.

Leo: "Etch the floor with magic lasers."

Poppy: "Broomsticks."

Devon: "And there are five of us. . . ."

"Let's do that," said Sparkle. "This is the sort of thing best solved by nonmagical means. The demon is more likely to pick up on a spell being cast. We have a greater chance of him sleeping through a few brooms being moved around a garage."

In the end, we got a broom, a mop, a shower curtain rod,

and a snow shovel that Sarmine had been using for who knows what in the basement. I knew there was a push broom just inside the RV garage. I would grab that.

This was the scariest part of the whole operation. If we got the pentagram around the demon before he realized what we were doing, then we were safe. Poppy could call him out of the gravy boat and he would be contained. He might not answer all our questions, but he would be contained.

I carefully turned the key in the side door to the garage. Through the little window, I could see the votives on the floor around the cauldron. The first six were burned out— Esmerelda's and Valda's shattered, Ingrid's apparently melted. Sports Team's looked as though it had been mauled. I hoped she had gotten away. The remaining seven votives were still lit white, tangible symbols of hope.

"Should we pretend we're here on other business?" I whispered. "Like last time?"

"Let's just do it," Poppy whispered back. "As silently as possible. You all ready?"

"No," I said. "But who is?" I clenched my hands into fists to stop their shaking. We were going to do this. On purpose.

"On the count of three," said Sparkle.

She counted, and on three I eased open the door and got out of the way, feeling around for the push broom. The others crept inside and arranged themselves into four parts of a pentagram. Devon's side looked like a floating mop.

Where was that broom?

"Uh-oh," said Sparkle.

"The lamp," hissed Poppy. "It's glowing!"

There was no help for it. I would move faster in the light. I flipped the switch on. The broom was on the floor in the middle of the melted packing peanuts, where Lily had dropped it. I raced for it, seized the handle.

"Cam!" shouted Poppy. "Cam!"

I flung myself into the remaining place in the pentagram. The brush whacked against Leo and the handle slammed into Sparkle's side. It was a testament to the gravity of the situation that she didn't snap at me. We pressed in together, focused on one thing only. *Would it hold?*

The lamp glowed bright red.

We weren't going to have to summon the demon.

He was coming out.

The air filled with sulfur and gunpowder and smoke, and then there was the elemental. He was seven feet tall, nine feet tall. He was every color of the rainbow. He dazzled up and down. I was having flashbacks.

"Who dares disturb my slumber?" he shouted in a tremendous, vibrating, sepulchral voice. It shook the RV garage.

"Um, we didn't mean to wake you?" I said. "It's just, we want to ask you—"

He whirled and glared. His rainbow light swooped straight toward me. I leaned back, arching, pressing my broom against the other two as hard as I could. "What is this?" he shouted in my face, great hot gusts of sulfur and steam. "What have you dared to do?"

"Pentagram," I squeaked.

He whisked around the star and came back to me. The bright shifting lights faded to a dim purple. His face solidified and he said grumpily, "Very well. Tell me what you want to know and we will see if we can reach an arrangement."

"You won't just tell us?"

"Why should I?"

"Because we have you trapped."

He smirked, and his next words sent chills down my spine. "Or perhaps you merely think you do. Your pentagram has certain . . . limitations, you know."

I looked sideways at the others. I didn't like the sound of that.

"Demon," said Poppy.

"My name is Hudzeth."

"Hudzeth," she acknowledged. "We have several things to ask you. We think that when Sarmine opened the box on Saturday, that she accidentally summoned you from the lamp. We think you hexed her and all the other witches in the circle. And—"

I couldn't bear it any longer. "Did you take my mother somewhere?" I said. Oh, how far I had fallen in a few days. Now I was busy *hoping* that a demon had taken my mother somewhere. Better that than that he'd obliterated her.

The demon slid over to face me. "So this is the witch whelp," he said. "Missing its mommy?"

"I want to know how to get her back."

He yawned. I didn't think demons needed to yawn, so he was obviously doing it to be super annoying. "So you're interested in making a deal with a demon, then."

Did that mean he *could* retrieve her? "So she's not . . . dead?"

A long pause, while the world hung in the balance.

"No," he said.

My heart began to beat again. She wasn't dead! The holo had misfired! She was alive! But where was she that she hadn't already come home? "Wh . . . wh . . . what would you take to bring my mother home?" I said. Stupid quavering voice.

"Oh oh oh, let me see," said the demon, mocking me. "Maybe just your life."

"That is too much," Poppy leaped in. "You can't ask that of her."

The demon shrugged. "Demons want bodies. You know that."

We did.

"But you haven't told us if you *can* bring Sarmine back," said Poppy. "And if you can stop the hex before it gets to . . ."

"Before it gets to me and Lily," said Sparkle.

The demon whirled, turning to look at Sparkle. "Yes, you were in the circle on Saturday, weren't you?"

"We need answers," said Poppy.

"And you aren't going to get any until I get a body," said the demon. "Snap snap. Pony up."

I swallowed. Maybe I could offer myself up for a short time—like a day. Maybe that would satisfy him. I had handled a demon inside me before. For ten minutes.

And then, from the other side of the pentagram: "I'll do it," said the invisible figure holding the mop.

The demon whirled. His eyes flashed green. "Well, well," he said. "Whom do we have here."

Audible gulp. "I . . . I'm Devon."

"Wait a minute," I said. "You can't have him." This was giving me serious déjà vu. "He has already been there and done that and he is *not* strong enough—"

The demon interrupted me. "Oh, I know about him. I know *all* about him." The rainbow shimmered and resolidified as a plump, smoky, hobbity sort of figure. He bounced on his toes in excitement and I reminded myself firmly that he was a killer elemental from another astral plane. "Estahoth has been dining out for months on stories of his time with Devon. Is it true that you front a band?"

"Yes?" said Devon.

"You sing?" said the demon. "You play the guitar? You make girls swoon?"

"Yes," said Devon, "yes," and "I suppose."

"Oh, he does do that," said Sparkle. She fluttered her eyelashes, and I don't have to tell you that the adverb to describe that eyelash flutter was *mockingly*.

"Now wait a minute," I said. "This is not a good idea."

"Hang on," said Poppy. "He's got that hex on him. This could be key to driving it out."

"Good idea," said Sparkle.

"Over my dead body," I said.

"I can arrange that," said the demon, and his pleasant hobbit face flashed razor-sharp teeth.

"Cam," said Devon. "*Cam.*"

The demon melted back, and the mop was speaking to me from across the pentagram. "Cam," he said. "I may be invisible. I may have stage fright. But I'm not *helpless.*"

"I never said you were. . . ." I protested, untruthfully.

"I *want* to help, just as much as Leo. You have to let people help."

"We are witches," said Sparkle sharply. "You are a guitar player."

"Witches are better able to resist demons," I said. "We have natural shields. You—"

"Have already done it once." He said it in a significant tone that made me stop and think. Was he trying to communicate that he thought he could better resist the demon since he'd done it once already? Maybe I was thinking about this all wrong. Maybe Devon wasn't a delicate flower, already weakened by one attempt. Maybe demon-carrying was like a muscle. The more you did it, the stronger you got.

Still, I was the witch. And as long as I was going to *be* a witch, then it was my job to protect him. "*I'm* going to invite the demon in, not you."

"Look, Cam," the mop said pointedly. "I trust you to get me safely out of this. And in the meantime, what's worse: a demon with mad guitar skills or a demon with mad witch skills?"

"The boy has a point," said Poppy.

"I can't let you do this," I said.

"I'm not staying if you don't," the demon said.

"At least have a time limit," I said desperately. "The demon—"

"Hudzeth."

"Hasn't promised us anything real. Just that he'll answer questions. I'm not giving up your life for some questions."

"Good point," said Poppy. "What about one hour, Hudzeth? One hour of freedom."

"One week."

"The curse will be over in a week and you know it. Five hours, and you also agree to take his hex off of him."

"One day, and that's my minimum offer," said the demon. "I'll throw in the hex removal for free." I suspected he thought a day was enough to worm himself inside Devon permanently. Devon had lasted three days at Halloween. But was he weakened or strengthened by that experience? Which of us was right?

"One day then," said Devon simply. "It's my turn to step up." Before I could do anything else, he dropped his mop with a clatter and stepped into the center of the now useless pentagram. The demon was right. Human pentagrams did have limitations. They were pathetic, really. I dropped my push broom to the floor. I couldn't do anything to stop this.

The demon flowed straight into Devon, a waterfall of rainbow light. As he did, Devon began colorizing again. Toes, feet, knees—up and up. It was as if Devon was an empty glass pitcher and the demon was filling him up with apple juice. No, that was a weird metaphor.

Devon's head snapped up. He was all visible again, and glorying in it. Light was in his eyes. A light of happiness, and confidence, and self-assured joy. "And now I can do this," he said, and he stepped across the push broom and kissed me.

14

Some Boys Have No Sense, That's All

"He really likes being visible," Sparkle mused dryly.

"I should try hexing and unhexing my next crush," said Poppy.

Their comments recalled me to my senses. We had been here before. This wasn't Devon anymore. It was Hudzeth.

"Very funny," I said, stepping back from the demon's embrace. "Now, can I talk to Devon, please?"

"This is Devon," said Hudzeth.

I waited.

"Oh, very well," he said with bad grace. The color disappeared from Devon.

"You're still invisible," I said.

"Apparently."

"You're otherwise fine?"

"I am," he assured me, and his hand found mine and squeezed it. That reassuring touch told me more than any words could. He really thought he could do this.

I squeezed back, then hollered, "Hudzeth!"

Devon colorized again. "Oh, goody, we're holding hands."

I let go. "You promised to take the hex off of him."

Hudzeth huffed. "Work, work, work. Maybe next time you'll avoid putting curses on us."

"On *him*, Hudzeth," I said. "There is no 'us.'"

"There could be," he leered again.

"I mean *you and Devon* are not an 'us,'" I said. "You are not a single entity and you are not going to—Oh, why am I wasting my time arguing with you? Fix him."

"Fine," he said, and Devon's face went entirely blank, with no one looking out of it at all.

"That's kind of creepy," said Sparkle.

"Is he going to faint?" said Poppy.

Leo dropped his curtain rod and caught Devon just as his knees sagged and he tumbled toward the ground. Carefully, he sat Devon on one of the patio chairs and kept a hand on his shoulder, keeping him propped up.

I ran to the sagging body, frantic with worry. Grabbed his hand. What was going on in there?

Finally, his eyelids fluttered and he opened them. "Holy Beedlezeth and Lucibub," the demon said. "What did you say you did?"

"An invisibility hex? Accidentally. Did you . . . ?"

He nodded. "I got it off. But that was strong. Don't do that again, okay?"

"I won't," I promised. "Not to a person, anyway." I realized I was holding Hudzeth's hand again, and let go. "Is Devon okay?"

"He is," Hudzeth said. "But I had to knock him out to remove the hex. He's sleeping it off."

I stood, eyes narrowing. "That's awfully convenient. Exactly when do you think he's going to wake up?"

Hudzeth brushed this aside. "This wasn't in some grand master plan," he said grumpily. "It's much easier to get around if the host body is there to help you."

"He's not a host body, he's—"

"I know, I know." Hudzeth sighed. "He'll be fine. Can I get going now?"

Protests rang out from all of us.

"I believe you agreed to answer some questions first," said

Sparkle. "To start with: Can you get Cam's mother back?" I couldn't believe Sparkle had asked that without asking about herself first.

"I cannot," he said. He raised his hand, forestalling my cry of despair. "But she is alive, and I can take you to her if the right circumstances occur. And that's all I'm allowed to say about that until the hexes are complete." But hope flooded my bones. Even if the demon couldn't get her, maybe I could. If I figured out the right circumstances, whatever they were. "What else did you want to know?"

"Sarmine wasn't the only one affected by that hex, right?" said Poppy. "I want you to stop it. Before it gets to my mother. And, uh, Sparkle."

"And Cam," said Sparkle.

"Yeah," I said.

"Ah, that might be more difficult," Hudzeth said. Regret tinged his voice . . . Devon's voice.

"Why?"

"Demons are bound to their contracts," he said simply. "I made this one a long time ago. I am compelled to finish it."

We looked at each other. It sounded like Present Hudzeth might regret what Past Hudzeth had done. But apparently that didn't matter.

"Look, you," said Poppy in a dangerous tone. "Devon traded twenty-four hours to you for some help. And this is what you've got? You can't get her mother and you can't stop the hex?"

"Devon traded twenty-four hours for some *questions*," said the demon. "And you're not asking the right questions."

We looked around at each other. What didn't we know? Everything, really.

But the first point of order was to figure out if Malkin had started this, or somebody else.

"Who put you in that lamp?" I said.

"Malkin," the demon said promptly.

"Okay then," I said.

"And three other witches."

"Wait, what?"

He raised a hand. "Before you ask, they were masked and it was thirteen years ago. I don't know which three they were. But one had a dog."

"Ingrid," said Poppy.

"Ah, yes, with the house on the mountain?" said Hudzeth. "That was satisfying." Right. This demon with my boyfriend's smile had exploded Ingrid's house. I leaned away from him. But he merely smiled cheerfully from the patio chair and said, "Next."

Poppy studied him. "We've found a possible link between the werewolves and Sarmine," she said. "And I'm told this coven has fractured several times over the treatment of Sentient Magicals."

"That's a missing link to Jim, too," Sparkle put in. It always fazed me to hear her drawing on her memories from her previous life like that.

"Is that the larger issue here?" said Poppy. "Are we on the right track?"

"Very good," said the demon. "Now ask me: Who has the most to gain if they get rid of everyone who opposes rights for Sentient Magicals?"

"Who has the most to gain?" I said dutifully.

He spread his hands. "Ah, that's the catch, isn't it?" Before Poppy could interject another scathing rebuke, he quickly continued, "Follow the money, see. Follow the power. Your father," and he pointed at me, "was trying to protect the Sentient Magicals from Malkin and her followers. And there are four key groups of Sentient Magicals, at least out here in the Northwest. The shifters—that's who Malkin was always after. The werewolves were controlled by that lady with the dog. . . ."

"Ingrid," I said.

"That just leaves the river mermaids and the Bigfoots," he said. "Find the witches who have such low ethics that they will divvy up actual people and you've got your four baddies." He flashed Devon's grin at us. "Now, I think that is in fact a bunch of answers. As soon as Devon wakes up, we have a lot to do—and so do you, because the three remaining witches will stop at nothing to get what they want. Come find us when you have their names." The door banged closed behind him—behind *them*, really. For the next twenty-four hours, that body was plural.

I surveyed the wreckage of garage. Brooms and shovels ringed the cauldron. The votives had been scattered in the chaos, but I could still see the remnants of their circle.

"Those horrible, horrible—" Poppy broke off.

"Witches?" I said dryly. The demon's reassurance that Sarmine was not dead was buoying me up. "Missing" was back to being a possibility. I could work with missing. I wouldn't retire just yet. "Well, come on, how can we figure out the other two witches? Time to pull up your notebook app again."

But Sparkle was looking ill. "I know one of them," she said.

We whirled. "You do?" Poppy and I said simultaneously.

"You sent me out to Unicorn Guy's house, remember?"

I did now. I had forgotten to ask about it. "What was his hex?" I said belatedly.

She shrugged. "I didn't stay long enough to see. But what I did see—" She broke off, and swallowed. "A swimming pool," she said finally. "He had just finished building a massive swimming pool in the field behind his house. He took me out on the back deck to show it off. I remember remarking that it was super deep. Good for diving, I said—only it was all finished and there was no diving board. I thought in the back of my mind that there was something else off about the pool, but I didn't put it together." She swallowed again. "The wall had no ladders."

All four of us had the same expression of horror on our faces.

"He's going to keep the mermaids there," Leo said.

"Watch them," Poppy said.

"But why now?" I said. "Why is he building this now? I haven't seen mermaids in . . . Actually, I've never seen mermaids. Esmerelda had a single mermaid fin last November. I remember her saying they were hard to source." I shuddered. The horror of it had kind of glossed over me when she said it. I mean, it was horrible, but I had kind of been thinking of mermaid fins in a hazy, something-that-had-happened-long-ago way. Some atrocity that happened in a different part of the globe. Not Unicorn Guy bringing mermaids right here to his paddock to . . . to keep like animals.

"He must expect to be gaining some very soon," Sparkle said soberly.

It was all the more important that we find that fourth name and solve the puzzle of what the witches were up to.

"But who would be managing the Bigfoots?" said Poppy. "It could be any of them."

"I know at least four witches who are interested in Bigfoot claws," I said. "We saw them Saturday night at the pizza place, chasing that poor piano player. The three Canadians and Claudette."

"Probably not Fiona," said Poppy, "because the hex already got her with that grizzly bear."

That nudged a thought that had been lurking ever since the demon had said there were four witches behind the spell, not just one. "But, by that logic, how could Ingrid be one of the bad guys?" I said. "The hex already got her, too. She wouldn't want her own house to be destroyed."

Poppy let out an exasperated sigh. "I should have seen that."

"Witches are always double-crossing people," Sparkle pointed out. "Maybe one of the others turned on her."

"She did look surprised," I agreed.

"Malkin's dead," Poppy said. "Ingrid was *supposed* to be dead. Whoever's left standing controls everything?"

"I'm the one who ate Malkin," pointed out Leo.

"I wish you'd stop saying that," I said.

"Unicorn Guy does not have the brains to mastermind anything," Sparkle said positively.

"Or he wants you to believe that," said Poppy.

"Have you met him?" said Sparkle.

"Claudette," I said. "She's near the end, and she is ice cold. I'd believe she could plot with her allies and then turn around and scheme to bump them off."

Sparkle rose. There was purpose in her face. "I'm going back to Unicorn Guy's house. He insinuated that he could use a partner in crime for some new venture. I'm going to see how much I can learn from him."

"I'll try to track down the piano player," Leo volunteered.

But there was a flurry of noes at that.

"You'd be in danger," I said.

"You're too valuable to let anyone know what you are," said Poppy.

"I let you help with the demon, but you're not getting anywhere near that mind-reading witch," said Sparkle.

"*Let* me?" Leo punched the air in frustration. "I can't sit here and do nothing while you girls protect me all the time."

There was a moment of silence. "I understand how that feels," said Poppy softly.

"Poppy," Sparkle said warningly.

"Look, Leo, there is something you can do," Poppy said. "It *is* dangerous, but it won't take you near Claudette. Your shifter skills might even come in handy."

"Anything," he said simply.

"When Cam and I escaped the explosion at Ingrid's house, we rescued four puppies. Real puppies. But she escaped with two puppies that I don't think are puppies at all."

"Werewolves," I said.

"People," said Poppy.

"Kids," said Leo. "Go on."

"If her allies really did turn on her—or even if she just thinks they have—then she won't have anywhere to go. I bet you anything she helicoptered home to her safe little mountaintop as soon as it stopped exploding. It's four hours away, but . . . you have a car. I can give you the address."

"A rescue mission," said Leo. "Good."

"She'll see your car," warned Sparkle.

"Hey, I can invisible that for you," I said, waggling my eyebrows. "*Permanently.*"

Everyone laughed.

"How about a 'do not notice' spell?" said Poppy. "*That* I can take off later."

"Sounds good," said Leo. "I'll take them back to my place and get Dad and Pops to puppysit."

"It's too dangerous," Sparkle said, unable to stop herself.

Leo took her hands. "I don't care," he said. "I have to do something. This is even more important than the future mermaids. These are *kids*, Sparkle. And she's got them *right now.*"

Sparkle's shoulders were tight. Leo had come to her once, looking for help, glad of her power. She was glad to *be* the powerful one. But she couldn't run everything for Leo. She had to step back and let him work, too. "I guess," she said slowly. "I guess the puppies might trust a fellow puppy dog more."

"I'm the perfect person for the job," he said. "Besides, the dads are softies. They adopted *me*, you know."

"Good point," said Poppy.

That left the finding of Sam to us. I looked at Poppy. "Home first," she said. "Mom thinks I'm at my regular after-school study club. If we don't get those bikes home, she'll confiscate my wand, and then I'll be no good to anyone."

"But . . ."

"We'll sneak out tonight," promised Poppy. "Somehow."

We piled back into Ingrid's SUV and dropped Leo and Sparkle off at Leo's convertible at school, with strict admonitions to keep us updated on anything that happened.

Poppy had the bright idea that if we loaded our bikes into the SUV, we could get them and the SUV home, and then we could use the SUV to sneak out. We drove at bike speed the whole way, making sure Lily's tracking device wouldn't notice anything suspicious. Parked the car a couple blocks away and biked the rest of the way.

Lily and Wulfie met us in the backyard. She was throwing a tennis ball for Wulfie and coaching him to bring it back with his hands, not his teeth.

She stood up when we arrived. "Oh good," she said. "Cam, can you take over this, please? And Poppy, can you make dinner for the three of you? I have . . . I have to go somewhere. I'll be back by midnight."

Poppy and I threw each other a glance. But all Poppy said was, "Hard to get anything done with a three-year-old around, isn't it?"

Lily laughed. "True."

We could see how it was. The lighter and airier Lily got,

the worse things were getting. If she didn't stop trying to keep things from us, she was going to explode. She washed the boy spit off her hands and headed off somewhere in the station wagon. The rear windshield looked fixed, but I couldn't tell from this distance whether Lily had discovered it and fixed it or that was still Poppy's illusion. I hoped it wouldn't rain on her. She would find out quickly enough then.

We were both starving. We sat down and fed ourselves and Wulfie some PB and Js. Wulfie preferred to take his to the floor and worry it in his teeth.

"How much longer is he going to be a boy?" said Poppy.

I counted back. "Maybe another day and a half? Where do you think your mother went?"

"Gee, it would be great if she trusted me enough to tell me," said Poppy. "If she could just remember that I'm not her little sister, and I'm not four years old anymore."

"Could be worse," I said. "She could send you a record of her spells and no further instructions on how to locate her or save the day."

"Mothers," she said.

"Yeah."

"So, this Sam guy . . ." said Poppy. "You said he was playing at the pizza place last Saturday?" She tapped her phone thoughtfully. "I wonder if we can use social espionage to get them to give out his information."

Social espionage. I knew one person who was really good at that. "I have his name and address," I said slowly. "Jenah wormed it out of one of his friends and gave it to me." I pulled the piece of paper from my backpack and handed it over to Poppy.

Poppy whistled. "Your friend has mad spy skills."

"Yeah," I said. "Yeah, she really does."

Poppy put the address in her phone and looked up, a grin spreading over her face. "It's the best possible news—he's a college student. He lives in this neighborhood."

It was in fact about time we got a break. We cleaned up our plates, grabbed a tennis ball for Wulfie, and walked the two blocks to Sam Quatch's apartment. It was close to where we had parked Ingrid's SUV. The rain of the past couple days had lifted—now it was merely the cool damp of early spring. Crocuses were poking between the roots of the trees, and daffodils were brave spots of yellow in the twilight.

Jazz piano drifted out of the open window as we arrived at the converted old Victorian. Jenah had found the right address all right, but did that mean he would help us? If Claudette and the Canadians chasing him were any indication, then he had every reason to be wary of witches.

The college-age boy who opened the door had light brown skin, black hair and beard, and a wary expression. A lot had happened since I had briefly seen him Saturday night, but I was sure he was, in fact, the piano player from the pizza place.

"Hi," said Poppy. "We won't keep you long. We'd like to talk to you about your life insurance policy." She drew her wand half out of her bag and showed it to him, her eyebrows raising significantly.

His face darkened and he began to shut the door on us.

But Poppy stuck her foot in. "Oh, good, I see you've dealt with my company before. We're here to help, but I am not going to talk about this on the steps. May we please come in?"

He drew back, his lips set in a grim line. With exaggerated courtesy, he gestured for us to come inside. We stepped into what I presumed was your average college apartment, messy with papers and textbooks and sheet music, furnished with a card table and a decrepit gold couch. The one nice thing in the room was a shiny upright piano against the far wall. Wulfie ran and jumped on the couch. And kept jumping.

Now that I knew what Sam was, I took a good look at him. He was on the furry side, sure. Not so much he couldn't pass for regular human. His lean arms were fuzzy, and he had a thick hipster beard. Or maybe I just pegged it as a hipster beard because he was also wearing a plaid flannel shirt. He was on the tall side, and his feet were on the long side, and they were stuffed into enormous black combat boots.

Basically, if you had told me a week ago that Bigfoot was alive and well and attending college in my city, I probably would have imagined him just like this. The only thing that ruined the picture was his hands. His long fingers were encased in a soft pair of white cotton gloves.

"Why are you wearing gloves?" I said.

Sam's face was suddenly livid. "Why? You tell me." He stripped off his gloves to reveal that every single fingertip had multiple Band-Aids on it. "I learned long ago that it doesn't matter where I go or what I do. Every so often, some witch shows up and demands an entire fingernail." He sat down on one of the card table chairs. "*Sometimes* they pay me for it."

Poppy and I looked at each other, horror in our eyes. *This* is what we had used to teleport ourselves.

"I thought Bigfoot claws were like a fingernail clipping," whispered Poppy.

"I'm just a *thing* to all of you."

I rubbed my eyes. Strike Bigfoot claws off the list of ingredients I was willing to use.

"And don't cry about it, either. I saw you at the pizza place. Spare me."

"I'm not," I retorted, and blinked furiously.

"All I want is to go to school, and get through my studies—"

"What are you studying?" said Poppy. It was clear she was as affected as I was, but she had better control over her feelings than I did.

He shot us a dirty look. "Jazz piano. And I have a concert coming up next week, and I needed that money. But the witch that caught me Saturday—was she satisfied with a toenail? Of course not." He tucked his hands in his armpits. "I've never had someone pull all ten at once." He leaned back in his chair. "So you're too late. You might as well go. Go on . . . get."

Silently, Poppy took a bottle of ibuprofen out of her messenger bag and passed it to him.

"Thanks," he said, and dry-swallowed two of them.

"Why . . . Wasn't there anything you could do to stop it?"

Sam gave me another dirty look. "As strange as I'm sure it sounds to you, this is preferable to the alternative. When the alternative is that someone else in your family tree has to suffer. But I wouldn't expect a couple of *witches* to know anything about protecting your mothers."

Ah. "We might know something about that," I allowed.

"Protecting," said Poppy. "Finding. Rescuing."

We wound down, all three looking at each other across the card table. I could see him considering the puzzle of us, filtering the actuality of us through his anger at what we represented.

"Poppy," I said. "Couldn't we . . . couldn't we do something about this?"

"Great minds think alike," she said. To Sam: "Give me your hand."

"What, you want my fingers next?"

She gave him a look, and he reached out, placed his hand in hers.

There was suddenly a moment when, I swear, the straight-A student of True Witchery noticed that Sam was cute, and the lumberjack mountain man piano player noticed that Poppy was cute. It was like this electric moment where you could feel the balance of the room shifting into new alignments. God, I was starting to sound like Jenah.

But Poppy merely said, "Phone, tell me the ingredients for Jenni's Totally Tubular Super Quick Regrowing of Your Awesome Manicure Spell."

"I take it you found that in another decade?" I said.

"Written on a hot-pink index card, stuffed inside a Wildfire teen romance," Poppy agreed.

The avatar recited the ingredients, and Poppy let go of Sam's hand and combined the ingredients on her phone screen. "Remove your bandages," she told Sam. She dusted her spell on the tips of his fingers, then delicately touched each fingertip with her wand. "Now hold your hands out." She came around the table and gently took each hand, one at a time. Carefully, she blew the ingredients off his fingers, adding her witch's breath to complete the spell. She looked at him, and I could almost see the electricity. "That, uh. Should do it," she said, maybe a wee bit flustered.

Sam reluctantly slid his fingers out of hers. Held them up.

We could all see that they were healed. Tiny nails were already starting to creep back, little moons at the base of each fingernail bed. "They don't hurt anymore," he said, and then, looking at Poppy with gratitude and disbelief: "Thank you."

Poppy shrugged. "I, uh. Should leave you my number. You can text me if it happens again."

"I will," he said, reaching for his phone.

"Although . . ." Poppy said, and she started to pace. "Maybe that's not what you want."

"No, I think I'd like that."

"I mean. As soon as they grow back, you're at risk again.

Would you like us to find a way to stop them from ever grow-ing back?"

Startled, he said, "Maybe." He caressed his healed finger-tips. "What's the point of having power that only other people can use? All they can do is take it from me."

That was one of those moments where I loathed my mem-bership in a group that contained all other witches. "I swear," I said, "Poppy and I will find a way to stop them growing *forever*, if you want. Then the witches will have no reason to bother you again."

"Could you do that?" he said. He was still looking at Poppy.

"We will try," she said.

"Er, it might be next week," I said, "because we have to res-cue her mom first, and, um, ourselves."

He sighed and held his hand out to us. "And you needed a claw for this?" he said. "To rescue the three of you?"

Poppy and I looked at each other in horror. "Oh, no," I said.

"We were just coming for information," she said.

"We didn't heal you just so we could take them from you."

"We're not *like* those other witches."

Sam spread his long fingers on the table. "Look," he said, and I think at this point I can stop telling you that this was said to Poppy, it was all to Poppy, and he never stopped looking at Poppy until we left. Which was fine and great, obviously, only I was starting to feel like a third wheel. "It would be awe-some to fix this problem permanently. I could get my life in order. I could focus on my career and not get derailed every couple months. If you can stop it, you can have anything you need in exchange."

"Information," I reiterated. "Just information."

"Look, here's what we need to know," said Poppy. "Who is it that's been coming?"

"There were several witches at first," said Sam. "When I was little. But when I was ten I made a deal with one of them and after that it was just the one."

"Which one?" I said.

"I don't know her name," Sam said. "But you saw her, Saturday. She has a French accent."

"Claudette," I said.

"That was easy," Poppy said. "Too easy?"

"It could be that some other witch has been casting suspicion on Claudette for a decade by mimicking her accent, so when we tried to solve the mystery today we would be confused," I said.

"Let's go with Claudette," said Poppy.

"She told me I was the only one who could protect my mother," Sam said. "She said she didn't want anything to happen to her, like the way my uncle Ed disappeared when I was little. She said if I gave her what she wanted, then in exchange she would keep other witches away from the two of us."

"Protection racket," said Poppy.

"So I made the deal. And it's never been particularly terrible, until this last year. She's been coming more and more frequently. Threatening me when my nails don't grow faster. Like I can do anything about that. I told my mom to go into hiding and not tell me where she is." He looked up at us. "Claudette can read your mind, you know."

"We're going to take care of her," Poppy assured him. I didn't know how we were going to do that, but I certainly didn't say it. Sam was looking at Poppy like she was the best thing to walk into his life, and I knew better than to interfere with a chance at a little happiness, even in the middle of tragedy and despair and woe. I had my own boy who was the best thing to walk into my life. If I could get the demon to walk out of his life first.

My phone beeped with a text. Poppy's *deedle-dee*'d. "Hang on," she said to Sam, and we both looked down to find a text from Sparkle. I was worried she was getting into trouble at Unicorn Guy's place, but it was something entirely different.

All over social media on WitchNet:
"Witches Chased by Single-Minded Predators
    in Strange Hex."

"It was one witch, earlier," I said.

Poppy was frantically Googling. "And now it's three," she said. "A lion, a tiger, and that grizzly bear. Tracking the trio of Canadians through downtown Vancouver. Their wands aren't working, and they're forced to use their wits."

"Such as they are," I muttered.

"The New England Coven has been summoned to help, since the Cascadia Coven is not responding. Well, yeah."

"But it's not midnight."

Poppy looked up at me, eyes wide. "Now that we let the demon out, he's not bound by the twelve-hour rule anymore. He has a human host. He has all Devon's strength to draw on. The hexes are speeding up."

"Hang on," I said. My phone had escalated to ringing. "Pink?" I said. "What's wrong?"

"Oh, Cam," said a small, scared voice. "My grandmother and I were eating and then a, a . . . a ghostly figure appeared. And it said, 'Witch Rimelda, prepare thyself! Your doom striketh at midnight!' in a really awful voice, and then it just disappeared. And her eyes went huge and she aged like fifty years and just fainted. I tried calling my mother but she said she wasn't leaving the house even for the queen of England and just hung up. Oh, Cam, I don't know what to do."

"Hang on, Pink," I said. "We're coming." I hung up and

turned to Poppy. "We've got to get out to Rimelda's," I said. "And we've got to warn your mother."

Sam looked at us blankly. "You're helping people. You really are different."

Poppy squeezed his arm. She looked small next to his lumberjack frame. "We'll be back to help you, too," she promised. She gave him her phone number, I scooped Wulfie off of the couch, and we hurried out of there, me catching her up on Pink's conversation as we ran.

We raced down the street to Ingrid's SUV, Wulfie joyfully leaping and yapping as we went. No matter how much you wore a small boy out, there was always more wearing to be done. Our car seat was with Lily, so I buckled Wulfie into the back, ordered him to stay, and hoped Poppy's "don't look at us" spell was still holding.

Poppy tossed me her phone as I got in the passenger's seat. "Will you text my mother for me?"

"What should I say?"

"Hexes speeding up," she said tersely. "Rimelda next." As an afterthought, she added, "Also say that we learned it on social media like good little teenagers, so don't get all huffy about it."

I typed that in, too.

"If she's home she'll know we're not," she said. "But one can hope. Anyway, if the curses are speeding up, she won't be around much longer to tell me what to do." She said it sarcastically, but I knew how she felt. After a moment, she added in a small voice, "I guess we did wrong to let the demon out."

"We now know the four witches who set up the original hex," I said. "We have a pretty good guess that Claudette may have double-crossed Ingrid and Unicorn Guy and added them to the hex. And, in other news, we know that all the Sentient Magicals are in danger."

"But what does that get us? I mean, really."

"More people to protect."

She nodded.

We drove in silence to Rimelda's house. Wulfie, for a wonder, conked out and began snoring in the back. It was twilight and getting to be his bedtime.

Poppy drove up the long gravel drive to Rimelda's. We found an anxious Pink waiting for us. She led us to the pool house, where her grandmother was sitting up on the couch, looking dazed.

"That was Malkin," Rimelda said to me. "That was Malkin. I saw her."

"Malkin's dead," I said.

"I know, I know. But it was her anyway. Some spell of hers."

I sat down on the coffee table next to Rimelda. "How much has Primella told you?" I said.

"We're all getting hexed. And mine's coming tomorrow night—right? Midnight, like the voice said. Nice of it to give me time to prepare," Rimelda added glumly.

"Okay," I said. "Two changes to that. The hexes are speeding up. Yours is coming at midnight *tonight*, I bet. Two hours from now. And the other thing: the hexes aren't random. The hex is going to be the worst thing you ever did to someone."

Rimelda was silent for a moment. "Well. It's been a good run."

Horror filled me. "You don't mean—You didn't kill anyone, did you?"

She sighed. "Who hasn't?"

Poppy, Pink, and I raised our hands.

"I've been carrying it around on my conscience all these years," said Rimelda. "I just never thought that defending someone would come back to haunt me."

Poppy and I looked at each other. "You mean . . . you didn't do it out of evilness?" I said.

Her wrinkled hands smoothed the afghan that Pink had placed on her. "No—no. But I never wanted to be that kind of a witch, you see. I didn't want to kill anyone. It was an accident."

"But then, you might be all right," I said. "I don't want to give you false hope—"

"We're thinking the spell is designed to punish anything bad you did *on purpose*," said Poppy. "That's our guess, anyway. How did it . . . how was it an accident, if you don't mind telling us?"

"It was a long time ago," said Rimelda. "My boyfriend was . . . well, he was a werewolf." A flash of defiance crossed her old face as she admitted her secret.

We shrugged.

"Hmph. That kind of thing is nothing to you youngsters, I suppose, but you have to understand . . . witches live a long time. My mother was born three hundred years ago, if you can believe it, and she had some very old prejudices. So she forbade it. And his parents weren't too happy, either. We were always on the run—never had help. And then Ingrid's mother sent someone after us to bring him in. Because, as far as she was concerned, he was just more breeding stock. Ingrid is just like her mother—two peas in a pod. We don't speak. At any rate. I tried to hide John, but . . . the thug found him. I tried to save him . . . there was a battle . . . I accidentally killed the thug."

I drew in breath. There it was.

"And I still couldn't save John," continued Rimelda. "He . . . he died in the fight." She made a face. "I guess I gave up on the struggle to be good after that. Except for when the coven gets up in arms about shifters and werewolves. I can't bring myself to vote to divide them up."

Poppy and I looked at each other. Poppy reached across and

took one of Rimelda's hands in hers. "We'll stay with you," she said gently. "We'll stay until midnight."

I took Rimelda's other hand, and she squeezed both of ours. I felt like, if she weren't a witch, she would have quavered, "Bless you, children." But she *was* a witch, and witches definitely do not quaver or say "Bless you." So, instead, she let go of our hands and said, more briskly, "Who wants to take a dip in the pool while we wait to see if I'm going to croak?"

Rimelda made a pitcher of margaritas and cast a spell on the pool to warm it up to hot tub temperature. Poppy conjured us both bathing suits. We politely declined the margaritas, so Rimelda drank most of the pitcher herself as she told us stories from the last century of being a witch.

She filled in details about the leaders of the Sentient Magicals groups. Apparently, after my dad had disappeared, they had all gone underground. Sam's uncle Ed Quatch had been leading the Bigfoots, and Jonquil's girlfriend Mélusine had been speaking for the mermaids. My dad, of course, had been advocating for the shifters, because it was too dangerous for shifters even to reveal themselves. Someone named Roberto had been the head of the werewolves—a "fuzzy hunk," said Rimelda—and that started Rimelda off on a new round of reminiscences about her fabulous romantic escapades, most of which had occurred in the sixties. I asked Pink if she wanted to cover her ears, but she said she'd heard it all before.

Rimelda had her fanny pack of ingredients buckled on and a good grip on her wand—"Hey, the voice said 'prepare thyself,'" she quipped—but mostly she used the wand to stir her drink and resalt the rim of her glass. Wulfie snoozed under Rimelda's afghan, and Pink sat curled up by her grandmother's side, unwilling to leave her.

At last it was 11:58 . . . 11:59 . . . and then the alarm on Poppy's phone struck midnight. It was a totally incongruous sound, a *deedle-deedle-dee* instead of the sepulchral *bong bong bong* that a midnight death toll should be. It in fact distracted me enough that I looked for the phone first, then heard the shattering sound of what I slowly realized was a glass pitcher of margaritas crashing to the cement. I whirled, seeking Rimelda in the dark.

She was gone.

15

A Phone Call from Sparkle

We took Pink with us, of course, and the four puppies from
Ingrid's. We couldn't not, even if it would require explanation.
But Poppy's phone started ringing on the way home and it was
clear there was going to be explanation, regardless. Poppy listened in silence to her mother's scolding and then dropped the
phone in her messenger bag without a word.

She parked the SUV in the driveway—in for a penny, in
for a pound—and we carried the puppies inside.

Lily sat us all down at the kitchen table. Wulfie curled up
in my arms, his curly head heavy against my chest. The puppies flopped on the floor. "Now, I want the whole story from
beginning to end," Lily said. "And don't you dare leave anything out."

Poppy told the whole story, with a few additions from me
and Pink. Lily sat through most of it, though at the part where
the demon went into Devon she got up and paced the kitchen
in frustration before sitting back down.

"I figured out the same thing you girls figured out," she said
to Poppy, "and I went to the garage tonight to contain the
demon in a pentagram. I would have gone sooner except for
Wulfie. I didn't figure there was a rush as long as I went before the next hex fired. The pentagram would stop the hexes
until Jonquil could help me deal with him. She has loads of
experience." She threw up her hands in frustration. "What on
earth possessed you to let him out?"

Poppy shrugged. I was ready to cry.

"We needed answers," I said. "And we weren't getting any. We put a time limit on him. He has to be back in the pentagram by four p.m. tomorrow."

"Oh, and I'm so sure you're skilled with making deals with demons now," said Lily.

I would have expected the sarcasm from Sarmine, but not from Lily. I bit back tears.

Lily rose to her feet and looked down at Poppy. Poppy stared mutinously back. "Give me your wand."

"No."

"I had this under control," said Lily, "and you have wrecked it."

There were angry tears in Poppy's eyes. She pulled the wand out of her bag and set it in Lily's hand.

Lily turned to me. "Your wand, please."

I passed it over, too petrified to do anything else. Angry witches would do anything to you.

"I don't have the authority to take yours," she said. "Sarmine would have my head if I did. But I'm locking it so my daughter can't use it." She made some passes over it with her own wand and handed it back to me. Poppy looked about ready to lose it at this new indignity. She looked like she was barely keeping it together.

"And now we're all going to bed," said Lily. "You have school in the morning. That is the only thing you should be worrying about."

I glanced at Poppy. School was so far down my list of worries, I doubted it would even make the top ten.

Lily made up the couch in the living room for Pink, and I carried Wulfie up the stairs to his dog bed. Poppy didn't say a word. But I felt her shoulders shaking silently with tears well after she was supposed to be asleep.

☾

The alarm went off—too early, as usual—and I shook Poppy's shoulder gently.

"Not going," she said.

"You have to go," I said. "You have that calculus quiz. And you—you *like* school. You want to get into Larkspur."

She rolled over and looked at me despairingly. "I can't do anything without my wand. I'm helpless."

"You don't need a wand to take calculus," I said. "Unless that's how you manage to remember all those derivative thingies."

It was a measure of Poppy's despair that she didn't even shoot me a dirty look for my feeble joke. "Of course not," she said. "But don't you see? With the wand I can protect myself from anything. If there were—oh, I don't know—an earthquake, a disaster, a car crash, even if I just forget my lunch, I have my wand, my ingredients, and my database of spells. I am always prepared. I can cope."

"Probably none of those things will happen today?" I said. "Anyway, I need your help. We need to corner Devon and get him to return to the pentagram and stop hexing people."

"You want me to go near a demon without my *wand*?" said Poppy. "Look, Cam, I can't protect my mother, I can't protect you, and I can't even protect me. I'm useless."

I stood up. "Poppy Jones, you are not useless," I said. "Now, you get out of that bed and quiz me on American history. I'm not going to be behind any longer."

It was the first smile I'd seen from her since Lily took her wand. It disappeared again right away. But she did get out of bed.

I went to pull my phone off the charger and found a missed call.

Poppy said, "Did you get a call from Sparkle too?"

Of course. Her hex was not due till noon today, but the demon was loose and the hexes had sped up. Hearts pounding, we listened to our voice mails. Sparkle sounded almost . . . excited?

"We were wrong about the hexes," Sparkle said in my message. "It wasn't the worst thing you've ever done! Because I didn't get food poisoning, or the mumps, or break all my toes!" I shuddered. "I lost one fingernail. The littlest one. Pulled right on out."

And you're excited by that? I thought.

"Cam, I know who I did that to," the recording continued. "I did that to a shifter, before I knew better, back when I was Kari. And I remember hearing who Esmerelda did that old and ugly curse to; I just didn't put it together before. She did it to a mermaid who wouldn't give her the scales she needed. The curse is only targeting the worst thing you did to a *Sentient Magical*. Poppy's mom is going to be fine."

I turned to Poppy, whose face was lighting with hope. "Your mom is going to be fine."

"My mom is going to be fine."

"Let's go tell her."

We raced to her bedroom in our PJ's (well, PJ's for Poppy, good old Newt Nibbles for me) and told Lily. She was sitting on the edge of the bed in her bathrobe, lost in worried thought. At our news, her face cleared in relief. "You're right," she said. "I know you're right. Because the curse that Valda did? That was to a shifter, a long time ago." She swept us into a hug. "Oh, girls."

Poppy turned to me. "And then, you'll be fine too," she said. "No backfiring hexes for you. You've never done anything to a Sentient Magical."

"Mm, love potion," I said. "But I asked him first, so hopefully that doesn't count."

"Wait, what?" said Poppy.

"Long story," I said. "But what about Rimelda? She said she never did anything to a Sentient Magical. Do you think she was lying to us?"

Poppy frowned for a second. Then she snapped her fingers. "She said she tried to *hide* her werewolf boyfriend. So maybe we were just seeing her get hid."

"That's possible," I said.

"Werewolf boyfriend?" said Lily

"Long story," we chorused.

"But look, if it's specifically targeting the worst thing we did to a Sentient Magical, then isn't it likely that someone on our side started the hexes?" said Lily. "I thought you said the demon pointed a finger at Malkin, Ingrid, Ulrich, and Claudette?"

I thought back to his exact words. "Technically, he only said they put him in the lamp," I admitted. "Not that they had come up with this hex."

"So who else *is* there?" said Poppy. "Someone outside the coven?"

I whirled. "Wait a minute. *You're* outside the coven."

"True," said Poppy.

"So *you* won't get hexed. You said at the beginning not to trust you. That you needed a grand magical working to get into Larkspur." My accusation was joking, of course. Mostly.

Poppy snorted. "So I'm Moriarty now? An evil genius who's been playing you while quizzing you on American history and feeding you frozen pizza?"

"I guess not." I wrinkled my nose. "Darn it."

"Not that I wouldn't like having this on my application for Larkspur," Poppy admitted.

"See? And it would fit all the facts so nicely. The bad guy is always someone who's been there all along, you know. Some-one you'd least suspect."

Lily held up her hands. "I didn't do it either."

"Darn it again."

"I've got it," said Poppy. "*You* did it."

"No."

"You and Sarmine?"

"No."

"You, Sarmine, and a partridge in a pear tree?"

"Oh, I know," I said. "Wulfie did it."

"On the full moon he turns into a criminal mastermind," said Poppy.

I laughed, then sighed. "We may not be able to solve this case before the hexes are done," I said. "But I still have to plan how to rescue my mother. The demon said he took her somewhere and he can take me, too. If I meet the right con-ditions, whatever they are. What?"

Lily was shaking her head. "I can't let you do that, Cam. You know it's a trap."

"Maybe so," I said. "But it's the only lead I've got."

"Now look," said Lily. "I *definitely* have never done anything to a Sentient Magical—not hiding them, not exploding their house, nothing. Therefore—"

"Are you sure?" interrupted Poppy in a small voice.

"What?"

"We found out how Bigfoot claws are gathered. Did you know?"

Lily was silent for a moment. Then: "I did know."

Poppy's face looked crushed. I completely understood. I dealt on a regular basis with the fact that my mother had dif-ferent ethics than I did. At least I was used to it.

"No one knew about that particular use for a long time," said

Lily, "So the Bigfoots had been mostly flying under the radar. But about the time everything exploded, thirteen years ago, and everyone stopped talking to each other is when Claudette started transporting everywhere. Slowly, the secret leaked to a few people, though it's still not common knowledge. A few years ago, the New England Coven led a raid on a particularly nasty witch back East and dewanded her, confiscated her ingredients. Jonquil was part of that. She sent the bag of Bigfoot claws on to me—she didn't want them. I didn't want them either, but . . ."

"You thought they might come in handy," I said. "And the damage had already been done."

"I wasn't going to buy any more," said Lily. "You know that."

Poppy nodded. "I believe you."

Lily glanced at her daughter. "But you would have chosen differently?"

Poppy shook her head. "I . . . don't know. I guess I have to think about it."

There was silence for a moment as we all wished there were easy answers to things.

Lily rubbed the bridge of her nose, where the glasses sat. "Let's return to the demon problem. It appears that I'm going to be around at the end of these hexes, and they're almost done. So whatever conditions the demon has for me, I'll meet them, and I will go rescue Sarmine. I have the experience and knowledge. I won't be walking in cold."

I admit, there was a feeling of relief at that, deep inside. The adults would handle it after all. Lily was going to be fine, and she would go fetch my mother. Poppy and I could go to school and worry about calculus and American history and who we were going to sit with at the lunch table. Maybe witches and nonwitches could share the same concerns after all.

"Now hurry and get ready for school, kids," Lily said. "I'll watch Wulfie and Primella. Poppy, a brief word. . . ."

I hurried back to Poppy's room and got dressed. Poppy came in a few minutes later, a funny expression on her face. "She gave me this," she said. She held up a gilded scroll. It read:

Be it Known that Poppy Jones is Hereby Entrusted with my Voting Rights to the Cascadia Coven.
Signed, Lily Jones

"It's a voting proxy," Poppy said. "Like Sparkle gave to her father to keep during the time she had amnesia. If something happened to Mom, I would be able to take her place in the coven until she returns."

"She *does* trust you," I said.

"As a last resort," Poppy said. Still, she held the proxy gently, like it was a fragile, beating heart.

For a change, we arrived at school with plenty of time. We locked our bikes to the rack. But Poppy didn't hurry away from me, hailing some friend and putting distance between us. She fell in beside me. "Where's your locker?" she said.

I told her, wondering at this strange new small talk.

"Ah," she said. "Mine's in the other wing."

That was the extent of our conversational abilities, apparently. We were out of context, and our other relationship didn't make sense here. I didn't know what else to say, and I didn't want to scare her off, so I held my tongue rather than say something dumb. We walked in silence to the center of the school, where we split off. "If you want, you can join me at lunch," she said.

"Oh!" I said. "I might," I said.

"If you want," she said.

"Sure," I said.

I found Jenah at our locker. The relief of having Lily back to solve things loosened my tongue. "Oh man, I have everything to tell you," I said. "You gather a posse for a few days and my whole life changes. But first, thank you for Sam's address."

"Oh, good," said Jenah. "Did you and Poppy go stop that Claudette person?"

I shuddered. "No, of course not," I said. "We just needed to ask Sam some questions."

"Oh," said Jenah. She seemed to be disappointed in that answer, but I couldn't help that. What could I do against Claudette?

"So, uh. How are things with you?" I said.

"I do have gossip," she admitted. "I spent all last night—when I wasn't coordinating Kit Kats—on social media."

"And?"

"You'll never guess whose videos finally took off."

"You?"

"*Devon.*"

"Devon."

"Devon."

"And these are, what, those music videos, or . . . ?"

"They *were* music videos. Just him and his guitar."

"And now?"

"They're still that."

"But."

"But now he's naked."

My screeched "*What?*" went through the roof.

"Calm down. He's got a guitar, you know."

"Strategically positioned."

"Exactly."

I took a deep breath. The demon was going to have a lot to answer for. "And I take it this has increased his points or hits or whatever it is you get on the Internet?"

"Through the roof. Thousands of shares. Millions of views. He has *spiked*."

"Spiked."

"He is on it. He is a rocket. He is a national treasure. He is stratosphere."

This was too much to deal with. Besides, I could barely imagine it. I mean, I was trying not to imagine it. My face was red. "But that's—Guys in the buff. Generally looks silly."

"Oh, well, he's not in the buff in all of them. That was just the one, for effect. To get the point across. The rest he's merely shirtless."

"Ah."

"Pair of jeans."

"Okay."

"Singing protest songs."

"You can stop there."

"The buff one was in the shower, so sometimes there's a towel."

"Just stop."

"And he's kind of laughing at himself, you know, which makes it even better—"

"Oh. My. God." I buried my face in my hands. Why hadn't I seen that this demon was equally interested in world domination—just in a different way?

"So," said Jenah. "I take it there was something you wanted to tell me?"

"I," I said, "am going to completely give up on relationships and become a nun."

"A nun."

"A witch nun."

"I don't think they have—"

"I'll invent them, then. A whole nun house—"

"Nunnery."

"And no boys. I'm done with them."

Jenah grinned. "I'll come join you. Sounds relaxing."

"Relationships are the worst."

"The worst."

I sighed and scrubbed my fingers through my hair. "Walk with me and I'll tell you my list of current woes."

"Woe away."

It was about this time that I looked at Jenah, really looked at her. "What are you wearing?"

"My old ballerina costume from *Swan Lake*," she said.

"Aren't you going to get dress coded for that?"

"We're going bigger today," she said. "All the Kit Kat kids. Can they really dress code all of us?"

"Jenah," I said. "They can and they will. Do you want to get suspended over a tutu?"

Jenah's face flashed with that righteous anger I had seen in the principal's office. But this time it was directed at me. "It's not *just* a tutu. I expected you of all people to understand."

I took a step backwards. "I do . . . I mean, I don't *not* understand, that is. . . ." I floundered.

"This is bigger than me," said Jenah. "When there is evil going on in the world, you have to stand up to it. You have to face it down. You are the one who has to make a difference."

"Now wait a minute," I said. "I haven't had a chance to tell you about my week, because you've had all those Kit Kats around, and my week has been way more dangerous and eviler than yours."

Jenah turned up her nose. "It is not a competition."

"Poppy and I have had to deal with witches and hexes and,

and . . . and *you* are having a grand old time running about in fluffy skirts. . . ."

"I have been trying to help with your problems," she pointed out. "*You* wouldn't let me."

"Trying to *protect* you, and the others—"

"Which doesn't change that I *am* working for justice in the small corner of the world I've got. What are *you* doing to make things better? Are you helping Sam? You actually *have* power. What are you doing with it?"

From down the hall, a melody caught my attention. Singing.

"If you'll excuse me," Jenah said coldly. "I have to go link arms and sing 'We Shall Overcome' now." She pushed past me toward the principal's office, and I stood there in the hallway.

It was totally unfair of her to criticize me while I was down. I didn't care what she said; my problems were way worse. And I *was* trying to deal with them. Why else had I been running around all week?

You were awfully happy to let Lily take over, a small voice said.

I was relieved, I told the small voice. And couldn't I be relieved when the adults were helping out? That's what adults were for.

Jenah did not make it to Algebra. Either the protesters were still singing or they were getting called on the carpet, one by one. The Devon/Hudzeth body was not there either. Were they busy hexing Lily? She was next. And what would the hex look like, if she'd never done anything to a Sentient Magical? Would it fizzle out in front of her?

My thoughts returned to Jenah and her accusation. What kind of action did she expect me to take? I admit, my brain was not super present in first-hour Algebra, or second-hour French, or third-hour English, by which time the wild Kit Kat rumors (*All* the cast was protesting! Naked! On the roof!) had been replaced by even wilder rumors about a certain young man whose music video "Take the First Step" was going viral.

During a particularly auspicious moment, when Mr. Kapoor was busy reciting from some script about someone named Mr. Smith going to Washington or something, my phone went off. It was from Poppy. Why would Poppy be texting me?

Before I could find out, I looked up to see Mr. Kapoor staring at me with an expression of disbelief. Mr. Kapoor *loved* his plays. He'd sneaked a lot of them into the curriculum. Reluctantly, I handed the phone over to him and tried to listen to him declaiming. The phone buzzed four more times, and every time he stopped and *looked* at me while the class giggled. I was so not used to getting texts that it hadn't occurred to me to turn my phone to "silent."

To Mr. Kapoor's credit, he seemed to think the looks and giggles were punishment enough. He returned the phone at the end of English, telling me politely to silence it from now on.

I obeyed immediately, and then hurried out the door. The texts read:

> my mom got the sign
> "yon doom striketh at noon! be prepared!"
> stupid witches and their ye olde nonsense
> I'm going home for lunch
> moral support and all
> you should stay and take your am hist quiz

So there we were. At noon, Lily would be prepared to have nothing happen to her and that would be that. Poppy could handle it—she had probably left already. I shouldn't intrude, even if I wanted. Maybe they could mend fences. Life was on the verge of going back to normal, and that was what I wanted, wasn't it? A normal girl. A normal world.

And I could round up a tutu and sit with twenty Kit Kat kids, or by myself.

❨

"There are many different ways to take political action," explained Jenah to a table of twenty Kit Kat kids and me. I wondered if all those Kit Kats had A lunch or if half of them were skipping. "First I tried showing the principal some facts and figures. I did it in a quiet setting where he wouldn't feel put on the spot. He had the chance to see that he had made a bad ruling and choose to reverse it."

"What did he do?" said Olivia.

"You know what he said? Some absolute nonsense about how I have a duty to not distract the boys. Me! I do not have any such duty. They have a duty to give me a good education, and I have the right to get it."

"Amen," said Olivia.

"Say the word and I'll draw you a cartoon about it," said Henny.

"Her cartoons are the best," said a cute Kit Kat boy sitting next to her. Henny blushed.

"Yes, please," said Jenah. "I'm sorry, but if you act like you live in 1952 you're going to get called on it."

"*The times, they are a-changing*," sang Bryan and Bobby.

"And by and large for the better," said Jenah. "Well, he had his chance to go easy."

I was feeling a little worried on his behalf. "Jenah. What are you doing now?"

She smiled wickedly at me. "We go big," she said.

"When protesters march at the capitol, *they* go big," said

Henny. "The biggest crowd. The flashiest getups. My grandmother, the governor, said her Secret Service people once had to whisk her through a crowd of fifty senior citizens dressed as *T. rexes*."

"And their point was . . . ?"

"We are having a dance-off to protest the dress code," said Jenah. "Friday morning, twenty minutes before school starts."

"You are totally invited," said Bryan.

"Bring your friends," said Bobby.

"Oh, boys, don't bother Camellia," said Jenah. "She has bigger fish to fry." This was said in such a light and airy tone that I couldn't tell if she had forgiven me or was being sarcastic. "The Kit Kat Krew has it under control."

A table of theater kids grinned at me. I admit, I maybe felt a teensy-weensy-whole-lot excluded.

"I suppose you're right," I said shortly. It certainly wasn't like I could discuss my witch life problems with them around all the time, anyway. I stood up. "Send me a letter and tell me how it all goes down."

❦

I took my lunch and found my quiet spot in the hedge. Pulled out the floppy disk, unpaused it, and commanded it to play. The holo was still white.

Right. Something had happened after Wulfie—perhaps Sarmine was forced into an epic witch battle with Ingrid. Well, I didn't have any better way to spend my lunch. The white light could play and play. I wasn't going to turn it off if there was the slightest chance of learning something.

My wait was rewarded. The white was replaced by our basement, yet again, and Sarmine in a ruffled salmon shirt and pencil skirt, drawing a blue pentagram. Who was she summoning now? She dragged a mannequin in a red shirt into the pentagram, and suddenly my face flushed and I went hot all over, the blood pounding hard in my chest.

I knew this episode. I was about to be very foolish. The shame of it, of watching myself, flooded me. There I was—could it be only four months ago? Standing on the floor, yelling at Sarmine that pigs were living beings too.

"Don't drip on my pentagram," Sarmine said icily.

I watched myself do a double take, then scoot back. The mix of emotions on my face—anger, confusion, et cetera—would be hilarious if they weren't so mortifying. Had I ever been that young and stupid? And since I obviously had, how come it wasn't longer ago and safely tucked in the past. Ugh, I hated watching myself.

Sarmine started working the spell to summon the demon. Now that I had heard Poppy talk about the theory, I recognized what she had said about working in N-space. Sarmine did seem to be concentrating on something she couldn't see. More spell, and then at last, in a rush of blue smoke, the demon Estahoth appeared in the pentagram.

I paused the recording. I knew what happened next and I couldn't bear to watch. I had brought Sarmine cow's blood instead of goat's blood for the spell. The mannequin failed to hold him. He rushed into me, and then, when I pushed him out, he went straight into Devon. Surely I didn't have to sit through all of this just to see my mistakes over and over again.

And yet I sighed and told the disk to resume. I couldn't turn away now.

The demon finally ran out the door with Devon, Sarmine swept coldly after him, and Past Cam sank to the floor to begin the unappreciated task of scrubbing out the pentagram. I told the recording to speed up times two, then times ten. The video kept playing while I scrubbed and scrubbed, and then swept the floor, and et cetera, et cetera. It was like Sarmine had figured out a way to punish me twice; first by making me do it, and second by making me watch it all over again.

At long last, Past Cam finished and went upstairs.

I slowed the recording down, watching. All was silent for five, ten minutes. With my luck, this disk was going to be entirely filled with me scrubbing the floor, and then floor, which was like the most boring video in the history of the universe.

Suddenly, Sarmine returned—still wearing that atrocious salmon shirt. Same day. She looked directly at the holo and said, "That wasn't what I intended, but will this be the thing to break you? We shall see." The picture went white; the scene ended.

Ugh. I leaned back, heart racing.

The holo was still white. I ate my sandwich, disheartened. Last October wasn't her last major spell, was it? In that case, did *anything* I'd seen have bearing on the case? Sure, the Wulfie bit was interesting, but come on. If that was the end, then I'd watched the entire holo and had nothing. Should I ditch school and play the whole thing again, more slowly, and look for clues? It was too bad I couldn't show it to Poppy— maybe she would see something clever I had missed.

And then the light rippled and Sarmine was standing in front of me.

She was in her workshop in the basement, holding a cardboard box. The same cardboard box she had produced during the coven, the one with Malkin's lamp in it. Was this a recording of the coven? No, it was in the basement workshop. It must be before the coven. *Use your brain, Cam.*

Sarmine carefully set the box on the floor. She drew a pentagram around it.

I sat back and hissed.

Sarmine *knew* what was in that box, or at least suspected it might be dangerous. She was being incredibly cautious.

She cut the tape and, with gloved hands, began to sift through the packing material. Then she stopped, rocked back on her heels. *She* hissed. She closed her eyes, her face blank. I could not tell what she was thinking, and she did not conveniently voice her thoughts to the empty basement. A pang hit me, realizing she had narrated less and less on the recording over the years. So different than her cheerful narration to Dad in the first few scenes.

Hands steady, Sarmine lifted the lamp from the popcorn. She placed it next to the box and stared it down. I could fill in her thoughts this time: *All right, Malkin. Let's see what you've got.*

She breathed once, stripped the gloves from her hands, and picked up the lamp.

Yellow smoke. Rainbow light. Darkness.

The demon poured out of the spout. His rainbow of colors filled the pentagram to the ceiling, a tower of light and flame. "Who has called me from the lamp?" he shouted. His voice rang at full volume in my ears—strange that nobody else could hear it. It was sepulchral, booming—the voice of a true elemental.

Sarmine is nothing if not brave. In a calm voice she said, "I am Sarmine Scarabouche. I trust Malkin has required you to do something horrible to me?"

A face formed, fire in its eyes. "Where is she? Is she here?"

"She is dead," said Sarmine.

The rainbow light and flame died away. In its place was a small, hobbity sort of fellow, standing inside the pentagram with a profound expression of relief. "Oh, thank goodness," the demon said. "She is absolutely the worst. She called me and made me do all kinds of work and then she and her friends stuffed me in this lamp to do one last thing. I had no idea how long I'd be stuck in here. She cheated me out of a body, too." He sniffed.

"What is your name?" said Sarmine.

He drew himself up. "Hudzeth, demon of the fifteenth layer," he said. "I am . . . not a very powerful demon, I admit. That's why she got the better of me." He eyed Sarmine. "Well, come on. I've got one last thing to do before I can be free, so I'd better get started."

Sarmine looked down her nose at him. "And your 'one last thing' is . . . ?"

"Take you to Jim."

16

A Bargain with a Demon

Sarmine went white, absolutely white, and she sat down hard. I felt the same, and was glad I was already sitting. "You mean he's—But why would she—" She stopped, composed her face, and tried again. "Why would Malkin arrange that?"

"Ah," said the demon, "It's not like she's arranged for you to return or anything. It's a one-way trip."

"You mean . . ."

He laughed. "Not that. I don't deal in euphemisms for *death*. I'd tell you straight up if that's what she ordered. Now look— what year is this?"

Sarmine told him.

He whistled. "Time does not fly when you're stuck in a lamp. So, about thirty years ago, Malkin summoned me. She was looking for a shifter and I couldn't provide her one. Every couple of years she'd call me back and see if I could help her locate one. Well, it got to be as how I started practicing. And then I could see them, kind of glowing out there. But by then I'd figured I didn't want to hand one over to her—I didn't trust her, see? Us demons share stories. I could tell she wasn't ever going to seal the deal by giving me a body, and I didn't want to get into any trouble I couldn't get out of. So I kept putting her off. I dunno why she didn't try for someone more power- ful. I guess I amused her. She made fun of how pathetic I was. But, every time, I'd learn things about the human world, and that made me more popular at home. So I kept coming back.

"But I got careless. She figured out what I wanted, over the years. My dream. And one day I accidentally let slip that I knew where a particular shifter was she was looking for. I clammed right up, but I know she went and . . . did something to them. Whatever happened, it did not make her happy."

I swallowed. Had the demon accidentally led Malkin to Leo's mom? That might have been around the time my dad had helped her escape into hiding.

"It was shortly after that that she called me, ranting about some coven. A witch and some shifter types were trying to upset her applecart."

"Jim," whispered Sarmine. "And the leaders of each of the remaining Sentient Magical groups. They disappeared shortly after he did—but they said they were going into hiding; they said not to contact them—"

"That's them all right. The mermaid, the werewolf, and the Bigfoot."

"And then what?" said Sarmine. I could hear the danger in her tone.

So could the demon. He flowed backwards. "You, uh, remind me of Malkin when you get that expression," he said.

"And then what did you do?"

"It's not my fault! She brought me my dearest wish! She kidnapped this up-and-coming rock star boy and dumped him in the pentagram with me—mine for the taking! What would you have done?"

"Hudzeth. What. Did. You. Do?"

The hobbity figure shrunk in on itself. "Something pretty awful," he admitted. I could see him sneaking peeks to see how Sarmine was taking this, which was not well. "They're all still alive, though. I can take you to them."

Hope. "Can you bring him back? I mean, bring *them* back?"

"One-way oubliette. In the demon realms."

Sarmine sucked in air. "That's why I couldn't find him. He isn't on earth to be found."

The demon raised his hands. "I did what I could! I made them a little pocket. It's not *too* hot, and I was able to slow time for them."

"Mermaid, werewolf, and Bigfoot," said Sarmine, ticking them off. "Mélusine, Roberto, and Ed Quatch. Not in hiding after all." Sarmine bit her fingernail, considering. "So if the four of them are there, then why isn't your contract done and you can go home?"

"Ah, that's the interesting part. It's, uh, not over. I can't break the contract I made, you know. I have to finish it out. Even though she tricked me—the rock star had such an ego I *couldn't* take him over. He dumped me right back in the pentagram and that was that."

"You are the worst at making deals ever," said Sarmine. "Well, what does the rest of your contract say?"

Hudzeth pressed himself against the other side of the pentagram, away from Sarmine's wrath. "That I have to take you and anybody else in the coven who ever stood up for the rights of Sentient Magicals to join them. In the oubliette of fire."

Sarmine stood and paced around the basement for several minutes while the demon looked hopefully in her direction. She stopped and looked at him.

He said, "So, uh, you'll come along like a good witch, then? I can fulfill my contract and go home?"

She snorted. Then paced some more. The demon deflated. I simultaneously felt sorry for him and wanted to smack him.

Finally, Sarmine stopped. She had reached a decision. She turned to the demon and said simply, "What will it take for you to make a bargain with me?"

"I'm listening," the demon said cautiously.

"You're a ticking time bomb," she said. "If I don't go with

you now, then someday someone will pick up that lamp without a pentagram around it and you'll come out and get me. Right?"

"Right."

She rubbed her eyes. "And anyway, if there's a chance I can save Jim, I have to take it." She started pacing again. "I just hope Camellia will understand. . . . I can't tell her before I go, because I know Claudette is a skilled mind reader. . . . I have a shield, but Camellia doesn't. . . ." She stopped. "What I need you to do is buy me time. Can you do that?"

"How much time?"

"A week, maybe?"

Hudzeth shook his head. "The compulsion to finish my contract is getting stronger, now that I'm out of the lamp. I can't wait that long. I can give you twenty-four hours."

She pursed her lips. "Not much time to find ingredients or make any kind of a plan. . . ." She looked directly at the camera then. I leaned back, my heart rate picking up. "You understand, I would need a lot of teleportation ingredients to bring everyone home," Sarmine said very clearly in my direction. "More than I have in my stores." I nodded back at her, even though she couldn't see me. I had the message loud and clear.

"Sounds logical," agreed the demon.

Sarmine turned back to him. "Twenty-four hours is just enough time to summon the coven. We need to figure out who did this, because it wasn't just Malkin. She had help." She shook her head. "There are so many terrible witches in that coven. Which ones were involved?"

He shrugged. "It was dark. They were masked. Also, it was thirteen years ago, and though some people might sit and dwell on their traitors for thirteen years, I've been writing songs. Do you want to hear one? It goes—"

"No no no no no," said Sarmine, "Thank you *very* much."

She sighed. "Can you keep the others occupied for a while? The ones that you aren't going to send to the oubliette?"

"I can," he said. "But I will need something for it."

"Letting you out isn't enough?"

"Look, lady, I disappear you and your allies and then I'm out of this lamp for good. I can go home, I can angle to get called by a better witch. . . ."

"Not if I lock up your lamp in a pentagram and let you sit here."

"You want me to do a lot of work," he said. "Keep a whole bunch of angry witches occupied? When some of them put me here in the first place?"

"Giving you a body is outside of my ethics," she said. I was rather surprised to hear that Sarmine had any ethics at all.

The demon stood there, a stubborn, waiting hobbit.

Finally, she sighed. "Look," she said. "Let me think about this for a minute. I think I have an idea, but . . ." She looked directly at me—no, not at me, at the camera. She crossed to it, her hand raised up—the screen went black. The floppy disk made a whirring noise and stopped. The recording was over, this time for real.

My blood pounded in my head. That was the missing piece, the tangle in the web.

There were *two* spells going on, not one.

Malkin had ordered Hudzeth to take a bunch of good people to the demon realms. And Sarmine had asked Hudzeth to hex a bunch of bad witches. Keep them occupied while she tried to figure out how to rescue everyone. She had waited, pretended to open the box for the first time at the coven, so the bad witches would see her vanish and think it was working as it was supposed to.

So who all was stuck in the demon realms?

Thirteen years ago the demon had taken one group of

people to his oubliette: Dad, Roberto the werewolf, Ed Quatch, and Mélusine. Then Malkin had trapped the demon in that lamp, keeping him in reserve for a day when she was ready to strike against the coven. My dad's disappearance had probably kept Sarmine on high alert—better to wait a while. Witches are willing to wait. They live for so long. And just in case Malkin died before the time was right to send Sarmine her nasty present, she had it set up as a death trigger.

And who had been taken this week?

My mom, of course. Rimelda—that's what had happened to her. She wasn't hidden or dead or anything else.

And all of the prisoners could be gotten out. Sarmine had, for once, entrusted me with helping carry out her plan. I was almost giddy with it. I bring her enough teleportation ingredients for everyone stuck in the oubliette and we could all go home. I could save my mother.

I got out my phone to text Pink the good news and saw a pile of texts from Poppy.

Noon had come and gone.

And Lily had vanished.

I flew home on my bike. Literally. I hoped no one saw me, but I didn't really care if they did. I had to get back to Poppy and Pink.

They were in the backyard, staring listlessly at nothing. Wulfie could tell something was wrong, that was obvious. He would come to their side and whine, then lope around the backyard, trying to throw himself the tennis ball. Back to Poppy and Pink.

"They are all fine," I said breathlessly, jumping off my bike and letting it fall into the yard. "My mother, your mother, your grandmother." Pink stood, hoping, hoping. "*And* we have the means to save them."

I caught the girls up on everything. "So all we have to do is figure out how many supplies we'll need," I said. "And then we'll get the three of them—no, there's more—" I stopped, all of it finally hitting me.

"Your dad," said Poppy. "You'll get your dad back."

I was as dazed as Poppy and Pink. I couldn't even imagine what it would be like to be at home with two parents, with Sarmine's sharp temper tempered by the kindness and empathy that everyone mentioned when they spoke of my dad. I didn't even know how to frame it in my mind.

"That's what your mom was saying on the recording for us to do," said Poppy. "Bring the jackalope whiskers and attar of roses and—" She made a horrified face. "A handful of Bigfoot claws."

I shuddered. "Sam is never going to believe we were telling the truth last night. About wanting to help him."

Poppy winced. "Okay, table that for a moment. Let's assume we can get all the supplies somehow. Even if we can, you burn through that stuff like crazy just to stay alive in N-space and not turn into, like, a heap of crushed molecules."

"Then . . ." I could barely say it. "*Are* they alive?"

"He promised us," Poppy said firmly. "Demons will evade like crazy but they won't break their contract. He said she was alive. But still. Humans aren't meant to exist in the demon realms. I don't know how we'll possibly make it back without a demon guide."

"And there's only one demon who knows how to find them," I said. "But I have to meet some specific conditions for him to take me, and I don't know what those are. Although I guess we know there's *one* thing a demon always wants."

"A body," said Pink.

"Yeah," said Poppy.

"I am not giving him Devon's," I said.

Poppy paced. "We may not have a choice. (A) I don't think he wants ours. He wants to be a rock star, not a witch. And (B) . . ." She trailed off, out of respect for me.

"You saw the music videos."

"Yeah. How's Devon going to let him go?"

"Call him," I said. "Ask him to come over. We need to talk to him."

Poppy obeyed. "He'll be over in one minute," she said as she hung up the phone, and the one great thing about demons is I knew that would be literally true. She looked down at her phone, then back at me. "Wait. Did you get a text about a coven?"

I looked at my phone and found I had one, too.

> Cascadia Coven called for this Friday at
>   midnight, at Ulrich's ranch.
> Let's try to solve this terrible business of
>   hexes, & additionally have martinis!
> By order of Ingrid Ahlgren, Claudette Dupuy,
>   and Ulrich Grey.
> <|:-)
> PS: If you don't come, we'll assume you
>   started the hexes and destroy you.

"Um," I said.

"I guess that proxy business really works," said Poppy. Her face looked drawn and tired. "And we have to go, or you lose your spot and my mom loses her spot. Things will just keep getting worse and worse for the shifters and everybody else."

"You got that place in the coven you wanted," I ventured. It was the wrong thing to say. I knew that, the instant I said it. This wasn't the way she wanted it, and Poppy gave me a look that confirmed it.

"My mom and I would have been *allies*," she said. "You have to have someone to work with, to make votes go your way. I believe in the political process and all, but if you think I could simply convince Ingrid, Claudette, and Unicorn Guy that they should give up being rotten people, then you are fooling yourself. Besides . . ."

"Your mom," I said.

"My mom!" wailed Poppy.

"My *mom*?" said Pink. She picked up her ringing phone with a hesitant, hopeful expression. "Okay," she said. "Okay. . . . Okay. . . . Really? . . . Okay." She put her phone down and looked at it as if it were a really confusing spell. "Um. My mom said she's sending me her proxy."

"Esmerelda said *what*?" I said.

"She says she's too hideous to leave the house and I'd better make her proud and not vote for anything stupid." She looked up at us, a crease in her forehead. "Do I have to vote the way she says?"

"If you have the proxy, you can vote the way your conscience tells you," Poppy assured her.

"Just vote the way *we* vote," I said flippantly. But Poppy was looking at me with a strange expression. "What?"

"Allies," said Poppy.

"Oh no."

"You, me, and Pink. That's three of us. Three of us who *could* make a difference."

"Three is not a majority," I protested. "We walk into that coven, they eat us alive."

"Ah! But are we only three?" said Poppy.

"Unless you count differently than I do," I said.

"You go talk to Devon," said Poppy, pointing past me. "Pink and I are going to look up some rules about parliamentary procedure."

I turned to see Devon walking up the driveway, a bouquet of tulips in hand.

"It's out of season for tulips," I said.

"Not in Brazil," he said. "I zipped there and back this morning."

"What, between pulling Sparkle's fingernail out and disappearing Pink's grandmother?" I said.

He looked wounded. "I *had* to do those things," he said. "I made a deal." He moved closer. "You wouldn't like me if I didn't keep my promises, would you?"

"I don't like you at *all*," I said.

He looked actually hurt at that, and I took pity on him.

"You know what I mean," I said. "I'm not *dating* you."

"Oh, but Cam. Cam Cam Cam. You could be, don't you see? Devon and I—we're melding. The best parts of both boys. And you . . . you know Devon is crazy about you, don't you? He always has been. Right from the beginning."

"Continue?"

He took my hand, and—ugh—I let him. I was starting to lose it, I think. "Look, Cam," he said earnestly. "I heard so much about you in the demon realm. Because Devon was crazy about you, and Estahoth felt all that. He said he was on the love roller coaster with Devon."

"The love—? Gross."

"A real emotion storm. He really got the sense of what it is to be alive, you know? Can't we . . . can't *you* take pity on me and give me one kiss? Let me experience what it's like to have someone love *me*?"

"I can't do that." I stepped away before I could do something stupid. "Don't you want people to love you for yourself? For *you*?"

His green eyes were pained. "Hard to do that when you're disappearing people for one witch and hexing them for anoth—" He broke off, the mistake plain on his face. "Uh. I mean."

Poppy and Pink returned just then, Poppy waving an old hardback book of parliamentary rules as she ran. The back door banged behind them.

"Confirmation," she said gleefully. "I have such a good idea—oh. Devon. I mean, Hudzeth. I mean . . . Wait, are we interrupting anything?"

I shook my head at Hudzeth. "You can stop pretending," I said to him. "I know you promised not to tell, but we know everything now. I saw Sarmine's recording. She let you out early and made a deal with you to hex all those witches."

Hudzeth sagged with relief. "Oh, good," he said. "I've never been good at keeping secrets. And I'm a little frightened of your mom, even stuck in the oubliette of doom."

"It was awfully nice of you to help her."

"I know, right? And for only a *chance* at a body. I can't tell you any other demon who would have taken that deal. But I trusted your mom and it all worked out. I think things work nicely when you can trust each other, don't you?"

Pink and Poppy and I stared at the demon. "Hudzeth," I said slowly. "Exactly what did my mom promise you?"

"Well, that Devon lived nearby, right? And that he was susceptible to demonic influences, having had a demon in him before, and he'd probably wander right into my grasp, yeah? It all happened as she said it would and—Oh, I wasn't supposed to tell you all that, was I. But you saw the tape. You said you saw the tape. It wasn't on the tape. She turned off the tape before she said that, so you wouldn't know. Oh, Fudgsicles."

"How could she have done that?" I said. "To me? To *him*?"

"It was only a *chance* at him," the demon backpedaled. "Only a chance."

"This is the last straw!" I shouted. "She can rot in the oubliette! I am never going to go get her! Never, never, never!"

That is when I finally broke down, throwing myself on the ground like I was Wulfie. All my unshed tears for her death came swiftly and thoroughly at her betrayal. How could she have done that? I howled out my misery until I finally wore down, hiccuping into the grass.

A light touch on my shoulder. Poppy.

She sat down next to me in the grass, right on her nice, neat slacks. She squeezed my shoulder and said, "I'm here for you, and I'm on your side. I will also list a couple facts and see if they help. One, she was trying to get eight people out of a trap. Two, she didn't have time to figure out a better plan."

Another figure sat down next to me. It was Devon, actually Devon for the moment, and he had a haunted look as he said, "She knew I had a weak point, and she exploited it." He looked down at his hands. "But she's not responsible for my having a weak point."

"And Hudzeth did help, as much as he could," said Pink. "He sent out warnings. My grandmother took her ingredients and wand because he had said to be prepared."

"Same with my mom," admitted Poppy.

I stood up, wiping my eyes with my sleeve. "Hudzeth," I said. "Come clean. What do those three wicked witches want you to do?"

"I'm old," he said in a quavery voice. "I've been weakened by my time in the lamp. I need a body or I'm going to waste away to nothing."

"The full story, please."

The quavery voice vanished. "I know how to track down all Sentient Magicals," he admitted. "I've been working on my ability in the lamp for the last thirteen years, and I can now do it. In exchange for me magically tagging all the Sentient

Magicals so they can be permanently tracked, the witches promised me I can pick one of the Bigfoots for a body."

"Hudzeth."

"I won't hurt it!" he said. "You know that. I'm just going to make it famous, that's all. Just like me and Devon have been doing. I'm a very good steward."

"You can't tag all those people."

He raised his hands. "Hey, I'm not the bad guy here. I'm just recording some information."

"It means their death sentence."

"You can't hold me responsible for that." His face was guilty but stubborn. A demon's Good Ethics list was absolutely not my own.

I groaned. "Then what."

Hudzeth volunteered, "But if you got me a body before the coven meeting at Ulrich's tomorrow, I could take that one instead. I would much rather have—"

"A body for free than a body you have to do work for, forever? Bully for you."

"Ask Devon," Hudzeth said. "Maybe he'll let me stay and we can avoid this whole unpleasant mess. We're bonding nicely." He shifted again, let Devon look out of his own body.

"He is better than Estahoth," Devon admitted. "We have the same goals. He's helping me do the things I wanted to do anyway. My anxiety feels so much better."

"Devon," I said. "You can push him out. Remember? You're stronger because you've done it before. You can do it again."

Devon kind of sidled away. "But then Hudzeth will be free to go to the coven tomorrow," he said. "Wouldn't you rather he not take that deal? I should at least work with him until next week, when all the witches have given up and gone home."

"And the week after that, and the week after that," I said. "If you start down that path, you will never want to make him go. And you can do it on your own, without him, Devon. You *can*."

An undecided Devon face flowed into a Hudzeth face, stubborn and self-satisfied. "If you'll excuse me, I have one more hex to cast. I need to take care of Claudette."

"And then you'll come back and we can go rescue my mother?" I said.

Hudzeth looked shifty. "Next, we're going to meet with a man from an indie label about recording our songs."

"And when after that?" I said bitterly. "Don't I even get a warning note?"

"Oh, do you want one?" he said.

A flapping piece of paper unfurled in front of me. "Camellia Hexar," it read. "Thy doom striketh at midnight."

"Midnight is a good time for dooms," Hudzeth said. "Besides, Devon has an invitation to play at a house party at nine and I don't want him to miss out on that." He waved fingers at us. "Toodles." And then he was gone.

Poppy and I stared at each other blankly.

"My brain. Is mush," I said. "It will never be unmush again. And I don't care if it isn't."

"Let's list out our problems," Poppy said.

"Our mothers are gone," I said.

"My grandmother, too," said Pink.

"Hudzeth wants to stay on earth and become a rock star," said Poppy.

"He's not going to take us to find our mothers," I said.

"So we'll wander through N-space looking for them, use up all our ill-gotten Bigfoot claws, and then burn to a crisp," said Poppy.

"Meanwhile, the bad witches got rid of all the good witches—"

"Sarmine, Rimelda, and Lily," put in Pink.

"So they can vote to make Sentient Magicals into property, and make it binding," I said.

"Then they'll trade a body to Hudzeth, and he'll work for them forever, until all the Sentient Magicals have gone extinct."

Pink shuddered.

"And that's why they called a coven for as soon as everyone was gone," finished Poppy. "'Try to solve this terrible business' my foot."

"But what can we do?" I said.

"If we could at least get our mothers back—" said Poppy

"Oh, I wish," I said.

"The three of them, plus you, plus Sparkle—theoretically, you might have a fighting chance to stop the coven from making those laws. Maybe one or two of the witches wouldn't show, what with the hexes and all. If Esmerelda keeps wimping out . . . then you'd be six, with Pink."

"You're forgetting I don't want to go to that coven at all."

"Theoretically," said Poppy.

"Well, *theoretically* we'd still have to get Hudzeth a body, or he'll just go back to the demonic realms, where any of those witches could call him and make him a deal in the future. We would only have postponed our problem."

"Hmm," she said, tapping her chin. "Where to get a body."

"And not Devon's," I said.

"When I don't know something, I Google it," said Pink helpfully.

"I think the Secret Service people come and get you if you Google *that*," I said.

"Too bad my avatar isn't a real help desk, like Devon thought," Poppy said.

"'Phone, where do we get a body?'" I said, imitating the requests Poppy had made to it.

"One that Hudzeth will use," said Poppy.

"One that he'll want."

"One boy. Requirements. As follows," said Poppy in a monotone, mimicking her phone. "Must be cute. Must be musical."

"Must be a rock star," said Pink.

"Must be human," said Poppy.

"Must be—"

"Wait a minute," I said. "Wait wait wait. Are you certain he needs to be human?"

"Well, we're not going to give him a shifter," said Poppy.

"Poppy," I said. "You want a big magical working for Larkspur. Do you think making a really cool app would do it?"

"I've already got my spell database," Poppy said. "But Larkspur has an amazing tech program. I'm probably not the only witch to think of it."

"How about an app that would hold a demon?"

17

Apps, Allies, and Turning Points in History

Poppy stared at me, her face blank. I didn't know if that meant she was thinking how great an idea it was or how stupid an idea it was. "Say that again," she said.

"How about an app—"

"That was rhetorical. Where's my phone? *Where's my phone?*" She opened her messenger bag, digging for it. "Hudzeth was in that *lamp* for years, and that's just a lamp. An app . . . an app could interact with the outside world. An app could make music videos. *Do* things."

"We'd still have to convince Devon that he's better off without a demon," I said.

She showed me the avatar again, the ponytailed black guy with the big smile. "Tell me that guy couldn't be a rock star," said Poppy.

"That guy could be a rock star," I said. "In fact, it would be a shame to leave him stuck in an app on your phone. I would like to see him be a rock star. *Everyone* would like to see him be a rock star."

"It's still a long shot," said Poppy. "Look, I can fix the app. It's just an extension of the code and spells I used to make it work with my wand in the first place. But . . ."

But Devon was flesh and blood, and the demon seemed to have his claws securely in him. "Yeah," I said. Would Devon even let the demon go?

But we would cross that bridge tonight. No, earlier. Four

p.m., when the demon's twenty-four hours were up and he *had* to return to give Devon a chance to say *No more demon, thank you very much.*

"And in the meantime?" I said. "What do we do now?"

Poppy straightened up. "We call our own coven," she said. "We call it earlier. They think they can use the disappearances to their advantage? Let's see if we can use the hexes to *our* advantage. We already know Esmerelda isn't bothering to show. Who else might stay home?"

"We . . . we do what? We call a coven *intentionally*?"

"You need three people to call one," said Poppy. "That's you, me, and Pink."

"I'm not asking *how* we call one, I'm asking *why*."

Poppy seized my hands. "Because this is our chance to do something. We're at an impasse until the hexes finish. Yours is the last one, at midnight tonight. Then Hudzeth will be released from his old contract and we can make a new deal with him to take us to our mothers. So right now, this is our chance to make a *difference*."

"But it's dangerous," I said, and my voice sounded whiny even to my own ears. "We're supposed to wait for our mothers. And *they* can work on changing these coven rules, and—" I broke off, looking at Poppy's expression.

Gently, she said, "I suppose I think that whenever you have an opportunity to make something better, you should take it."

I closed my eyes. People had been telling me that a lot lately. Especially Jenah. Maybe there was a reason I hadn't been able to hear it. "I'm scared," I finally admitted. "I wish you were the one on the coven, not me."

"I am for tonight," Poppy said. "I have my mother's proxy."

"Me too," said Pink.

Deep breath. "I'm not saying I'm up for this, but . . . what time would you want to call it?"

Poppy lit up. "We still have to gather ingredients, in case we can convince Hudzeth to take us to the oubliette, and we better get all our ducks in a row before yon doom striketh, whatever it is. . . ."

"Invisible turnip," I said, because jokes are the best way to deal with dooms.

Poppy checked the time on her phone. "Let's call the coven for the same time your mother did. Eleven thirty tonight."

"They'll chew us up and spit us out alive," I said.

"Not if we take reinforcements," she said.

Poppy immediately texted the coven about the new, improved coven time, called by us. Then she took her phone up to her room and fixed the demon app. There was a small explosion from upstairs during the process. I didn't ask. Finally, she, Pink, and Wulfie walked over to Sam's, leaving me her phone with the app on it to show Hudzeth.

After that, it was 2:45 p.m. and there was still one last thing I had to do before the demon meeting at four.

Go back to school.

I grabbed my bike from the backyard and headed out.

There was someone I had to see.

I waited at our locker for her. She was, of course, not alone—Henny and Olivia were still following her around like puppies. I swallowed my nerves and pride—hey, look at that, maybe I had just as much social anxiety as Devon—and said, as warmly as I possibly could, "Hi, Henny and Olivia, it's nice to see you. I hope rehearsals are going well?"

They looked at me like I had fallen from another planet.

"May I please speak to Jenah alone for a moment? I will return her to you in mint condition."

Olivia actually laughed at that.

Jenah smiled. "I'll see you at rehearsal," she said to them, and they waved and headed off. She raised eyebrows at me. "Yes?"

"So, when I get stressed I become kind of a jerk," I said.

"Mm," Jenah said.

"I'm sorry."

"Me too," she said. "I could tell you had something going down this week, and I could have tried to make more time for you."

"Also, you were right, and your dress code thing is super important. Even if it's not life-and-death, it, uh. It takes courage to do what you're doing. I'm glad you're doing it."

"Still time to join us and help save the day," Jenah pointed out. "Friday morning dance-off."

I shuddered. "But, look Jenah, the thing is, I also . . . It's been a weird week. I've been doing all these things I don't normally do. Like I was in a car with Sparkle and Leo and Devon and Poppy, and I had this strange moment where I felt, I dunno, like part of something so much bigger. . . ."

"Why do you think I like theater?" said Jenah.

"And you seemed to have that, and you were hanging with all those Kit Kats—"

"And you felt left out."

"I guess so."

"I told you at the pizza place," she said. "Our lives don't have to diverge unless you let them."

"I wanted to tell you everything—I still do—but you were so busy—"

"And you were busy with Poppy," Jenah said calmly.

"We just . . . have so much in common." I lowered my voice. "It's not *just* her mom. She's a you-know-what, too."

"Iiiinteresting," said Jenah.

"That's probably a secret," I said hastily.

"Silent as the grave. Look, Cam." Jenah had a serious face now. "How many close friends have you had in your life?"

"Um." Sparkle when I was five. And then mostly—"Mostly you," I admitted.

"Well," said Jenah. "I think you are making a new good friend."

"I am?"

"Letting someone into your life? Sharing feelings with them?" I shuddered, and Jenah laughed. "It's okay," she said. "You might soon have *two* good friends."

"Huh." I said. "Really?"

She shrugged. "Only you and Poppy can answer that for sure." She smiled and touched my arm. "I have to run to re-hearsal," she said. "I promise we'll hang out soon."

I felt a little fortified after that. Jenah was right. Maybe you could gather new friends without losing the old. Maybe you didn't have to start over, like Sparkle, to make changes in your life.

And sometimes, maybe you could make changes to improve other people's lives, too.

I biked over to my house and got there a little before four.

I pulled out Poppy's phone to look once more at the app we were going to offer the demon. The cute avatar came right up when I touched the icon, and it grinned, waiting for me to ask a question. It looked like a pretty sweet deal to me, compared to being stuck in demon fire forever. But would Hudzeth take it?

I closed the app and stared at the phone. Unlike mine, Poppy's phone connected to both WitchNet and the real world. I could do something on this phone I'd never been able to do before.

Look at Devon's music videos.

Heart beating, I opened up the top-ranked one. "Take the First Step."

He was in jeans in this one—just jeans—sitting on a beach somewhere. Must be nice to have demonic teleportation handy all the time. The sun was setting pink behind him. Between the beach and the jeans, the words of the protest song slipped down like butter. The confidence fairly radiated from his face and posture. He cared about what he was singing. That magnetism was what was making the song go viral—everything else was just the hook to get your attention.

His song was a call to action. What Jenah had said. What Poppy had said.

I closed the video and put the phone in my pocket.

It was time for me to listen.

And time for Devon to listen, too.

The rest of the early evening was a mixed bag. The first scene went something like this:

Me: So, Demon, do you want to live in this app?
Demon: I'm signing a music deal with Devon. Also, no more witches, forever, you suck.
Me: I hope your music videos tank and you turn into a turnip.
Demon: *sticks out tongue*
Demon: *vanishes*

Shortly after that, Leo arrived, with two puppies in the backseat of his expensive car.

Leo: So, first I turned into a dog . . .
Puppies: arf arf arf

Leo: And they totally came with! I'm like their big brother.
Puppies: lick lick lick
Leo: Did you know Ingrid's collars have two settings?
Human or wolf.
Me: Wow, that could be really useful for the werewolf
community. . . .
Leo: Also since I petted a werewolf I can turn into one
now!!11!

I sent Leo off to take the puppies to his house to play there.
That collar definitely held promise. I wondered what it would
be like to have my little brother around *all* the time, and not
just three days a month.

And finally, Poppy came back with Pink and Wulfie and
Sam.

Poppy: *produces Tupperware of ten Bigfoot claws*
Me: Gee, I hope you found a pain-free spell or some-
thing. . . .
Poppy and Sam: *smooch smooch smooch*
Pink: *makes gagging noises*

I put all the teleportation ingredients in the old fanny pack
that Sarmine had given me long ago, and strapped it on.

We dined on sandwiches and tap water and, as night fell,
we began organizing for the night's main event. Pink took
Wulfie upstairs to read to him till he fell asleep. The rest of us
went to the RV garage. The destroyed votives were replaced
with new ones. Mine was the only one still intact and lit. I
didn't like the idea of extinguishing it, so I set it aside and got
a new one for the coven tonight. I did not have Sarmine's spells
for fancy chairs and green fog, so we left it as a dimly lit

garage with a bunch of mismatched chairs forming a circle. Poppy produced a packet of inferior Parmesan cheese and we cast my new invisibility spell on a couple of Sarmine's old bed-sheets and handed them out to our allies. Pink was super impressed by the bedsheets and commented several times about how non-eely they smelled.

Devon/Hudzeth showed up about eleven. Their gig had gone well and the two of them were completely uninterested in splitting up the act. I gave them a bedsheet, wondering how it would be to date someone who was someone else half the time. I hoped it didn't come to that.

It was 11:20 when the first witch showed. "To your places, everyone!" I said. "Be absolutely quiet, and don't come out from the bedsheets till I call you!" They scattered, and then I caught the flash of a sequined skirt as a dark-haired girl walked to the RV garage. "Never mind, it's Sparkle." Which was good, as I had been getting worried about her out there at Ulrich's house all on her own. "What happened with Uni-corn Guy?" I said as I let her in. "Did you find out what his hex was?"

Sparkle sighed. "He might have *plans* to gather mermaid fins, but I gather he hasn't actually been that monstrous so far. At least, all that happened for his hex was a bunch of video cameras showed up at noon and started recording him in the shower. Because he is a disgusting perv. I didn't think that was sufficient justice, so after I verified that yes, the new pool was for the mermaids, I, uh, pushed him into it."

"And there was water, or . . ."

"Yes," she assured me. She grinned. "But no ladders, remem-ber? There's a sunbathing rock in the middle, so he won't drown, but he can't climb out. Someone can go over tomor-row and throw him a rope."

"Sweet justice," I allowed.

It was 11:29 now and I was starting to hope that maybe no one would show.

"So we can just vote on new laws and pass them?" I said to Sparkle. "Like, you and me? That would be two-oh, easy. Change everything for the better."

"Have to have a quorum of the coven here to vote," said Sparkle. "Seven people minimum."

I sighed. It was annoying to have to hope that not all of the witches were taken out by Sarmine's karma hex.

"They have a good incentive, though," said Sparkle. "If they don't come, they lose their place. So they'll try."

Right about that time, the door to the garage slammed open. In came the trio of Canadian witches. Sports Team was wearing a different sportsball shirt. Leggings was still wearing leggings. Boring Skirt had found an equally boring skirt. It was all very kind of them, I thought.

They did look a little hectic from their day of being chased by wild animals. Sports Team had an arm sling, Leggings was covered in bandages, and Boring Skirt was limping. Their robes were half on, and only Boring Skirt had remembered her mask. Come to that, I had no idea where my coven costume was. I was wearing jeans and a freshly unicorn-spritzed Newt Nibbles T. It had been through a lot.

Sports Team grinned triumphantly as they marched up to their places in the circle. "Thought you could do this without us?" she said. "Guess again."

"Delighted to have you here," I said, fairly truthfully, and gestured them inside with a flourish.

There were five coven members now, standing in a loose circle around the cauldron. The thirteen votives were dark.

I picked up my wand and stood at Sarmine's place at the

cauldron. I was terribly nervous. Why couldn't Poppy be doing this? She liked this stuff. But she was in the back corner of the garage, silent and secret under an invisible bedsheet.

"I, uh, call you to order," I said.

"This isn't a meeting of the Girl Guides," sniped Leggings.

"Girl *Scouts*," said Boring Skirt. "This is America, you know."

"I mean . . . By the order of Hikari Tanaka, Esmerelda Danela, and myself, Camellia Hexar, I call this meeting to order." I tried to emulate my mother's ringing tones.

"Don't you know the spell for the little gavel sound?" said Sports Team. "I like when Sarmine does the gavel sound."

I ignored that, because obviously I was going to have to start ignoring them or I was never going to get through the night. "Please initiate your votives so we can begin."

The five of us bent down to touch our wands to the candles. "Camellia Hexar," I told mine, and it obediently lit up white.

I stood. "Now, for the first item of business, I'm going to take roll call to see if we have a quorum present."

"Can't you count?" put in Boring Skirt.

"Sarmine Scarabouche?" I called. No answer, obviously. Her votive remained dark. "V. Valda Velda?" I said, and my heart was thumping. "Esmerelda Danela?"

That was Pink's cue, and she handled it perfectly. She slipped out from under the bedsheets, a tiny girl in solid black, and walked straight to her mother's place.

"We're using midgets now?"

Pink produced a scroll from her sleeve and unrolled it to display the official proxy seal. She dropped it in the cauldron and a poof of smoke went up and her light flashed green. Accepted.

"Present," said Pink.

"You're still not at seven," sniped Leggings.

But I was breathing easier, now that I had seen that the cauldron accepted Pink. "Ingrid Ahlgren," I called. "Ulrich Grey. Sports—I'm sorry, what *are* your names again?"

"Fiona Laraque," said Sports Team.

"Jen Smith," said Leggings.

"Penny Patel," said Boring Skirt.

I tried to commit those to memory, but I wasn't sure if they stuck. I had too many other things on my mind. I called out Rimelda Danela (gone) and Hikari Tanaka (present), and then we got back to Lily Jones. Poppy stepped forward with her own proxy seal. She dropped it in the cauldron and—*poof*—she was accepted too.

"You were saying . . . ?" I said to Leggings.

Ingrid glared. The balance of power in the room was shifted—I could feel it in the air. There were four of us now: me, Sparkle, Poppy, Pink. Three of them.

"Seven makes quorum," I said. "The coven is complete." My heart was beating fast. "The next order of business." I took a breath. "I move that we redefine what *coven* means."

"Seconded," said Poppy.

"Oh my god she's her mother's daughter," said Sports Team. "Are we going to be here all night with definitions and spreadsheets?"

"Witches make sweeping rules that benefit themselves and nobody else," I said.

"You can't really be suggesting we let in humans," said Leggings.

"No," I said. "But there is another group of people within the magical community who have no representation. Sentient Magicals."

Boring Skirt gasped in surprise. Leggings laughed and howled and slapped her thigh. Sports Team picked up a chair and threw it to the floor to relieve her feelings.

"Per Beezlebub's Rules of Disorder," I said, as Poppy had coached me, "I now open the floor to general discussion, criticism, and insults."

"We've spent the last century making rules to divvy up Sentient Magicals, you goose," said Leggings, still laughing. "You don't think they'll like hearing that."

"No, because I think they'd like to put a stop to being divvied up," I said.

"It would be one in the eye for Ingrid," Boring Skirt pointed out.

"Sure, and then we'll let chickens vote on whether to be eaten," said Sports Team.

I looked again at the clock. My doom was creeping ever closer and I had to get this done by midnight. "Discussion over," I said. "It's going to a vote. All in favor of allowing Sentient Magicals to join a coven?"

My light lit green. So did Sparkle's, Pink's, and Poppy's. It would be four to three, and nothing they did would matter. Sports Team threw another chair.

"They'd have to join under normal rules?" said Boring Skirt. "Overthrow someone, or be appointed by a majority?"

"Of course."

She shrugged, and her light lit up green. I was surprised to see her on our side at all, but witches are nothing if not unpredictable. She must have decided it was more amusing to watch the expressions of indignation on Sports Team's and Leggings's faces.

The cauldron spit up a green glow. "Motion carries," I said. I glanced out the garage window. By the coven rules, the other witches still had a chance to show. As long as the coven was not completed. Nominations could happen, but they might not be binding if the original witch showed up.

I hoped Sarmine would forgive me, but I needed to play it

safe, and there were two witches I thought were definitely not going to show tonight. Sarmine could sort out her position in the coven later. "On to the next item, then. I nominate Leo Crawford to fill the empty place of Sarmine Scarabouche."

"Seconded," said Sparkle.

"Now, wait a minute," said Boring Skirt. But it was too late—it had been too late from the moment Pink and Poppy got those proxies.

Leo turned from a mouse in the corner to a large, naked boy—I wished he would stop doing that—and Sparkle threw a robe on him.

"Floor open," I said, but they were stunned. "Floor closed. All in favor?"

Four green lights to three red. Leo was in.

"And finally, I nominate Samuel Quatch to fill the place of Rimelda Danela."

He threw aside his bedsheet and walked to Rimelda's spot. Five green lights to three red. Bigfoot was in.

We were winning. We were driving them back. We were six to three now—nearly a majority. Eleven forty on the clock. *Keep going, Cam.* My heart beat faster. "And finally, I move to give full protection to Sentient Magicals—"

The room erupted, or at least the three middle-aged witches did. "Now, wait a minute—See here—"

It didn't matter how much they fussed. There were more of us. I just had to get through this.

"You can do it, Cam," Poppy whispered next to me, and I kept going.

"Full protection," I shouted over the uproar, "to Sentient Magicals, including that—"

"Cam," said Sparkle. "Cam!"

The door flew open, and in stalked the three worst witches. Ingrid's hair was half crisped off, but she was here. She moved to her place, her dog at her side. Unicorn Guy limped behind her, on crutches, his ankle in an ACE bandage and a sneering look of triumph on his face. Claudette was wearing gloves now. I assumed that, like Sparkle, she had found out what it was like to lose a fingernail—probably twenty, in her case. Certainly there was no snapping her way around the garage. She *walked* to her place, gloved hands sneaking into her purse to rest her fingertips against a blue cold pack. Suddenly we were nearly at a full coven again. Six of them. Six of us. We could no longer carry the vote.

Leggings looked like the cat who had caught the canary. "Say that again," she purred, "about the protection of Sentient Magicals."

The newcomers swiveled to look at me. My mouth was dry. "I move to uh . . . to uh . . ."

Next to me, Poppy's voice cut cleanly through the garage. "To grant full protection to Sentient Magicals; that the sale of nonvital items such as hair and scales shall be strongly regulated; that the sale of vital items such as bones shall be completely prohibited, and their possession punishable by dewanding."

"I open the floor," I said weakly.

"I will never pass that," spat out Claudette. "*Jamais!*"

"Child, do you understand how vital Bigfoot claws are to teleporting?" said Boring Skirt, more kindly. "You'd never make that stick."

"As I understand it, any coven law is enforceable by any witch within the coven's area," said Poppy. "You are all deputized to go forth and rat out your fellow witches. Further, covens will frequently form a brute squad to go forth and—well. Enforce some things more forcibly."

"And once an idea starts, an idea can spread," rumbled Sam. "It can make a difference."

"Naive children," scoffed Sports Team.

"You've got children of your own," Sparkle shot back. "What kind of world do you want to leave them? One where you hunted the shifters to death?"

"Where you mutilated the Bigfoots?" said Sam.

"Don't forget the werewolf puppy kennels," said Leo.

"But you don't understand," said Leggings. "This is the way things have *always* been."

"And the way they're going to continue to be," Ingrid said sharply. She raised her arms dramatically to the room. "Yes, I've been spearheading a long-forgotten plan of Malkin's this week. Frankly, I thought it would never come to fruition. I'd forgotten about it. But Malkin once called a demon named Hudzeth and set him to a near-impossible task: to be able to always and instantly call up the location of every Sentient Magical in the world. The demon has completed this task, and now, due to an *excellent* contract of Malkin's, he will live in that lamp and share that information with us forever."

Way back in the corner, I saw Devon start. Oh, Malkin had been clever all right. She never played anyone fair if she could help it. She would love to see Hudzeth feel this extra twist of the knife from beyond the grave.

"Bigfoot claws are vital for teleportation," Ingrid continued. "Mermaid fins are one of the most potent items used for spells to contain dangerous creatures. I use them all the time just to leash my werewolves," and here she stroked her dog's head in a significant fashion that nearly made me retch. "And we all know about the many uses of shifters." Her gaze swung to pinion Leo, who swallowed, but held his ground.

"That's not playing fair, Ingrid," put in Sports Team.

"You shouldn't have risked yourself, child," Boring Skirt said to Leo.

"I am merely being logical," said Ingrid. "If we don't make

use of this information, then someone else will. My were-wolves are well treated. Ulrich will care for the mermaids. Claudette has allowed the Bigfoots all *kinds* of freedom. Much of this will continue. But I will not let sentiment stand in the way of protecting ourselves and our country. It has always been a race to get to any discovered Sentient Magicals first. And now I simply intend to win that race, for all of us. The Cascadia Coven will be the most powerful in the world."

Ingrid swung her head around to glare pointedly at Poppy, at Pink, at me. "And if you don't like it," she said, slowly and coldly, "then I have a willing demon who will drop you in a nice, contained oubliette of fire . . . *forever.*"

There was silence in that garage. Pink was trying hard not to cry, and I wasn't much better. I was appalled. This was the plan Malkin and these witches had set up years ago, to systematically get everyone out of the way who opposed them, and then to coldly and ruthlessly turn groups of people into *supermarkets*, for their personal use.

I was at a loss. How did you fight an evil, an organized evil, like that? Whether or not they got the coven to agree with them, they were clearly going to summon Hudzeth in another minute—probably torture him out of Devon if nothing else—and then the three of them would control this information forever.

Whereas all our side had was a ragtag scattering of *individuals*. If we could get the whole coven to agree that Sentient Magicals had rights, then at least we would have the backing of the other covens out there in the world. The Geneva Coven would support us, I felt sure. If we passed it. One step forward was small change, but it would make a statement, it would take a step down the right path. We would have the power of the coven to enforce our new rule. But how? How to do anything at all, when doing even a little thing would make

anything right here, right now, in this garage. But make no mistake,
we would all meet with mysterious accidents in short order.

And then Wulfie and Leo and Sam would have even fewer
people to keep them safe.

"And now, I think, it's time to vote," said Ingrid. I could see
why she wanted to vote now. Six to six was a tie, and a tie
meant the motion would fail. Things would go on as they
were. "Perhaps someone would care to second me—"

"Wait," said Sparkle. "I have something else to say." In that
silence, Sparkle took the floor. "You all have to understand,"
she said. "I have a unique position. It is so hard to move beyond what you were told was normal, when you were little. We
live so long, and our childhoods were very long ago. We forget
that the world moves forward, the world changes. If you don't
change with it, if you stick to your old ways of doing things
just because they are familiar, then you are holding the entire
world back from being better."

Boring Skirt was looking at Sparkle. Sports Team was looking at Sparkle. Everyone was looking at Sparkle, in shock.
Hikari had been on their side, once. Sparkle was not. *Hikari*
could have gotten out of here unscathed. Sparkle was putting
herself in jeopardy right along with the rest of us.

"I am not special," Sparkle said. "I was as blind as anyone.
What I learned as a teenager from my ancient great-aunt was
just . . . *truth,* was just *the way it was.* But one thing different
happened to me. I took an opportunity—for all the wrong
reasons!—but I took the chance to forget my first life and
start over, sixteen years ago. Even a single generation makes a
tremendous difference in the way you see the world. You all
have this capacity for change. You just need to wake up and
see the world with new eyes. You need to *do better.*"

I looked at Sparkle with amazement. I had never heard her

speak so passionately about anything. She had clearly been doing some soul-searching in the last few months.

"You make a good point," Sports Team admitted.

"Fiona," said Leggings.

"Well, she does," said Sports Team. "I have a daughter—*and* a son. I can't tell you how many times I've told my son that he can be anything he wants to be in the witch world. But where are his role models to emulate?"

"Hey now," said Ulrich.

"The world is changing, that's all," said Sports Team. "And sometimes for the better."

"My twelve-year-old has been after me to stop teleporting," admitted Boring Skirt. "What would she say if she were here now?"

"What would she say?" scoffed Ingrid. "She's not in charge—you are. The job of parents is to oppress their children as long as possible. The job of kids is to gain enough power to eventually overthrow them. That's how I got started in *my* business."

"I don't know," said Sports Team. "Maybe I'll abstain. Times do change, Ingrid."

"It's six to six," scolded Leggings. "Not voting is the same as giving it to them."

"If you're threatening me, I'll hex your minivan," said Sports Team.

Hope surged. Maybe we could win this. I opened my mouth to call for the vote—

And the door burst open one last time, on a cloud of cigarette smoke.

Valda.

Her sharp eyes took in the situation as she stomped to her spot in the circle. Her light lit up white. She was admitted. The coven was complete. No more spots open, even if I had

Wulfie or someone else here to fill them. The best I could do at this point was call for a quick end to the coven ceremonies, to lock in the two boys in their new roles.

But even if I did that, we were only ousting Sarmine and Rimelda, who had been on our side to begin with. And there was no guarantee that Esmerelda would let Pink stay. This was as good as our numbers would get, without more overthrowing. I stood there, unwilling to draw Ingrid's wrath yet unwilling to go down without a fight.

Around the room, my gaze met my friends and allies, old and new. Poppy. Sparkle. Leo, Sam, Pink.

And in the back corner, Hudzeth, his bedsheet thrown aside, watching me out of Devon's eyes, waiting to see what I would do.

Each drop of rain will raise the sea . . .

The demon would take me to my mother *if certain conditions were met,* he had said.

I finally knew what that meant.

And it dovetailed with what I was about to do.

Because the thing is, at some point you've got to do something about what you believe in. You've got to stand up for truth, and justice, and all that stuff. You can have all the ethics lists in the world, but when it comes down to the end of things, sometimes you have to just do what is right. And what is right might be hard to figure out, and it may not be black and white, and it might not be easy to do. You have to pick up and muddle through, and you'll make mistakes, but it's better than doing nothing. You might accidentally hex your boyfriend when you were trying to help him. You and your friends might loose a demon when you should have contained him in a pentagram. And your mother might even put your boyfriend in jeopardy for a chance to save a whole bunch of people.

Because the reverse is an even bigger mistake. Failure to

act is a mistake. Letting the world go to hell in a handbasket is a mistake.

Sometimes you have a small moment where what you choose to do will make a big difference.

I rose to my full height. My fingers trembled on my wand. "You," I said to Ingrid, and to Claudette, and to Ulrich, "are terrible people, and I will do anything in my power to stop you. I stand with Sentient Magicals, and I will work against you. I may only be one little person, but even one person can choose to stand up to evil when they see it. And oh boy, do I see it."

Ingrid made an angry motion, stilled the dog at her side. "You'll regret this, you whelp," she said.

"Perhaps," I said with dignity. "But first I have some business to take care of." I turned to the silent boy waiting in the back corner. Even if he didn't want to take me, he *had* to now.

Because I had stood up for Sentient Magicals, to the whole coven.

There was only one person left from Saturday's spell to get hexed or vanished, and that was me. I had declared where I stood. It was my turn to go to the oubliette of fire.

"Hudzeth," I said. "I'm ready."

He moved to the front, dark and silent, his hand outstretched to mine. The witches who had wanted him looked on in growing surprise.

"You'll come back," commanded Ingrid, flustered. "*Naturally* we can improve on that terrible old contract of Malkin's, find you a body—"

"Looks like she's already found him one—"

"So much for *her* ethics—"

The babble around me rose as Hudzeth/Devon crossed toward me, the echoes ringing in my ears. No, it wasn't that at all. It was the clock, finally striking midnight, and there was Poppy, turning toward me, eyes worried, hearing her phone chime in my back pocket. The three Canadian soccer moms, thinking over what I had said. Valda, sharp eyes turning toward me, watching my expression go blank—

Devon took my hand—

And then it was all fading, fading. . . .

This was what it was to vanish, to disappear. This was what Sarmine had felt, and Rimelda, and Lily. Everything was growing very warm. Perhaps I was actually burning up in a fire. Perhaps he had consigned our mothers and grandmother to the flames; perhaps everything he had said was a lie. . . .

It was hot. So very, very hot.

We were in the demon realms now, just as when Poppy and I had teleported to Ingrid's. The demon was taking me to the oubliette, pulling me along, faster, faster. Devon's face was flushed with fear as he looked around, going deeper into layers he didn't belong in. I knew those green eyes so well, I could read them. Fear and—guilt? But who was feeling guilt, Devon or Hudzeth?

I looked at his eyes through the heat and the steam, and one thing finally became apparent to me. The demon had said that, if I met the conditions, he could take me to my mother, with the ingredients she needed to come home.

He had never said that her plan would actually work.

Here was the pit, the abyss, the one-way oubliette approaching. Other demons, presumably worse demons, reached their hands out for warm human bodies. Coward Hudzeth was ready to drop me and go. He would be gone, done with all of us, and then there would be nine bodies in the trap. No guarantee that we could ever get out. I suddenly saw that now.

"Devon," I said to Hudzeth. We were right on the edge, and I spun in his arms, cozying up to him. "Before we go into the pit . . . just one little thing, one little thing for me to remember you by."

His eyes lit up, and he pulled me close. So delighted to finally get that kiss.

"Devon," I murmured, and then my lips were touching his. "Stay with me." I locked my hands tightly around him and toppled us over into the pit.

☾

A voice, calling to me. I was feeling so hot and squashed. Flattened, sideways, thinning, drawing out, and that voice calling me back to life: "Cam! Cam!"

I opened my eyes to see the face of my father.

18

N-space

"Dad?" I was saying, and then, as joyfully as Wulfie ever could, "Dad Dad Dad Dad Dad!"

He swept me into a hug. I had thought I might not actually know him. And yet I did. Somehow I did. He pulled back to look at me. "It seems like one year since I left—not thirteen. You were so little. It's a good thing your mother got here first and had a chance to catch me up."

"I have a brother," I said. It seemed important to get that out. "Um. Did you know?"

"I'm delighted," Dad said, squeezing me again. "And Mélusine is making Lily catch her up on all the stories of Poppy."

I looked around at that. The oubliette was basically a large rocky cavern, except there were flames licking all the walls, and the walls went up and up until they disappeared from view. There were a few arches in the rock, which I hoped led to things like bathrooms. The only light was from the fire, which cast strange shadows and made the shape of the cavern seem to continually shift and change.

A few steps down, there was a rocky pool carved out of the stone. A pretty mermaid, blue haired and generously curvy, sat there, eager face turned toward an animated Lily. That must be Jonquil's partner, Mélusine, and Lily catching her up on everything that had happened in the last thirteen years. Rimelda was perched on the stone equivalent of a poolside chaise lounge, fanning herself with her fanny pack and complaining about the heat to two rather fuzzy middle-aged guys—Ed Quatch the Bigfoot and Roberto the werewolf.

Sarmine was smiling, for a wonder, and looked—well, not twenty or anything, but not sixty, either. She hugged me, too, and then she said, "You two can do more catch-up later. The first thing is to get out of here. Camellia, did you bring the teleportation ingredients? We had some here"—and she flicked a glance at Ed—"but not the quantity that we'll need to rescue everyone."

I unbuckled the fanny pack and held it out.

"Excellent. I knew I could count on you." Sarmine took a deep breath. "This isn't going to be easy. We are deeper in demon territory than any witch has ever gone. It's going to take every bit of this mixture, everyone's concentration, and a whole lot of luck. But there is nothing to do but make the attempt."

She combined the whisker and attar of roses and the precious claws that Sam—and Ed, apparently—had sacrificed for us. It made a good-size quantity, but I knew how quickly it would burn up if we got off the trail. She smeared some of the oily mixture on everybody's palms and kept the remainder in her fanny pack, ready to distribute again when necessary.

"Ready?" she said. "Don't let go." We linked hands, and she touched her wand to her palm.

Nothing happened.

Sarmine tapped her wand, shook it out. Tried again.

Nothing.

A snort from Devon, and Sarmine whirled, fear and anger on her face. "What is this? Are you who I think you are? What do you know about this?"

"All you witches think you're so clever," sneered the demon. Hudzeth contorted Devon's face with anger. "You tricked me in here"—he pointed at me—"and now we're all stuck. Sure, you've got your ingredients to cast your spells. But spells don't work in this pit. You can't cast anything. Malkin had me build that in when I set it up."

Sarmine's face was white with fury. "You never mentioned that."

"You never asked."

The others, who had been looking hopeful, were now looking worried. Mélusine the mermaid was clutching Lily's hand, despair in her expressive face. Rimelda's grumpy expression said that she had always expected something like this. She handed her fanny pack to Ed Quatch and flapped her hand at him till he started fanning her.

"Are you saying you can't leave, either?" said my dad.

"Not unless I leave this body," said Hudzeth. Devon's face bore a most un-Devon-like grumpy pout. "Humans can't do *anything* in this pit."

And Hudzeth didn't want to give up his body.

I was hopeful that the demon actually *could* get us out of here. But *would* he?

"Hudzeth," I said slowly. "I'm beginning to think you're not quite as weak a demon as you claim to be." This was not flattery but truth, and I meant it.

The anger melted away. He blushed Devon's blush and looked down. "More of a nerd than a thug," he admitted. "Spent the last thirteen years studying things. When I wasn't writing music."

"This pit is impressive," I said. "Malkin told you to contain them. And to make it so they couldn't cast spells. But you also—what? Slowed down time for them? Banked the fires so it wouldn't get *too* hot?" It felt like a hot summer day, all right. But I wasn't dying.

"Didn't want them to suffer like I was," he muttered. "Hated being stuck in a lamp."

"I think you have the same problem as Devon," I said calmly. "You're afraid."

Both halves of Devon looked at me mutinously. "Not afraid," they said.

"You want to coast on Devon's talent," I said to Hudzeth, "and you, Devon, want to coast on his charm. When *I* think you both have those qualities, all by yourselves, if you can learn to trust in them."

"Well . . ."

"You said it to me right at the beginning," I said to Devon. "Before all of this happened. You said you couldn't make the audience care about *something so silly*."

He furrowed his brow. "And . . . ?"

"You're not self-conscious when you believe in what you're doing," I said. "That's the missing piece. Sure, relying on the demon makes everything easier. But that's not why you were able to make those videos. I heard the song. You were singing about something you cared about. That was important to you."

"But I feel like I *should* be able to sing about butter," said Devon, with a wistful expression. "Nnenna does."

From the hot tub, Mélusine pronounced dramatically, "You are an *artist*. A *true* artist does not waste their time on fluff. An artist follows their *vision*."

I caught my mother rolling her eyes.

My dad, more gently: "Everyone is different."

"You said it in the car," I said. "It's something you have to do by yourself. Not with the demon." I made a face. "Also, you will literally be stuck in this hot pit forever if you don't."

Devon breathed. His eyes changed color.

And then, quite suddenly, he was standing next to a hobbity Hudzeth, who looked dejected about the whole thing.

"Please?" he said to Devon, and he tried to poke his finger into Devon's palm.

"No," said Devon firmly.

I squatted down next to Hudzeth. "And now, how would you like to try this app?" I said. "Free rein over the Internet. Super easy to go viral when you already live there, and everything is virtual anyway."

Hudzeth looked up at me. "I don't think you understand," he finally admitted. "It's not just the hordes of adoring fans. Fans aren't the same as . . . Oh, you don't understand. I'll be *alone*."

As he had been alone for thirteen years in that lamp. And maybe, in spirit, before that. "You'll be in Poppy's phone," I said. "And it sounds like you have a lot of knowledge about shifters that could be invaluable for us to help them. If you want to *help* us in the future, I don't think you'll lack for friends again."

He reached out to Poppy's phone.

And then the demon poured in through the port, into her phone, into the app. All the words and numbers on the screen rippled in front of me, and I imagined the demon trying to find what set of coding meant "avatar."

I wondered if I needed to pull up the app and somehow guide him into it with my voice, but before I could, Poppy's cute avatar popped up on the screen. He smiled at us, and the rakish smile was million-watt. This guy could be a phenom, was all I was saying. He strutted completely off the screen of the phone and then came back on the other side.

"How does it feel?" I said.

"Pretty good," he said. The robotic sound was gone from the voice now. He nodded a few times, shook his ponytail, considered everything. "Really good."

"But can you access all your power from there?" said Dad.

"If I can't, I'm getting back in the boy," said Hudzeth.

"You just try it," said Devon.

"You had all your power when you were in Devon, on the surface," I said. "You would have had it in that mannequin Sarmine made for another demon once."

"The theory is sound," agreed Sarmine. "What?"

"Everyone grab hands," I shouted. "We're getting out of here."

I held my hand out for Devon. Ed Quatch took his hand, and Sarmine took his, and then Dad, and then Lily. Lily linked her other arm with Roberto, who carried Mélusine in his arms. I held the phone aloft. "Everyone think of Sarmine's backyard!" I shouted.

"I don't know what that looks like!" shouted somebody.

"Then think of me!"

The rocks shook threateningly around us. The fire blazed, not wanting to let us go. The phone nearly slipped from my grasp as the demon shot us all up, straight through all the layers, straight out of the oubliette.

It was hot and horrid and miserable and I could feel my sweaty palm loosening its grasp. "Don't you dare," I told myself, and clung on with all my might until all eight of us, plus a possessed phone, popped out of the air, one by one, rolling across Sarmine's backyard and gasping.

Dad swept me into another bear hug. Then he seized Mom and whirled her around, kissing her. "I thought I'd never see this place again," he said. "Never see either of you."

"Oh, Jim," she said, and her face was the happiest I had ever seen it.

Ed Quatch found the garden hose, turned it on, and began gulping water from the nozzle. He doused Mélusine's tail and held the nozzle to Roberto for his turn. I could see they were going to be doing that for a few minutes.

Me, I hurried back to the garage.

Poppy and Sparkle had been holding down the fort admirably in the ten minutes we were gone. I strongly suspected an all-day filibuster would never fly in the witch world, as witches would get bored and leave, and to heck with the rules.

But Poppy and Sparkle *had* held them for ten minutes, apparently by the time-honored trick of getting the villains to elaborate on their plans. Ingrid probably also thought the demon would come back after he had completed his task, despite what she had let slip about contractually leaving him in a lamp.

I figured it would be reasonably hard for Hudzeth to be forced to fulfill the rest of that terrible contract to tag all Sentient Magicals if Ingrid wasn't around to make him.

I looked around to see who I could spare. Ed Quatch was well watered now, shaking droplets out of his black hair. I motioned for him to come join me. Then I flung open the door to the garage.

All the witches turned.

You know, it was really a delightful moment, to see the look of shock and dismay on the faces of Ingrid and Ulrich and Claudette. I was back, and nobody had expected that. And behind me—Ed Quatch, who nobody had seen since he crossed them, thirteen years ago.

"It can't be," said Ingrid, dumbly.

"*Merde*," said Claudette.

Maybe it was kind of fun wielding power. For good, anyway.

I handed Ed the phone. "Ed," I said, and pointed dramatically at Ingrid. "Will you and Hudzeth please take this wicked witch and drop her in the demon's oubliette."

"Gladly," Ed said, and from the phone I heard the chortle of a vastly amused demon.

Ingrid shrieked, "No!" But before she could do anything, Ed seized her arm with one hand, and with his other hand, held the phone high. Hudzeth guiding them, they vanished into N-space.

Roberto, shaking water from his hair, put a comforting hand

on Ingrid's pet werewolf, calming him. I was glad he would be around to help rehabilitate Rover and the two puppies.

Claudette stepped backwards. "I, *euh,* have been meaning to abdicate anyway," she said. "Quite busy . . . dedicating my life to my gardening. . . ." She snapped out of the garage in a puff of rose smoke.

Only one left to worry about. I turned my contemplation to slimy Ulrich, looking at me wide-eyed from his crutches. "This was Jim's spot," he said, groveling. "I was just holding it for him. It's all his again."

"No more swimming pools?" I said to him.

"I'll turn it into a splash pond for the unicorns," he promised. He limped out the door as fast as his crutches could go.

That took care of them—for now, anyway. But some of the original coven was back from the oubliette now, and not all our changes would stand. My head was spinning and I couldn't keep track of who was in and who was out. The witches were standing around in clumps, everybody catching each other up on things. Lily was returning Poppy's wand to her, and I definitely caught the words "proud of you." Pink was hugging her grandmother fiercely.

A freshly rewanded Poppy came to my rescue. "Everyone take your places," she said. "Let's see where we are now."

We arranged ourselves in the original circle. Sarmine, Valda, Pink, my dad. The three Canadians. Rimelda, Sparkle, Lily. Me. Everyone else crowded into the corners of the garage, among the brooms and paint cans, while Mom and Dad beamed rather foolishly at each other from across the circle.

It was a lot better and, at the same time, it wasn't. Poppy wasn't on it, the one person most qualified to wield a spot righteously and well. And we had lost all the Sentient Magicals that had been the true beginnings of a more inclusive coven.

I looked at Sparkle and Poppy in despair. I knew this was

the psychological moment to make changes. But now the makeup of the group had shifted again. And while I felt reasonably sure we had formed a group whose majority would not actively hunt down Sentient Magicals, would their tolerance extend to inviting them into our group?

"Hey, Leo," said Sparkle. Her voice sounded kind of funny, in a *don't say anything and I can get through this real quick* sort of way.

He bounced to her side.

"So, I'd like to abdicate in favor of you," Sparkle said. It sounded super offhand, but I was sure this was not the case. "I suppose I can nominate you in my place? I mean, you'll take it?"

"Are you sure?" said Leo.

She shrugged it off. "You're the shifter, not me," she said. "You're already in jeopardy, since everyone saw you. You'd better keep the benefit of helping change things. It's pretty tedious and all. . . ."

She wasn't fooling Leo. He looked in her eyes and said, "Yes. I will."

Sparkle made the nomination and it passed. I could see the shifting expressions on the faces of the old coven members who had just returned from the oubliette—confusion quickly changing to acceptance, as their votives lit up green.

I sneaked a look at my dad and saw far more than acceptance. That was definitely pride on his face. I was following in his footsteps. He grinned at me, and I beamed back.

The room was silent, and everyone was staring at me. Why was everyone staring at me? I looked at Sarmine to confirm Leo's nomination, but she raised her eyebrows expectantly at me.

Right. I was the one who had called the coven.

And Sarmine believed in me enough to let me finish what I had started.

I took a deep breath. Nerve-racking, doing something when

the master of it all is standing right next to you. "Eight to three," I said. "Motion carries."

Sparkle took Leo's hand, and together they placed their hands on her votive next to the cauldron. The glow changed from white to green and back to white. Sparkle drew back, giving Leo room to stand by himself in the circle. She really was serious about a new path in life. It was too bad; this Sparkle would be an asset to the coven. But I respected her for what she was doing.

Rimelda raised her wand. "Primella told me there was one other Sentient Magical who joined the coven, in my place, while I was away. Who was that?" She peered around until Sam stepped out of the corner, raising his hand, with its beginnings of new nails. "What's your name, young man?"

"Sam Quatch," he said warily.

"Very well, Sam. I'm old and cranky and tired of doing nonsense like this when I could be relaxing by the pool, thinking up hexes for people who actually deserve it, like politicians and reality TV stars. I'm abdicating in favor of you, so you'd better do a good job, young man."

"I—I will," he said, startled. We voted him in, he took Rimelda's place next to Leo, and she went and sat on the piano bench to enjoy the rest of the proceedings.

After that, the numbers were in our favor again. We took a vote and quickly installed Roberto the werewolf in Ingrid's old place, and then we tried to elect Mélusine, but she absolutely would not.

"I trust Roberto to look out for our interests," she said, in her dramatic way, "but the thing I am doing next is going home and asking Jonquil to marry me. You may elect a mermaid the next time a space opens up."

"I promise," I said, and then, with glad heart, I turned to the one person I wanted to be on the coven more than any of us. Honestly, if Mélusine *had* wanted a spot, I might have stepped down for Poppy. And yet I was glad it hadn't come to that. Because I thought we could do more good together.

We elected Poppy easily, and then I yielded her the floor. This was her area of expertise.

"And now," said Poppy, and there was a smile playing around her lips, "we call for the vote again."

The thirteen of us gathered around.

"But first," she said, "masks." I reached for my nonexistent mask, and then I realized she was gesturing at the older witches, who were pulling them on out of habit. "*No more masks*," she clarified, and reluctantly the masks went up and off. They could see which way the wind was blowing.

"Lights," she said.

The garage lightbulb had gotten broken at some point in the scuffle, but now, all around us, witches raised their wands, lighting the old garage.

Poppy spoke in a strong, clear voice. "I move to grant full protection to Sentient Magicals; that the sale of nonvital items such as hair and scales shall be strongly regulated; that the sale of vital items such as bones shall be completely prohibited, and their possession punishable by dewanding."

It carried, ten to two. Valda was never going to be anything other than nasty, but it was possible we could work on Leggings, I thought. I wondered if we needed to find a way to recall terrible witches, next, or if we were just going to have to accept a few of them in the name of democracy. Though, in that case, we really needed to establish an election process. . . .

"Pledge with me," Poppy was saying, "that we will all work together to end this violence. End this destruction. We can do better." And all around the circle the young voices rang out.

I will!

I will!

I will!

Epilogue One

Friday morning, twenty minutes before class.

The schoolyard was filled with boys in leotards. I was beginning to see what Jenah had meant about going big. There were girls in athletic clothes, too—some of them in dance costumes, but many of them in baggy clothes—big, saggy basketball shorts and loose T-shirts. The boys were the ones Jenah had specifically asked to wear form-fitting leggings and midriff shirts, and they had come through handsomely. The senior class vice president, a six-foot-tall boy with a beard, went leaping past me in a tutu and pink leg warmers. "I'm never taking this off," he hollered at Jenah as he *jetéd* past.

"You see?" she said. "We're showing the administration that gender-specific clothing policies aren't going to fly here. They'll have to outlaw yoga pants for everyone—which they might—or no one. Either way, it has to be consistent. That's all I want."

"All?" I said.

"Well. And a scene. Who wouldn't want to make a scene, given half an excuse? And this was the perfect excuse." She pulled out a real, live megaphone from somewhere—well, probably from Sparkle—and shouted, "Listen up, everyone! The dance-off begins on the quad in three minutes, right after the one and only Devon performs for us! Come show us your stuff! The Kit Kat troupe will get us started." Right on cue, the Kit Kat kids flowed past, every one in more-outlandish dance gear than the last. Henny and that cute Kit Kat boy were arm in arm, and so were Bobby and Bryan. Olivia was carrying Jenah's ballet bag for her.

Everyone was working together, and down on the quad I heard no hesitation as Devon started into his song. It was the same one he had been singing on the beach video with Hudzeth, but with no partly naked gimmicks now. Well, as far as I knew. He sang with conviction:

> A single rose can feed a bee
> Each drop of rain will raise the sea
> Every forest starts with a tree
> The first step is up to you

Voices rose as people joined in the chorus with him. Each individual. Each together.

If there was one thing I had learned this week, it was that everyone had their own story. Jenah's story was not mine this week. She was the hero of her own personal journey, which had started with an unfair ruling and ended with a climactic dance-off on the high school quad. I was the smallest of small parts in her story this week, the minorest of side characters. My journey had been . . . well, maybe a little more epic, and involved new allies, new worlds to explore. It didn't matter. One did not trump the other, and did not need to. We were still best friends, and that never needed to change. When I needed her, she helped me. And when she needed me, well . . .

I had told Sparkle to magic me up the fanciest of dance costumes. The most dramatically sequined. The most show-stopping, attention-calling, frankly embarrassing getup of getups.

As I pulled it from its duffel bag, I saw that she had come through splendidly.

There was an enormous hot-pink tutu flocked with bows and stars. I put it on. A silver-sequined short cape. I put it on. A four-foot feathered headdress that should have weighed fifty pounds but clearly had been imbued with some sort of Sparkle magic and was light as one of its own hot-pink feathers. I put it on, too. I did not look in a mirror. There were limits.

"Jenah," I said with dignity, as a thousand leotarded teenagers ran gleefully past us, "I am ready to help you save the day."

She turned from her megaphone to see me. She did not laugh, because she is a True Friend. But she beamed from ear to ear as she squeezed my hands. "Thank you," she said.

Epilogue Two

Saturday morning, surprisingly late in the morning.

It was good to be back in my own familiar bedroom, with a familiar puppy dog–shaped boy curled at my feet. Well, there was one change to the room. I had taped up Friday's American history quiz next to my bed. After all, it isn't every day you get an A-plus on something. Maybe right now Jenah was taping the new gender-neutral dress code ruling up in her own room, so she could be reminded of her success. Poppy was right. It was very bolstery to look back at what your past self had achieved . . . with the help of some friends.

There was another change, too. Dad had put his foot down and said I deserved a real phone, like normal teenagers had. Right now it had a pile of texts with Devon about a date. A real date, tonight, with pizza and a movie and no witches.

Except for me, of course.

Dad was downstairs flipping pancakes and singing old pop songs. I had never heard anyone downstairs singing old pop songs. Come to that, I had never gotten to sleep in until nine a.m. There were changes coming to the house. Maybe even kindergarten, in a couple years, for Wulfie, using those collars Ingrid had developed. I rubbed his belly, considering it, and he pawed the air in his sleep, content.

I also considered the brochure in my hands.

Picture yourself at beautiful Larkspur College!

Choose from our wide variety of interesting
courses, such as:

- Hexes: A Fascinating Study of Witch Retaliation!
- Demons & Their Summoning: A Practical Lab!
- Shifters: Allies or Ingredients? An Exploration of
  Ethics!

Sarmine came in to say "Pancakes," then saw what I was
flipping through. She sat down next to the bed, pushing salt-
and-pepper strands of hair back into her bob. "I suppose you
want to go to Larkspur now," she said.

"I've got a whole year to come up with a grand magical act,"
I said.

"You don't think rescuing your parents from the demon
plane cuts it?" she said. "Or installing a bunch of Sentient
Magicals in a witch coven—an innovation I'm not entirely sure
about."

"Oh, we've only just begun!" I said. "Shifters and werewolves
and so on are just the beginning. The elementals need their
say, too—demons, dragons, phoenixes. I think Hudzeth could
end up being a useful member of the coven, don't you? Poppy
says she can rig up a projection holo so his tiny size on the
phone screen won't hold him back. And then I contact Moonfire, invite the dragons on board—maybe even get Jenah to
be their spokesperson. . . ."

Sarmine looked dazed. "This new generation," she murmured.

"Seriously, Mom, I've got a whole year to plan," I said. "Just
see what I come up with next."

~~CAM & POPPY'S~~

~~POPPY & CAM'S~~

OUR APPENDIX OF SPELLS
AND OTHER EPHEMERA

Cam's Incredible Invisible Spell

- Crushed watermelon seeds
- Saffron
- Unicorn spritzer
- MYSTERY INGREDIENT

Take the exact right amount of all these ingredients and combine. Sprinkle on item you wish to make invisible. (Note: Does not work on witches.) (Also note: *Do not get on a regular human.*) Invisibility spell is basically permanent. If you manage to work this spell, and need something un-invisibled, please contact Poppy at poppyjones@spellmail.com for the antidote.

Poppy's Astounding Re-visible Spell

- Peeled banana skins
- Cinnamon
- Unicorn spritzer
- MYSTERY INGREDIENT

Take the exact right amount of all these ingredients and combine. Sprinkle on item you wish to make visible again. (Note: Only works on objects—cloaks, sweaters, cars, etc. If you have turned a regular human invisible using Cam's Incredible Invisible Spell, then you will need to contact a demon. Good luck.)

Final Hex List

1. Sarmine Scarabouche—Vanished.
2. V. Valda Velda—House tried to destroy her.
3. Esmerelda Danela—Old and ugly.
4. Ingrid Ahlgren—House exploded.
5. Ulrich Grey—Cameras in bathroom.
6. Fiona Laraque—Grizzly chased her.
7. Jen Smith—Lion chased her.
8. Penny Patel—Tiger chased her.
9. Rimelda Danela—Vanished.
10. Hikari Tanaka—~~food poisoning, murder, idk~~ nope! fingernail pulled out.
11. Lily Jones—Vanished.
12. Claudette Dupuy—Twenty nails pulled out.
13. Camellia Hexar—~~backfiring hex?~~ Vanished! On purpose!! To SAVE THE DAY!!!

ACKNOWLEDGMENTS

This book's thanks start with Caroline M. Yoachim and Stephanie Denise Brown for their invaluable help reading drafts of the book. To Tinatsu Wallace, who explained to me how chapters work. To Meghan Sinoff, who explained to me how puppies work. To Melissa Connolly, who explained to me how parliamentary procedure works, and then watched as I let the witches trample all over parliamentary procedure.

To Derek Künsken, thanks for checking Claudette's French. You get your own paragraph because the above paragraph is funnier the way it is and I couldn't fit you into it.

I couldn't do this without the help of Ginger Clark, Holly Frederick, and Nick Beudert at Curtis Brown, who steered me through many adventures this year.

I am incredibly grateful for all the support I've gotten at Tor/Tor Teen, including but not limited to: Melissa Frain, Desirae Friesen, Patty Garcia, Amy Stapp, Amy Sefton, Todd Manza, and Marco Palmieri. Many thanks to Emma Goulder and everyone in the Tor art department for the wonderfully wicked covers of Cam.

(While we're on that subject, if you want to know more about the disastrous pool party at Rimelda's house, where Cam first met Pink, go find "That Seriously Obnoxious Time I Was Stuck at Witch Rimelda's One Hundredth Birthday Party" on Tor.com. It's a prequel to all the books, and has amazing cover art by Chris Buzelli of Pink facing a giant inflatable kraken.)

I went on a remarkable number of book-related adventures for *Seriously Shifted*. Thank you so much to Rosanne Parry for connecting me to fab Portland store Annie Bloom's (you can now order signed/inscribed copies of my books through them!), Kate Ristau for connecting me to the wonderful store that is Another Read Through, and Jason Gurley for connecting me to the Barnes & Noble Bridgeport.

I had an amazing time at BEA, Norwescon, Westercon, WorldCon, PNBA, OCTE, Orycon, and Wordstock, and am deeply appreciative of the hard work that went into running those conventions.

I had a remarkably good time dancing onstage at the Nebulas in Chicago, and I have to say a special thank-you to the security guard at Chicago Midway airport who, upon hearing that I had lost my driver's license, waved me through after studying my picture on the jacket of *Seriously Wicked*. (True story.)

I had an extra fabulous time at Houston Teen Book Con, and I want to give a shout-out to all the students I met there: those who helped run it, those who attended, and those who came up to say hi. You all made it seriously awesome.

Thanks as always to everyone who had me out for a reading/signing/general hootenanny, including Peter and Renee at Powell's, Duane at U Books, Maryelizabeth at Mysterious Galaxy, Kristy at Corvallis Library, Mary at Grass Roots Books, Marchelle at B&N Bridgeport, and Elisa and Cal at Another Read Through. (Whew!)

A special thank-you to Matt Haynes and everyone with the Pulp Stage (Kaia! Racheal!) for both supporting my books and producing/performing in my plays for so many years now. It has been a wonderful journey.

Thank you to Cynthia for the delectable supply of baked goods, and Jenna, Kim, Tracy, Jill, Dale, and everyone else for the photos and social-media support. (As I type this I have finally acquired a real phone, guys!)

A random but heartfelt thank-you to a nice man named John I met on the train during last November's book tour, who showed me that there were people working for good in the world, at a time when I was very grateful to hear it.

An extra-special thank-you to my dad, who, besides reading drafts and listening to me brainstorm, had strong opinions about what should happen with Cam's dad.

As always, a sincere thank-you to Eric and the rest of my marvelous family, who are always there for me, who help me (so! much!), and who believe in me that I can do the thing.

To all of you who have read this far, I want to tell you, very sincerely, that I, too, believe in you. You can make a difference. You can do the thing.

Portland, Oregon
January 2017